THE LIFE AND DEATHS OF BLANCHE NERO

a novel

Ken Brigham

The Life and Deaths of Blanche Nero

For information about this title, contact the publisher:

Secant Publishing, LLC
P.O. Box 79
Salisbury MD 21803
www.secantpublishing.com

ISBN 978-1-944962-14-2 (hardcover)
ISBN 978-1-944962-16-6 (paperback)

Library of Congress Control Number: 2016937928

Printed in the United States of America
Design by: Kit Foster Design

To Giorgio Crivelli, engineer and sculptor,
who opened my door to Venice.

Everyone tends to remember the past with greater fervor
as the present gains greater importance

—Italo Svevo in Zeno's Conscience

There are two parts to my story, each born of violence—acts of man and of God. Venice, La Serenissima, that most serene republic, is where the parts converged. That is where I was moved to write down what I remembered of my eventful and enigmatic life. And it is the place where the enigma was resolved, where I learned, belatedly, to laugh and cry and love.

Blanche Nero
Venice
Winter, 2005

When Isolo San Michele goes suddenly dark of an evening, its stately face abandoned by the setting sun, the sighs of long-departed souls resting there creep across the soft green swish and slap of the lagoon. Those dead souls live still in their legacies and in the soul of La Serenissima—that most serene republic—but they are at rest. Rest. Only a privileged few brave souls find rest before keeping their inevitable date with the Angel of Death.

On a winter afternoon, San Michele goes dark suddenly and the chorus of dead souls' sighs rises above the clack-clack of the vaporetto and the low rumble of the many-tongued interlopers ambling about the Fondamente Nove. On such an afternoon, there is a promise of serenity in that place.

Serenity is place. An obscure internal place at the center of the self's maze of dead ends and switchbacks. A paradox concocted of equal parts hope, ambition, experience, and fate obscures the path to the center of the maze. That place is not easily gained.

Serenity is also an outside place on this planet where universal rhythms converge in ways that can only be felt from the center of the maze.

Discovering both places and coming together with them is finding Serenissima.

CHAPTER 1: JUSTICE'S HEAVY HAND

I dressed in my best clothes to attend my father's murder. My mother didn't tell me to do that. After all, I was fifteen years old, poised expectantly on the brink of womanhood and perfectly capable of deciding things for myself, thank you. Mother didn't tell me much at all except to get dressed, that we were going to see my father killed.

"Justice, Blanche," was all Mother said when I asked questions about it, "an eye for an eye."

Daddy killed his only friend, hacked him to death with an army surplus machete in the middle of the cornfield behind our house in Almsboro. The two of them were cutting cornstalks after harvest and arranging the severed stalks into the shocks that decorated the field in the fall and winter. Apparently they were in the middle of the field, out of sight. Nobody really knows what happened. Having done the deed, Daddy came to the house and called Sheriff Hansley without speaking to Momma or me.

He sat down to wait for the sheriff and said, "I killed Old Man Flaherty in the cornfield," speaking to the empty space in front of where he sat rather than to me or Momma.

Old Man Flaherty (I never heard him called by any other

name) had moved into a small house on a dirt lane off Hardin Pike only recently. He was a wiry, somber man. His age was indeterminate but the mileage showed. Shortly after arriving, he seemed to go out of his way to befriend my father. Flaherty lived alone and kept pretty much to himself except for the time he spent with Daddy. I don't think Daddy had made any friends in Almsboro until Old Man Flaherty arrived. Now I think that it should have seemed a strange and unlikely friendship to us, but it didn't. It was whatever it was. Old Man Flaherty was rarely mentioned in our household.

Momma was a nurse and was familiar with death, including violent and senseless death. She worked a lot of extra shifts in the small and poorly equipped emergency room in Haightsville about ten miles up the road toward the river; the ambience of that little town did not foster amiable interpersonal relations. In the fifteen years of her marriage to my father, she had never known him to be violent. However, she was all too aware that she didn't really know my father very well at all in spite of the years they had lived together. There was more pragmatism than passion in their partnering. She had sensed he had something of major importance to resolve and suspected that he had spent the better part of their time together looking for the right opportunity. Maybe he found it.

Daddy continued, still talking to the empty space. "I called Ben Hansley and he's coming to take me to jail."

To this day I am baffled by my mother's response. She didn't cry, didn't really seem all that upset.

She asked, "Why did you do that, Gianni?" her voice calm and steady.

"It doesn't matter why, Michelle," he answered, now looking

passively at Momma. "I did it and I'll pay the price for it."

Daddy hired the only lawyer anywhere near Almsboro, an aging man with the unlikely name of Calibrini whose tiny office was perched over a feed store in Haightsville. He was thin and disturbingly shaky. He was rumored to be "shell-shocked" from his service in the war. But the lawyer probably didn't matter anyway since Daddy pleaded guilty to a charge of murder. Even under pretty aggressive questioning by the presiding judge, Daddy refused to explain his actions. He just said, "I did it, Judge. I have always believed in justice and having lately become a murderer doesn't change that. I'll pay for what I did."

The judge replied, "Do you realize, John Nero," everybody in the room knew each other plenty well to use first names, but the judge used Daddy's anglicized given name and Italian surname for emphasis, "that you could be electrocuted for this?"

"If that is just, so be it," Daddy said.

When they read the sentence, the room was as silent as death. No weeping. No histrionics. Daddy stood by his trembling lawyer, stone-faced. Mother and I were on the bench behind them. If my mother reacted at all, I couldn't tell it. Taking her cue, I, too, showed no reaction.

As we were leaving the courtroom, Mother turned to me and said, "He looked more at peace than I've ever seen him. He was going to do something like this sooner or later. It was in his blood."

I had no idea what she meant by that at the time. I didn't ask her to explain and she didn't volunteer. But her statement stuck in my mind. It also struck me that I shared his blood.

If there is any way to kill a human being, legally or otherwise, that is aesthetically tolerable, it is not electrocution. Legally sanctioned premeditated murder by electrocution was done in an even more depressing annex to an abysmally depressing state prison.

Dressed in my best clothes and having carefully styled my longish hair, I sat in the passenger seat of my mother's decaying Nash Rambler, staring straight ahead and wondering what I was supposed to be feeling. The bland gray prison edifice loomed on the horizon. The long gray walls stretching across the gently rolling hills reminded me of pictures I had seen of the Great Wall of China, except for the coils of razor wire and the intermittent turrets with armed guards, their nervous eyes constantly scanning the grounds. What I think now, reflecting on that scene, is that it had no human dimension. We were automatons going through the motions programmed by others or by circumstances outside ourselves. Or hard-wired within ourselves. The hard-wiring still troubles me.

I laughed. A small nervous laugh at first that grew into something even less appropriate and heartier.

"This is like a bad movie," I said, embarrassed a little at my inappropriate affect.

"This is no movie, Blanche. You can't imagine it away," Momma responded, aware of my tendency to find respite in an imaginary world when the real one didn't suit me.

After a short pause, I asked, "Why do you think he did it, Momma?"

"I have no idea why and, like he said, maybe it doesn't matter. At least not now. Maybe he couldn't help himself. It's often hard to make any sense out of what people do."

"Do you love him?" I asked.

"Did I love him, you mean?"

"Well, he's not dead yet."

"He's dead, Blanche, has been for a while as far as I'm concerned. This little performance we're about to see is just going through the motions of making it official. If you're looking for reasons that you can live with, believe that your daddy killed Old Man Flaherty because he had to kill someone he cared about in order to finish the business of his life, and Old Man Flaherty happened to draw the short straw. I guess you can't ignore unfinished business that important forever."

The "execution suite," as it was called, bore not the slightest resemblance to anything that could be accurately described as a suite. The space consisted of two rooms, a small viewing room, and the execution chamber. The viewing room looked through a plate glass picture window into the execution chamber anchored at its center by the electric chair. The chair resembled a crude and hideous throne presiding over the entire suite. It sat on an elevated platform—dark unfinished wooden frame with leather seat and back and straps on the arms and seat for securing the victim for his final life experience. The seats in the viewing room were actually church pews discarded by a local Methodist church and donated to the state. I thought it ironic that we sat in church pews to watch them kill my father. Maybe there is something about violent death that is akin to a religious experience, but it didn't feel that way to me.

There was no way to dignify that scene. I still believe that taking a human life is an obscene and base act, no matter how it's done and regardless of any pretense about the common good. But I'm also fascinated by why we keep insisting on doing it….and by our methods.

We sat in the church pews alone, me and Momma. The curtains across the viewing room window that blocked our view of the execution room slowly retracted. The effect was like we were watching a movie or a stage play. I guess we were doing that. We watched two uniformed guards escort my father into the execution room from the small antechamber where they had administered a sedative. He didn't look at us. His face was placid, almost beatific. He didn't resist as they strapped him into the chair and placed the electrodes. He looked straight ahead as he had done when confessing his crime to me and Momma, like he was staring into another world. Maybe he was, either a past or a future one.

Having secured my father in the electric chair, the two attendants gave the straps a final tug to be sure they were intact and tight enough to withstand the violent electrogenic spasm that would be my father's final physical activity. They left the room. After what seemed to me like a long time, there was a loud thudding sound as the circuit linking my flesh-and-blood father to several thousand volts of electrical current was closed. His body lurched wildly. As I reflect on it, his movements resembled a grand mal seizure, limbs straining against the straps, face contorted, urine flowing down the leg of his prison uniform into a puddle at his feet. His body went limp. The curtain across the viewing room window closed abruptly. My mother and I looked at each other, locking eyes for a moment. The show was over.

At that instant I resolved to do something with my life that would nullify that experience. Something that valued people more than justice. Mercy more than sacrifice, I remembered from one of the few sermons to which I had been exposed. I resolved that to myself. But I still felt a morbid attraction to people killing other people for whatever reason.

Both Old Man Flaherty and Giovanni Nero were dead. I didn't know whether Daddy's family in Italy knew anything of this. If Mother informed them, she never told me so. I don't even know for sure if she knew how to contact his remaining relatives, if there were any. Her Canadian forebears would not have approved of her choice of this husband. And, truth be told, she wasn't that interested in his ethnicity or his history in Italy before he emigrated. I was surprised when she told me that, surprised at how little there was that interested her.

We sat opposite each other at the kitchen table in our modest (even by Almsboro's modest standards) clapboard house. A nearly finished bottle of cheap Chianti sat between us, nestled in its plastic fake straw basket. Momma stopped on the way home from the killing of my father and bought two bottles of the wine. She justified buying the wine and sharing it with her underage daughter as a tribute to my father's Italian heritage—a wake was an appropriate tribute and age was not an Italian criterion for consuming wine. She justified buying a cheap Chianti by pointing out that it was, after all, Italian and its cost was consistent with our financial situation.

"So," I said, "you never answered my question about whether you loved him."

"I don't know how to answer that," she said, swirling the wine and staring at the glass of red liquid like it was an unfamiliar object. "I think so, at least as best I could and in the beginning."

"What was the attraction?"

"Opportunity…and laughter. He made me laugh a lot."

"Not lately," I observed.

"No. And when the laughter died, pretty much everything else died too—anything to do with feelings."

"So why did you stay together?"

"Blanche, you will learn at some point that you do some things because you need to, some things because you want to, some things because you choose to for practical reasons, and some things because you don't really have a credible choice. For me, it was the latter with your father."

Since then I have spent precious few nights free of dreams or nightmares—sometimes pleasant, more often terrifying, awakening me, trembling uncontrollably, in a drenching frigid sweat—having something to do with the seminal events of that day. Steeled by that experience, I have done some things I thought I needed to do, many things for practical reasons, a few things just because I wanted to (not always my wisest choices). After all that, I decided to write it down. It felt as though I no longer had a credible alternative.

Serenity is what I'm looking for, lately in La Serenissima herself, Venice, that most serene republic. I spent my life looking for it everywhere else I could think of so why not the Fountainhead. Maybe coming here was foolish, bearding the lion in his den (my father was born around here someplace). I guess we'll see whether that is the case, whether my Jacobean wrestling match with the Angel of Death is destined to go on forever. But it's not so much the Angel of Death that I fear. I've spent my life wrestling with that guy, watched a lot of people die. I may even have helped some of them along. You win some you lose some. Death is a worthy opponent. What terrifies me is the memory that my father found his serenissima only by killing his best friend. Murder that Mother said was in his blood. I share that blood. The one time when I thought I was in love, I ended it peacefully out of fear that allowing it to run its natural course would risk my doing something violent. That relationship made me aware that I was capable of violence. That frightened me. Although I depended on violence among others for professional satisfaction and a livelihood, it still scared me.

So at last, approaching the end of my sixth decade of life, I'm giving it my best shot. I've taken my long-overdue sabbatical from the medical college. It was a timely escape from the post-Katrina rubble of The Big Easy and Charity Hospital (The Big Free). I come seeking serenity in Venice, the Fountainhead. I sit in a place that is little more than a stone's throw from and with a bird's-eye view of Isolo San Michele, the Death Angel's Victory Garden. I come hoping to discover my private serenissima. I've tried my best to stack the deck in my favor. I am writing it all down in hopes that I'll discover something unexpected. I've tried everything else I can think of.

CHAPTER 2: A CHANCE ENCOUNTER WITH MORTALITY

From that early morning in Piazza San Marco when we first met until the day I killed him, I was constantly aware that Ludo was dancing with the Angel of Death. It may have been that the two of them—the Death Angel and Conte Lorenzo Ludovici,—were just biding their time, waiting for me to arrive and complete the ménage à trois that we became for a few months. They were lovely months.

I startled awake at four in the morning enshrouded in the fog of terror that always came after the familiar dream. It was not yet daylight but a soft glow from the lights along the *fondamenta* filtered through the window curtains. I lay still for a while gathering my wits. I heard the rumble and clunk of a reluctant roll-aboard being dragged by a tourist trudging down the fondamenta heading for the early morning Allilaguna Linea Blu waterbus to the airport. Leaving Serenissima.

After a few minutes, I gained enough control of my mind and body to get out of bed. I pulled a curtain aside and looked out into the still-dark morning. I was always an early riser, an inclination reinforced by a lifetime accommodating the demands of my chosen profession. I dressed and walked outside. I looked across at San Michele, floating ghostlike in the dark lagoon. I walked through the deserted streets without any real destination in mind, relishing the penetrating silence. Venice is silent in those early hours like no other place. The morning mist crept up from the water and smeared smoky haloes around the canal-side lights. The haloed lights reflected in the placid water surrounded the space in a soft, silent glow, the darker side of the legendary Venice light.

I didn't deliberately head toward the piazza. If I believed in such things, I might think that I was led—or driven there—by those nebulous forces that cavort impetuously about that city— spirits or whatever. I might believe that the different paths taken by Ludo and me on our walk that early morning were destined to intersect at the specific spot in the Piazza San Marco where we met. At that time of morning, it is the most beautiful spot in the world.

"An enigma of Venice," a voice spoke from behind me, a man's voice, the English beautifully embellished with the lyrical rhythms of Italian, "is that human beings created this. It is as though our forebears outdid their God."

I had not been aware of the stranger approaching from behind me. I stood stock-still with my back to the basilica, to the right of the campanile, looking into the rectangle of the colonnaded edifice that defines the margin of the piazza on that side. I was mesmerized by the sight . My heart raced. My breath came in short gasps. There is a frightening timelessness to the view from that spot. I guess what I felt was awe, although I had no other experience with such a feeling so I'm not sure if that's the right description. Every time I return to that spot, I have the same feeling, undiminished from that first time.

The piazza was deserted and I suppose I should have been startled by the stranger's comment coming without warning from so close behind me, but I wasn't. Even then, there was something pleasant and comforting about the sound of his voice.

My attention still fixed on the misty row of timeless colonnades and the complex of feelings that the scene stirred in me, I answered simply, "Yes."

When he didn't respond, I turned to face a tall gentleman standing, feet apart, both of his gloved hands resting on an ebony walking cane planted firmly before him. A black and white harlequin statuette, head thrown back, masked eyes gazing heavenward, perched atop the cane's polished black shaft. My intruder's hands caressed the statuette.

"*Buon giorno*, signora," he said, looking directly at me, "I did not intend to intrude on your private admiration of the crown jewel of our city. If I spoiled the moment for you, I apologize. But since I have done that already, let me wish you *bienvenuto*, a heartfelt welcome to La Serenissima from an authentic Venetian...Conte Lorenzo Ludovici, at your service, signora. Such a pretentious title. Do call me Ludo. My former friends all called me that."

Taken aback by his rush of words and the incongruence of the situation, I didn't respond immediately but looked him over. He was a handsome man of substantial years. He was tall and stood erect, his back poker-straight. He swayed a little as though he needed the assistance of the cane to maintain the pose. He was hatless and his shock of white hair ruffled in the morning breeze. A close-cropped gray beard rimmed a strong face—regal cheekbones, decisive chin, the classic Roman nose, and smooth brown skin of his ethnicity. The dark green cashmere topcoat hung a little loosely on a surprisingly delicate frame. A long tan scarf was looped in the Venetian style about his neck. His striking smile was a declaration, a statement of both fact and promise.

I said, "Buon giorno, Ludo," returning the smile and feeling in some way connected with the warmth emanating from his words and from his smile.

"And what brings the lovely American signora out into the cold at this hour, might I ask?" he said.

"Am I so obviously American?"

"I mean no offense, signora," he replied, "but of course you are American, although I would guess that you have some connection with our city that is more than the curiosity and self-importance that often brings your countrymen here. Is that not so?"

I answered just, "Yes," although I was tempted to say more, to tell this stranger the whole story, to spill my unsettled guts to the unknown Conte Ludovici right then and there in the middle of the Piazza San Marco in the magic predawn Venice chill.

Without warning or permission, he moved the ebony cane to his left hand and took my arm with his right, gently grasping my elbow.

"Shall we take a small walk?" he asked. "Dawn will soon steal across the city. To watch the stealth of morning light gently nudge away the darkness is to experience one of our city's many secrets."

He guided me beside the basilica and into the *sestiere's* maze of narrow streets. He walked slowly and with some difficulty, leaning alternately on the cane and on his tightening grip on my arm. He coughed occasionally, a dry hack that I had learned to associate with too many cigarettes smoked for too many years. I later learned to my dismay how wrong that diagnosis was.

"And may I ask your name, Signora Americana?" he asked, guiding our path through *sestiere* San Marco.

He was guiding us as though he had a destination in mind although we strolled along casually, our pace betraying no sense of purpose.

"I am Blanche Nero," I answered.

"Oh no!" he exclaimed, "You cannot possibly be both Blanche and Nero; you must be one or the other. So is the Signora Americana the lovely French *blanche*, innocence as pristine as the driven snow, or the Italian *nero*, dark passions lurking deceptively behind a lovely mask poised to strike at the unwary victim? Pardon me please, signora, if I lapse into melodrama. It is one of the few pleasures that I can still enjoy."

I laughed, feeling more lighthearted than I had felt in a very long time. Ludo smiled again his declarative smile and squeezed my arm. He coughed again, this time emitting a series of hacking sounds that seemed to come from somewhere deep in his chest.

"Well, not innocence for sure," I said. "If I was ever innocent, I don't remember it. I've always thought that innocence was a lot less valuable than it was cracked up to be. Besides, I think my namesake was Tennessee Williams's New Orleans Blanche, not the innocent French variety. As for Nero, you may be onto something there."

"Ah, yes, the lovely and fragile Blanche DuBois who depended on the kindness of strangers, as I recall. I can appreciate that. I too have benefited from the kindness of strangers although one could argue that there were often less than completely generous motives at play. But Nero…was your father Italian?"

"Yes, he was Italian, born somewhere in or near Venice. I don't know much about him."

"As I suspected," Ludo said with an air of satisfaction, "the lovely Signora Americana comes to our city for her own private reasons. Perhaps I can help if your reasons are not so private as to exclude a harmless and rapidly aging gentleman.

"But enough of this for now. Would you care to join me for an espresso at my home? It is very close. The coffee will repel the morning chill and we can watch the dawn illuminate the lagoon from my window."

"I'd be delighted," I answered.

I *was* delighted to encounter this charming man so unexpectedly. I didn't anticipate then what was to come of this apparently accidental collision of two solitary souls in the early morning. Insomnia has its consequences.

To my surprise, Ludo guided us toward Cannaregio, the *sestiere* where my small apartment was located. We wandered across Campo Santa Maria Formosa, along the narrow *calle* beside a beautiful hotel housed in an elegantly restored palazzo, through Campo Santa Marina to Campo Sante Giovanni e Paolo and down along the Fondamenta Mendicante that ran beside the Ospedale Civile, the city hospital that occupied one of the truly grand fifteenth-century edifices in Venice. This was the route directly to my apartment. We crossed the bridge that marked the boundary between the *sestiere* Castello and Cannaregio and onto the Fondamenta Nove that fronted my apartment.

We didn't speak again until we arrived at the front of the palazzo beside the Ponte Mendicante. Ludo stopped at an unobtrusive door that opened directly onto the fondamenta and fished in a pocket for his keys. The entrance to my ground-floor apartment was just around the corner off a small *corte*. To my amazement, it appeared that Conte Lorenzo Ludovici lived on the floor (or floors, I didn't know how many yet) above my ground-level apartment. The coincidence made me begin to feel a bit leery of the count. Was this a setup of some kind? Was I about to discover a Venetian secret that I hadn't bargained for and didn't care to know?

He opened the door and we climbed the short flight of marble steps to the first floor.

"Welcome to Ca' Ludovici," Ludo said, motioning me toward a large ornate sofa that fronted the window overlooking the lagoon and San Michele across the way. "Let me take your coat and I'll make the coffee."

He took my coat and left the room. I wandered around the large space, perusing the art, the furniture, getting a feel for the place. It was a large room on the first floor of the building, the floor called the *piano nobile*, the main room of the classic Venetian palazzo. The furnishings were elaborate, several couches and large chairs scattered about. On one wall was a huge tapestry, obviously old and probably original and expensive. I didn't know much about Italian art of any kind so I wasn't sure. Italianate paintings, mostly portraits, hung on two of the walls. The large window overlooking the lagoon was framed by heavy velvet drapes. A burgundy awning shaded the balcony outside the window. The place reeked of old money and decaying ostentation. I didn't like the feel of it. It was the kind of place that might hold generations of dark secrets. Perhaps my newly discovered count was their keeper (or their perpetrator—who knew?). It felt like a place where the privileged might hole up to waste away and die.

When Ludo returned to the room carrying a silver tray with two espresso cups and a slim bottle of clear liquid, he had removed his coat. He wore a heavy sweater that didn't hide the fact that he was alarmingly thin. He was tall and angular. He moved slowly and with some apparent difficulty but there was an aristocratic grace to his movements. He placed the tray on the small table in front of the sofa and sat down beside me.

"Here we are, Blanche Nero," he said, then quickly added, "I simply cannot call you by such an incongruous name. Let me see…perhaps I shall christen you thoroughly Italian as Signora Bianca e Nera, white *and* black, not the clashing oxymoron *white black*, and without the unattractive dilution of our lovely language. So the reality of Signora Bianca e Nera will be a living chiaroscuro, light and dark, the one enhancing the other as in the works of some of our Venetian master painters. But I am taking liberties, aren't I? Well, I choose to see you as Signora Bianca e Nera but if that does not please you, I shall keep that to myself."

I didn't know how to respond. This strange and exotic man was recreating my person as he wished to imagine me. I liked that because it saved me the risk of revealing anything true about myself to him. Let him invent me as he chose. I wouldn't be responsible for Signora Bianca e Nera. She could be a pleasant diversion from my apprehension about uncovering the real Blanche Nero and the roots from which she grew.

"If you want to see me as Signora Bianca e Nera, that's fine with me," I finally responded.

"The coffee!" he said, "I promised it would fend off the morning chill and here I blather on letting it get cold. Ah, well, I find that a generous portion of grappa does wonders for an espresso in the early mornings. It renders the temperature of the coffee irrelevant."

Ludo poured a generous portion from the bottle into each of the cups and handed me one. He took the other and gestured with the cup toward me. I returned the gesture and we drank. The sharp taste of the grappa mixed with the lukewarm espresso felt warm indeed. The memory of the morning chill vanished, disappeared suddenly as if by magic. Maybe it *was* magic. Maybe I was being treated to a magician's prestidigitation. If Ludo could so easily produce the Signora Bianca e Nera from the raw material of Blanche Nero, disposing of a morning chill should be a trivial trick.

We sat on the sofa looking out the window as the daylight emerged.

"Are you really a count?" I asked.

He drained his cup and refilled it with grappa, holding the cup in both hands and rolling it between his palms.

"Ah," he answered, "but of course I am a count. From a long line of counts that will, to the everlasting disappointment of my dear departed father, end with me. I am the last of the Ludovicis. My father's disappointment notwithstanding, I take some pleasure in my place at the end of that line. The Ludovici heritage has given me a comfortable life, but there is much in that name to regret. The world will not be poorer for the loss of the Ludovicis.

"But I am sounding maudlin and that is inappropriate for a

gentleman in the presence of a lovely signora. Tell me something intimate about yourself, something you swore you would never reveal. I can be trusted with your secret and I do so love secrets. Let's make a bargain. Tell me a special secret about yourself and I'll do the same."

I laughed.

"Why would I tell a secret to a total stranger?" I answered.

"Oh, but who could be a safer audience?" he said. "Certainly not one who knows you, or thinks so. Secrets can only be safely shared with strangers, my dear."

"I watched them kill my father," I said.

I didn't plan to say that and as soon as the words were out of my mouth I was terrified. Since I escaped the tentacles of Almsboro years earlier, I had never discussed that event, had never so much as uttered those words to another living human being. Why, in God's name, did I choose to reveal that seminal event in my life to this total stranger?

"Ah," the count sighed," Ah...now there is a secret."

For the first time since we met in the piazza, Ludo seemed at a loss for words. A rim of morning sun was rising into view to the right of San Michele, casting a bright streak of light across the lagoon toward the fondamenta. Ludo refilled my cup with grappa and I took a couple of large swallows of the harsh warm liquid. It felt good. We stared at the rising sun for several minutes without speaking.

Finally, Ludo said, still staring at the rising sun, "Perhaps we will have some time to talk further of your secret if you wish. We will see. Meanwhile, I owe you a secret, do I not?"

"Yes," I answered absently.

I was still tremulous from my impulsive and frightening

revelation. I could not imagine what secret of Ludo's would matter much to me. It had been a pleasant morning up until then and I didn't like this turn of the conversation although I shared responsibility for it.

"I am dying," Ludo said, "as you may have suspected. I am not exactly the picture of health. My secret is the reason I am dying. It is a secret for reasons that I will not reveal to you just now. The secret is that I am dying of the terrible plague called acquired immune deficiency syndrome—AIDS."

I was too familiar with AIDS, the Death Angel's diabolical trump card. I hated that disease.

I reached for Ludo's hand without thinking and held it. His hand was soft and wasted. I could feel the hard, smooth contour of carpal bones through his parchment skin. We looked at each other for a long moment.

Ludo was dancing with the Angel of Death and I was being lured into the dance with them.

Signora Bianca e Nera is cordially invited to join Conte Lorenzo Ludovici in his terminal dance with the Angel of Death. No reply is necessary.

CHAPTER 3: THE KINDNESS OF STRANGERS

L egend was that Almsboro acquired its unusual name by accident. Apparently an enterprising horticulturist, years earlier, had decided that the location was ideal for cultivating European palm trees. He bought up several acres along State Highway 19 and planted the trees with the goal of capturing the landscaping market for that somewhat unusual species. That was before anything else of significance existed in the area. He made a sign of metal letters screwed to a wooden board and mounted it beside the road near the entrance to his palm farm. PALMSBORO, the sign announced. After a few years, the farm failed and was abandoned and as the sign deteriorated, the first thing to go was the *P*. It rusted and fell to the ground leaving only ALMSBORO. When people began to move to the region and establish the rudimentary town, they assumed from the sign that the area had been named Almsboro by some unknown pioneer and that became the official name. A county-maintained sign declared that fact to people traveling Route 19. It seemed to me that names should be conferred deliberately and that acquiring one by accident must say something about whatever the Fates intended for the place.

Almsboro existed at the time of my birth there and to this day, if it still exists (I honestly don't know if that is so), only because of the XXX video store and topless bar that lured the truckers down the single interstate off ramp that led to the town. *Town* is hyperbole. Almsboro consisted of three churches, two stores, one bar, and a public elementary school…and the Twilight Fantasy Club with its neon LIVE GIRLS GIRLS GIRLS sign near the interstate exit, which attracted the strangers whose contributions to the local economy were, and possibly still are, responsible for Almsboro's continued existence.

In reality, the promise of multiple girls at the Twilight Fantasy Club was an exaggeration on most nights. And *live* could be considered in that instance a relative term: technically true but only just. They lived and breathed but without much enthusiasm for either of those activities. *Girls* was also a significant understatement of the chronology of the female patrons and employees of the Twilight Fantasy Club; they were a well-seasoned lot. I went there occasionally on a lark with one or another of my high school boyfriends just for the hell of it and because nobody checked IDs. My presence gave the truckers a little something extra for their money and I didn't mind that. The truckers were good for the local economy so maybe I was doing my duty as a responsible and caring citizen of Almsboro by adding a little something to their enjoyment.

The truckers, lured by the somewhat exaggerated promises of the Twilight Fantasy Club's sign near the interstate off ramp, also dropped a few bucks at Pat Ryan's Tavern (*Pat's Place,* the sign said) and sometimes filled up with diesel or bought some baloney, mayonnaise, and Wonder Bread at one of the two general stores that marked the north and south borders of the town—Scott's Grocery on the northern border and MacGinnis's Market on the southern. The sparse collection of other institutions (the three churches, Pat's Place, and the elementary school) was scattered along the mile and a half of two-lane Route 19 that separated the two general stores. The patronage of the truckers was, percentage wise, a significant fraction of the less-than-burgeoning Almsboro economy. Their generosity was probably the difference between life and death for the little town.

Mother and I and, until recently, my father lived in a little white clapboard bungalow just at the intersection of Route 19 and Hardin Pike. That crossroads, exactly halfway between Scott's Grocery and MacGinnis's Market and just around the corner from Pat's Place, was the precise center of the town of Almsboro. I thought it ironic that the single murder ever to occur in Almsboro was committed at the very center of the town (what would have been its metaphorical heart had the town been sufficiently large and vibrant to justify the metaphor). I also think now that the town was never the same after my father's parting shot at a society with which he had never made peace. He killed more than Old Man Flaherty in that cornfield.

I began seriously plotting my escape from Almsboro on the day of the ceremonial murder of my father. I became at that time especially interested in how we wound up there. I thought that if I knew the route in, I might more easily identify a route out.

My inquiries into our family history took the form of conversations with my mother. My mother usually worked the night shift in the ER in Haightsville. Our presence in the little house at the crossroads overlapped for the couple of hours between when I arrived home from school and when she had to leave for work. We usually ate an early dinner together. I would engage her in conversation over dinner and afterward while we cleaned up.

From the time of my father's death until I left home for college, those few hours each day were the total contact time between me and my mother. She worked the night shift seven days a week. She arrived home from work sometime late, after I had gone to sleep. I arose in the mornings, made my breakfast, and left for school without waking her. She was awake when I got home from school. We had dinner together. We talked a while. She left for work to repeat the cycle. I was on my own every night and much of the day on weekends since she slept late even when I was not at school. I probably would have behaved differently during those teen years had I been more closely supervised, but I doubt that the eventual outcome would have been much different.

Those dinner conversations were excruciatingly painful for both of us. While my father was alive, at least for as long as I could remember, our family led a remarkably nonverbal existence. There was little conversation at meals. I can't remember a conversation among the three of us about anything significant. My mother would occasionally ask me about school offhandedly, or compliment me on another straight-A report card. But there was nothing about the history of our family or anything that would give me even the slightest clue to who I was and where I came from. My father rarely spoke at all and when he did, he spoke in unrevealing, short declarative sentences ("I am going out." "I am going to bed."). You get the idea.

I believe that lack of information more than lack of affection (although maybe it was some of both) was responsible for my determination to explore every possible switchback and blind alley of my psyche. I hoped that if I amassed a sufficiently large catalog of experiences, something that made sense would emerge from my experiential miasma. It turned out that I was wrong about that. But I have to admit even now that my approach to searching for personal maturity made for an interesting trip. Nearing the beginning of my seventh decade of life, I am prone to some nostalgia for those reckless and heady days.

After my father's state-sanctioned murder, I felt a need to force the issue for pragmatic reasons—I needed a way out of Almsboro. I had no intention of depending on the kindness of strangers to make a life for myself. I would figure out the emotional stuff on my own. But I needed some historical information and when I first tried to engage my mother in meaningful conversation, it was painful for both of us.

"So, how did you meet Daddy?" I asked one cold winter evening, still sitting at the kitchen table and staring at the remains of our simple meal.

My mother sighed and looked out the little window over the table at the field of decaying corn stalks. She stood up and went to the window, her back toward me. I could feel the tension between us. I was assaulting territory in her memory that she had chosen to isolate behind a wall of time and resolve.

"He was a patient in the ER," she said.

"In Haightsville?"

"No. In those days I was working in the ER at the university medical center in the city."

News to me. I never knew that she had any connection to the university.

I was even then thinking about the university as a possible avenue for my escape from Almsboro. I was smart and some of my teachers had encouraged me to aim at college, maybe even beyond. They were troubled by my incongruence, a pretty and brilliant bad girl, and the more perceptive of them probably thought I'd better use my brain to get the hell out of there or my body was likely to wind up someplace I didn't want to be.

"The university?"

"Yes."

"What were you doing there?"

"This in painful, Blanche," she said, perhaps the most personally revealing statement she had ever made to me.

When she returned to the table and sat opposite me, I could see that her eyes were wet. I had never seen my mother cry. She had endured the murder of my father without shedding a single tear that I knew of. Given that, I assumed that she was incapable of crying. Maybe incapable of feeling any emotion that strongly.

"I'm sorry," I said.

"It's okay." She reached for my hand across the table and held it loosely. "It's just that there is a lot of the past that I don't want to think about. We are where we are. Does it matter what happened before that?"

"It feels like it matters to me," I answered looking directly at her face with the defiance of a daughter who had been held for more than a decade and a half at emotional arm's length.

I had no great affection for my mother, and my number one priority was getting past this part of my young life and getting to some other place. What other place was yet to be determined, but it was going to be another place from where I was.

"Okay," she said, "here's the story. Before I married your father, I was married to someone else."

More news to me.

"I met him," she continued, "when I was a nursing student at McGill. He was a surgical resident, a stunningly handsome French-Canadian. I was smitten. We got married. When he finished his residency, he came to the university here for a fellowship. I graduated from nursing school and came here with him taking a job in the university ER. Not long after we moved here, he discovered someone else that he liked better than me. He left me with a permanently broken heart and a determination not to let that happen again."

The moisture left her eyes and she let go of my hand. Her face took on the vacant, stolid mien with which I was familiar.

"So why Daddy?" I asked.

"It may be hard for you to imagine, but I was lonely, and he was cute and witty then. I had him as a patient in the ER when he presented with a broken arm that he got from falling off a tractor on this very farm. He flirted with me. I gave him my phone number and he asked me out. I also wanted to get away from the university, away from too many reminders of irretrievable pleasures. Moving out here seemed like an escape. And he made me laugh then. I married your father before I knew that I would never really know him. Maybe I didn't want to. Maybe we were a good match that way. Once we were married and ensconced in Almsboro, I took the job in Haightsville and he tended the farm. Whatever pleasure there was at the beginning went away, evaporated, the fog of self-deception burnt away by the cold, stark light of reality."

I was surprised at how articulate my nonverbal mother was capable of being.

"What reality?"

"Two realities. You and the realization that something unnamed was wrong; the nameless dread, I called it. You because neither of us had a clue what to do with a child. The nameless dread because it hung there between us, ominous and unspeakable. I honestly still don't know what it was."

"Why Almsboro? Daddy came from Italy, didn't he?"

"Yes, he emigrated from Italy after the war but I don't know why Almsboro. He never explained that to me. He didn't talk much to me or anyone else about his past that I know of until Old Man Flaherty moved in. They seemed to have something in common, some kind of connection that I didn't understand. Maybe something to do with the war. I overheard Flaherty say something about the war once but I didn't catch exactly what. There might also have been some connection with that lawyer, Calibrini, in Haightsville. I'm not sure. Your father didn't tell me much about himself and I guess I really didn't want to know anyway. I just wanted some peace."

I can understand now the value of peace, and the need for it, but not then. I wanted action. Peace was the furthest thing from my mind.

"Peace?"

"Yes. Peace. You wouldn't understand yet. Maybe some

day."

The conversation was enlightening but did little to alter the emotional expanse that separated my mother and me. That expanse persisted to the day she died. Neither did the conversation explain our way into Almsboro very well. The only two people who might have done that, my father and maybe Old Man Flaherty, were both dead. I was beginning to think that there was a plan there. Maybe my father needed to obscure his route into Almsboro for some reason, cover his tracks, and had to kill Old Man Flaherty and assure his own demise to accomplish that. No more tracks for Giovanni Nero. The enigmatic Johnny Black's trail ran headlong into a dead end. I would have to blaze a trail out of Almsboro without the advantage of knowing the way in.

I thought more and more about the university as an Almsboro escape route. At some point, I concluded that education was my best chance. I was blessed with a really good brain. The fact that I also had a good body that I and several of my male classmates frequently enjoyed was just recreation. Over those high school years, I grew a sense of purpose that was stronger than the pleasurable passions of youth. I enjoyed those all right, but I came to believe that pleasure was evanescent, temporary, to be savored in the moment without expecting more of it. The stuff that was likely to last, endure, didn't always feel good. But then there seemed to be so little space between pain and pleasure.

So little space between pain and pleasure, love and hate. In a way my life was suspended between Almsboro and Haightsville—the kindness of strangers and the violent consequences of darker human passions, the Twilight Fantasy Club, and the Haightsville ER. Part of what I needed to understand was why I felt so intensely drawn to both extremes, why I felt there was so little distance between them. Or maybe why didn't make a lot of difference. But there was something deeply unresolved that I needed to uncover and confront.

CHAPTER 4: MY TICKET OUT OF ALMSBORO

To the best of my knowledge, I personally created the solitary road from Almsboro to Knoxville to Nashville to Baltimore and thence to a career as an academic trauma surgeon. I blazed the trail. I doubt that any previous resident of my vestigial hometown ever considered the possibility of such a route. If so, they left no tracks. So I built the road out of Almsboro through those other places and thence to a career that concluded in New Orleans at Charity Hospital, the Big Free, in a surreal post-Katrina world where it was impossible, even for one as well trained and experienced as I was, to distinguish between the Angel of Mercy and the Angel of Death. I built that road, laid the paving stones one by one, laid them with my own hands, in a pattern of my own design.

The high school I attended was in Haightsville, a twenty-minute ride on a dilapidated school bus from my home in Almsboro. I hated the school bus. Riding it was a depersonalizing experience—the last thing I needed. I needed personalizing experiences and was doing everything I could think of to create them. But the bus was the only way for me to get to school.

Getting home was another matter. Several of the upper-class boys had their own cars and I knew most of them quite well. It wasn't hard to convince one of them to drive me home. They commonly competed for the privilege. Often, I would invite my driver of the day to return later after Mother had left for work to share a personalizing experience. As far as I was concerned, it was a pleasant way to compensate the boy for helping me to avoid the school bus ride in the afternoon. I thought of those evening trysts as carfare. I was determined to pay for what I got. I granted favors; I didn't accept them.

The closing bell for the final period of the day rang out on a warm spring afternoon during my senior year at Haightsville High. As I gathered my books and started to leave the room, the teacher, Mr. Tilden, called me aside.

"Blanche," he said, "you're wanted in the principal's office."

It was a summons with which I was not unfamiliar. It was usually an occasion for a semi-explicit lecture about my multiple relationships with persons of the opposite sex. But I had been pretty good lately.

"Do you know why?" I asked.

"Actually I do know why, but the principal wishes to address the issue personally with you," he said.

Damn! I thought, what in the world could motivate Old Pillowtits—the nickname given to her by the boys that I also adopted; it seemed so appropriate—to want a one-on-one with me now?

I thanked Mr. Tilden and made my way down the hall to the principal's office.

"Miss Nero," Old Pillowtits began.

She had let me cool my heels for a bit in the outer office

before bringing me in and sitting me down in front of her large desk. I was generally not affected one way or the other by a command appearance before Pillowtits but for some reason, I felt apprehensive that afternoon. I wasn't frightened or anything like that, but I felt a sense of an impending something that I couldn't define.

"You are the most difficult student I have ever encountered in my nearly thirty years of teaching." Clearly steamed, Pillowtits resorted to a familiar opening line. "How in the world a precocious, undisciplined, boy-crazy slut," she continued, her face flushing beet-red, "and I use that foul term advisedly, can be the most outstanding student academically in this school escapes me."

She hadn't used the *S*-word with me before but had hinted at it strongly enough. I wasn't shocked. As the term was commonly used, it fit me pretty well in those days.

Pillowtits shook her head. She was working up a good case of exasperation.

"Where are you going with your life, Blanche Nero?" she continued.

"I'm not sure," I answered, "but it will be a long way from here."

"Believe me, that can't happen soon enough as far as I'm concerned." She sighed the words, heaving the pillowy contours of her substantial chest.

"However," she continued, "the reason I asked you to see me was to do my duty as principal of this school. I am to inform you, and heaven knows I would never have predicted this," she continued, clearly anxious to get this unpleasant duty over with, "that you have won the National Merit Essay

Contest. You are the first student from this school ever to receive such an award. I wish I could feel more pride in that fact than I do. The prize is a full scholarship to the state university. And may God help the state university," she concluded, rolling her eyes skyward and waving her arms in a gesture meant to emphasize her exasperation with the situation, with me.

I wrote the essay as a research paper on modes of enforcing capital punishment, state-sanctioned murder. It was not about capital punishment per se. It did not consider legal or moral aspects of state-sanctioned murder. It was about technique. How it was done, not why or whether. I carefully researched the various ways that socially sanctioned executions had been carried out, beginning with early civilizations and continuing up to the present time. I landed telephone interviews with several judges, executioners, lawyers, and pathologists. I argued the pros and cons of various techniques, explored the meaning of cruel and inhuman punishment in the context of legal executions. Given my family history, it was a cathartic exercise for me. That was the reason I wrote it. I didn't expect such an unusual approach to the assignment to fare so well in the competition.

But I was elated. Step one on the road out of Almsboro. If I had any remaining doubts about my brain being my ticket out, they vanished that afternoon. I marveled at the irony of my father's fatal gesture making possible my entrée into a world beyond Almsboro. It was the only thing I could think of that I should thank him for.

I passed by Mr. Tilden's room on the way out of the building. He called to me through the open door.

He sat at his desk in the empty classroom. He may have been waiting for me; I'm not sure. Mr. Tilden was my science teacher and I liked him. He was young and good-looking. He had an unusual accent and a quaintly formal way of speaking that didn't fit the way he looked or his age but was oddly intriguing. He was an occasional object of my fantasies, but it hadn't gone beyond that.

I went into the room and sat down in one of the chairs in the row directly in front of Mr. Tilden's desk. I crossed my legs, deliberately allowing my skirt to migrate far enough north to display a significant amount of lower extremity skin. I don't know why I did that. Force of habit, I guess.

"So, good news, I hear," he said, unable to resist eyeing my legs.

"Great news," I replied. "My ticket out of here."

"You are a fascinating young woman, Blanche," he said.

He got up from his chair and walked to the blackboard. He turned around to face me and rested his hand on the chalk rail.

"Fascinating," he continued. "So many options for you, so many. At some point, you'll have to plot a course. And that will require making choices; I suspect difficult choices for you. You will probably have to give up some things you enjoy, make some compromises."

"Maybe," I said, "maybe not. I've done pretty well so far by ignoring most of the rules. Maybe I'll do it differently from most people."

"Well, maybe," he said, sitting behind his desk again. "But be careful. Pay attention. Society's rules exist for reasons that may be more practical than ideological but there are reasons."

"Society's reasons haven't done much for me," I said,

crossing my legs in the other direction and allowing my skirt to migrate a bit further north, the hem inching a bit above mid-thigh.

There was a long pause during which Mr. Tilden made no effort to hide the fact that he was admiring my exposed legs. I smiled at him.

"You have lovely legs, Blanche," he said. "Lovely legs. They should carry you far and well if you have the insight and determination to keep them headed in the right direction. That seems to be an issue for you."

"You're wrong about that, Mr. Tilden," I answered. "These legs are stronger than you think. Anything wrong with being strong and smart and also pretty and sexy?"

"Not necessarily," he said. "But it is vanishingly rare for a young woman of your age to be able to handle such a potent brew of gifts without losing her way. Do you have any idea where you are going, Blanche?"

"Well," I said, "it looks like to start with I'm headed for the state university and who knows where beyond that."

"A good start. And also good to start thinking where beyond that very early in your academic career. You will find that it can be difficult to change courses midstream. I rarely advise students at your stage on career choices. It is generally premature to do that, and also a royal waste of time. But since you are a truly exceptional case, unique in my experience, I think you might benefit from establishing a destination very early. It might help you to keep those lovely, strong, sexy legs headed in the right direction. A career in medicine might be a fitting goal for you." He paused and wiped his forehead with the back of his hand. "A doctor. That's what you should aim for. You are exceptionally strong in science and the medical profession will tolerate your, shall we say, behavioral eccentricities, overlook or perhaps even admire them. A doctor, Blanche. Give that some thought as you plan your college career."

I would be lying if I said I hadn't thought of that possibility. Occasionally when I wasn't in the mood to deal with a ride home with one of the boys, I would go after school to the Haightsville ER and just hang out for a while. There was time enough after my last class before the school bus left for me to hang out there for half an hour or so. I'm not sure what drew me there. Maybe I was trying to get a handle on who my mother was and thought that hanging around where she worked might provide a clue. It didn't. From where I am now, I could also be convinced that there was even then a germ of something that grew into my fascination with the doings of the Death Angel. There must have been something strong enough to pull me there in spite of the fact that it meant that I'd be forced to endure two depersonalizing rides on the school bus in the same day.

Mother had introduced me to one particular ER doctor, Dr. Edelman, whom she seemed to know well and sometimes he would take time out to talk with me. I liked the apparent chaos of the ER, the action. The idea of being in charge of that scene was appealing. I had imagined myself in such a role, imagined that as a distant and unrealistic dream. But Mr. Tilden gave me permission to believe that it might actually be possible.

A few times I have been impressed with the power of a brief conversation or an apparently trivial experience to impact my life. That conversation with Mr. Tilden late on a sunny afternoon in his empty science classroom at Haightsville High was one of those times.

Obviously relishing a final glance at my legs as I got up from the chair, Mr. Tilden said, "I like you very much, Blanche. I really do. We are both probably fortunate that my inclinations to physical passion tend more toward those of my own gender. But you are a beautiful and obviously desirable young woman. One can only hope that your exceptional brain will engage sufficiently to keep you from the tragic path too often trod by beautiful young women passing through this institution. Do pay attention, my dear."

I thought that was a needless warning. I don't think anyone understood that I had no intention of trodding any tragic path. And I could not possibly have paid any closer attention. It was just that I was intent on blazing my own trail. I was unencumbered by what other people did, by expectations. I didn't know then exactly where I would wind up, but wherever that was to be, I would not get there by accident.

So, I had a ticket out of Almsboro, but I had to extricate myself from the place before I could use it. It turned out that the very thing that earned my ticket out—my brain—was responsible for complicating my exit.

Tradition at Haightsville High School (or maybe custom is more appropriate—tradition implies more history and permanence than there was reason to expect of HHS) was that the graduating senior with the highest grade average over the four years there was named valedictorian. And the valedictorian gave a speech at the graduation ceremony. A lot of parents and a few students thought that was a big deal. I didn't and I'm sure my mother didn't. I doubted that my mother would give up a shift at the ER to even attend my graduation. I might not attend myself.

Apparently when it dawned on Old Pillowtits that I had the highest average and would be named valedictorian, she blew a gasket. She convened the faculty (I learned this later from Mr. Tilden) and declared that naming me to that honor would be an eternal blight on the school. She would not let that happen. She had an abiding commitment to the honor and integrity of HHS and was determined to protect the reputation of the institution from the behavior of a tart like me. Well, at least she didn't declare me a slut to the entire faculty; at least that's what Mr. Tilden said. He described the meeting to me in colorful and possibly somewhat embellished detail.

"It was one of my finer moments," Mr. Tilden said. "'Let him that is without sin among you cast the first stone,' I said, rising in indignation at the miscarriage of justice that was being proposed and daring to use the words of Jesus Christ Himself, a personage the principal frequently invokes to support the behavioral norms she attempts to impose on her charges. 'If sexual activity,' I continued, 'among the student body is to disqualify them for academic honors, the pool of candidates for such awards may be smaller than you imagine, Madame Principal. And what about our precious boys? Blanche Nero could not have committed her alleged acts of sexual indiscretion alone, could she? Whose sons are players in this little episode? Are we to treat our best student shabbily because of her gender?' I got a little carried away. I was very pleased with myself. I fear that may have been a bit too obvious. At any rate, Babe Hedgepath seized the tone of my little speech and threatened to make the unjust treatment of Blanche Nero a cause célèbre. Needless to say, that did not sit well with our principal but it pleased several of the other female teachers. Blanche Nero as cause célèbre. I love the irony of it."

Babe Hedgepath (unlike the other teachers, she insisted that the girls call her by her first name) was a broad-beamed woman in her mid-forties with meaty thighs and close-cropped hair. She was the girls' gym teacher and my only exposure to her was in gym class. (*Exposure* is the right word since she often hung around the girls' dressing room when we were changing clothes, eyeing with obvious interest the exposed anatomy of her students.) She had always been nice to me, but then she was nice to all the girls. She seemed to me an unlikely champion.

Later that evening, there was a knock at our front door. Bobby Terwilliger had given me a ride home after school. He returned later after Mother left for work. We were sitting on the couch in the living room. We were fully dressed (or more accurately, redressed) and enjoying a glass of wine pilfered from my mother's modest stock, quietly savoring the moment. I could not imagine who would be knocking at the door at that time of evening.

I opened the door to confront none other than Old Pillowtits herself. Neither of us spoke. She looked past me, spying Bobby lolling on the couch fondling his glass of wine. Still feeling the calm satiety of the moment, he was unfazed by the surprise appearance of the principal. Realizing the implications of the scene—the son of the county superintendent of schools caught all but *in flagrante delicto* with her nemesis, Blanche Nero—Pillowtits's face took on an appearance of sheer terror. Without saying a word, she turned on her heels and lumbered to her car, the tires spitting gravel as she sped away. She was no doubt anxious to escape the implications of her unanticipated discovery. But, as Pillowtits would come to realize, implications of discovery, once made, are not so easily escaped.

I still don't know what possessed the principal to visit my home that evening. She never mentioned the episode to me and I felt no need to pursue it with her. Mr. Tilden said later that she might have wanted to placate me in some way that would allow her to avoid giving me the award but he wasn't sure. Whatever her reasons for coming to my home that evening, she was certainly not looking for what she found.

The following day at school, my selection as valedictorian of the graduating class at Haightsville High School was quietly announced. Mr. Tilden and Babe Hedgepath were the only teachers to offer me their personal congratulations.

Contrary to custom, the graduation ceremony was held in the afternoon that year and my mother was there, dressed in her nurse's uniform so that she could make it to work on time for the night shift. My valedictory address, pretentiously titled "Individuality and the Futility of Nuance," was politely received. I was required to vet the address with Pillowtits beforehand and so wrote it out as a short essay. The message was basically that potential was a highly personal thing to be realized only by escaping the ambiguity of collective expectations, something like that. I ended with an exhortation to self-discovery and decisiveness. "Discover what your personal *it* is and do it." I said. I was probably exhorting myself more than my classmates. Unlike me, most of them had, early in their budding adulthood, relinquished their future to the expectations of others or to the limited possibilities of their history.

Reflecting on the occasion, I thought that I had the advantage of having been left to my own devices prematurely. I was armed with a unique view of what I could realistically expect of other people and of society in general. Switchbacks and blind alleys? Sure. But I had the advantage of having learned where a lot of the blind alleys were. I was confident that the road ahead was unlikely to present me with any major surprises.

CHAPTER 5: THE THREE OF US

Each time I saw Ludo, I was more aware of the presence of the other member of our ménage à trois. I saw him almost every day for those last few months. We would meet on the fondamenta for an early morning walk or meet for lunch someplace and visit a site that Ludo felt revealed something special about his city. He was determined to introduce me to Venice, his Venice, not the "gaudy whore invented by guide books and travel writers" (Ludo's words). When he used those words, he quickly added, "Not that there is anything wrong with gaudy whores. They too have a place and my city is quite happy to accommodate them. She may even tart herself up in that guise for the *Redentore* celebration or for *Carnivale*. But she is not at heart one of them."

"What are you writing, signora?" Ludo asked one morning over coffee in my little flat.

Our morning walk had been longer than usual and Ludo looked exhausted by the time we arrived back at the Ponte Mendicante. I asked him into my place for coffee. He hadn't seen the place previously. I forgot about leaving my writing book open on the table. He glanced at the open page as I made coffee.

"I'm trying to recall my life and writing it down seemed like a good idea when I started," I answered. "I'm not so sure about that now. It's harder than I expected."

"Ah, signora," Ludo interjected. "One must be careful about writing things down. Words once written are said forever. I much prefer the quicksilver of the elusive spoken word that vanishes as quickly as it comes. I detest permanence and the illusions it births. Whoever invented the illusion of immortality should be drawn and quartered in a public place. We Italians have some historic experience with drawing and quartering those who displease us in public places, you know."

I laughed.

"I can't imagine my gentle Conte Ludovici contemplating such violence," I answered.

I used the possessive *my* without thinking. I had started to feel more than a little possessive of Ludo.

"I may be less gentle than you perceive me, signora," he said. "But, another matter," he coughed, covering his mouth with a bony hand. "About your name. I can no longer think of you as Signora Bianca e Nera. There are two reasons. First, I wish something more familiar than signora, if you will permit that. And second, I have yet to see your dark side, your *nera*. From now until I have reason to do otherwise, I will think of you as simply Bianca. I realize that I am taking liberties with your name again and perhaps in some other areas as well. But since I am already doing that without your permission, you may as well grant me the additional liberty to call you by that name. May I please call you just Bianca?"

He looked directly at me, imploring with his eyes. He

flashed his declarative smile.

I thought about that. We were both perfectly comfortable with my calling him by the familiar Ludo. Why was I reluctant to accept the same familiarity? I think I feared losing myself in the contrived hodgepodge of changing names that Ludo seemed intent on inventing. I wanted to know Blanche Nero, the real one. I thought that there was something essential about my name. What I was about was serious to me. He may not have seen the dark side of Blanche Nero, but my dark side was there and still troubled me in the night. I marveled at how lightly Ludo carried the Ludovici legacy, his fatal sentence, and who knows what other accumulated loads of his history. I may even have envied the apparent lightness of his heart. But his lighthearted approach to his persona, unlike the virus in his blood, was not infectious. Or perhaps I was immune.

But how could I refuse my dying count with his bright declarative smile this small liberty?

"Of course, Ludo," I answered, "although I fear you're falling prey to an illusion of your own making. If the illusion pleases you, I'll be your Bianca."

"Thank you, Bianca," he said. "You have the enduring gratitude of the somewhat meager remnants of a venerable line of Ludovici nobles," said with a theatrical bow.

There was a long pause in the conversation as I served the coffee at the small table next to the kitchen alcove. I took a bottle of grappa from the shelf and poured a generous amount into each of our cups. Grappa with our morning coffee (*corretto*, the Venetians call it) had become a habit, a sort of ritual, since that first coffee we shared in Ludo's house on a cold morning. I'd become fond of the habit and often indulged it even when I was alone.

"Why do you need to reinvent me, Ludo?" I asked.

"Reinvent? Oh no! I wish not to reinvent you, but to reveal who I perceive you to be. And perceptions change. If I am truly honest with you. And I confess that honesty runs counter to a core principle of my life. I resolved long ago to be consistently dishonest with my fellow persons. It is a useful principle for the most part. But here is a small bit of honesty. Distance. I fear closing too much the distance between myself and Blanche Nero. I fear that for both of us. And so, I indulge in this little game of musical names. It is a harmless game, I assure you. Surely with less potential for harm than the alternative."

"Is Blanche Nero really that frightening?"

"Blanche Nero is the most frightening woman I have ever met in my much too brief life, mi amore," Ludo responded.

He gulped a large swallow of the grappa and coffee and turned to look out the window.

I would learn later that there was good reason for Conte Lorenzo Ludovici to fear getting too close to Blanche Nero. There was good reason for both of us to fear closing that distance.

"Can we go across to Giudecca?" I asked.

It was a beautiful sunny warm day and Ludo and I walked all the way from Canaregio, through *sestiere* Castello and San Marco to Dorsiduro and now strolled along the Zaterre that fronted the Giudecca canal facing south. I looked across the canal at the row of shops, restaurants, and other low buildings along the waterfront, punctuated by the distinctive Palladian outline of the Redentore at the center and San Giorgio at the near end of the island. I had never taken the short vaporetto ride across to Giudecca and it struck me that this lovely afternoon would be a good opportunity to do that. Ludo was not enthusiastic about the idea.

"If you wish to visit that place," he said, more than a hint of disdain showing in the choice of words and in how he said them, "I shall be pleased to wait for you. I am certain that I can locate an amiable spot in the sun and a glass of wine with which to amuse myself."

"Why wouldn't you join me?" I asked, genuinely puzzled by the very un-Ludo-like attitude that he had assumed.

"A visit to Giudecca, my dear Bianca," he answered, "is not likely to contribute to a discovery of the true Venice that I wish for you. That island is technically part of Venice, but there is nothing authentically Venetian there. I fear, my dear Bianca, that that island and its people have greater affinity for dark than light, for *nero* than *bianco*. If," he continued, recouping some of his customary verbal flair, "this swath of canal and its borders were a painting, it would be a chiaroscuro, the dark of the Giudecca contrasting with the incredible light of the Zaterre."

His comment made me acutely aware of the light, that Venetian light that transforms ordinary into magnificent, homeliness into beauty. I turned my face toward the sun and closed my eyes. I felt beautiful for a moment. That was a strange feeling for me. I had always known that I was pretty and I suppose I felt that. But not beautiful. That was another feeling altogether.

When I opened my eyes, I realized that we had stopped walking. Ludo stood a little way apart from me and looked intently at my face. He didn't smile. Neither of us spoke but just stood there looking at each other for a few moments. He took my arm and we resumed our stroll along the water.

"And I should add," Ludo continued as though that strange vignette had not interrupted him, "a visit to that island will do nothing to advance your quest for self-discovery. Alas, Bianca, I suspect that road will lead you in quite another direction."

I didn't respond. I decided to drop the idea of visiting Giudecca although Ludo's aversion to the idea puzzled me. His allusion to my path to discovery was also puzzling. Was he playing some kind of game with me? If so, why? I could think of no reason why he would go to so much trouble to befriend me unless it was genuine. But if Ludo wasn't for real, I was not yet prepared to discover that.

"Shall we have a small libation at the Riviera, Bianca?" Ludo said.

The Riviera was a small trattoria and bar on the Zaterre where we had lunch sometimes. There were tables outside on the canal front. We sat and ordered a glass of wine.

Ludo seemed more pensive than usual and more than a little tired. We had walked a long way. Although we walked slowly and stopped frequently as always, Ludo seemed exhausted by the effort. I thought that I could see him slowly deteriorating, losing his battle with the virus, yielding to his partner's lead in the death dance.

Sometime shortly after meeting Ludo, I promised myself that I would not try to be his doctor. If there was to be a relationship of any kind, it would not be that one. I forced myself not to inquire about his medical care. I rarely even asked about how he felt. I was determined to accept him as he was or not at all. And not at all was no longer an option.

But my resolve weakened a little in the face of his obvious deterioration. He was failing too rapidly. There were medications that could hold the virus at bay if not eliminate it. I worried that he was not getting proper care.

I said, trying hard not to sound too concerned, "Ludo, are you taking the medicines? There are very good ones now, you know."

"Those infernal pills!" he declared. "I have the pills. But there are so many of them and to be taken with such exasperating regularity. Bianca, although it may not be obvious to you, I am not a person of rigid habits. I will not relinquish my freedom to the tyranny of those damn pills!"

"The virus is a more exacting tyrant, Ludo," I said, "but I won't trouble you further about it."

We sat quietly for a while. We sipped the dry red wine and relished the warm sun. A gondola, its two occupants locked in a passionate embrace, ghosted along the canal. As it passed close in front of where we sat, the gondolier's stiff pose was silhouetted for an instant against the distant shadow of the Giudecca façade, a snapshot no less vivid for its reproduction on a million postcards.

Still gazing out across the canal, Ludo said, "How is your writing coming along, Bianca? Your life story, you said. I envy you a life story of such interest that you choose to live it over. I cannot imagine reliving a life without the privilege of revising it. And knowing how it turns out? I would feel too intensely the curse of a Cassandra, knowing what was to be but helpless to prevent the disaster that seems to be our human destiny one way or another. But perhaps I have become too cynically enmeshed in a history quite different from yours."

"Well," I replied, "I finished a couple of parts. But what you say is true. When I started, I didn't realize that writing it down would be like living it over. That's not at all what I had in mind. I thought that I might discover something important that I'd overlooked on the first time through, something that would help me make more sense of it."

"I wish you well, my dear, but I long ago gave up trying to make sense of our brief sojourn among the living. I have come to believe that it is what it is and that our best revenge is to relish beauty and pleasure wherever we can find it for whatever time the Fates see fit to grant us.

"But how have we allowed ourselves to lapse into such a melancholy conversation? Shall we brave again the babble and clatter of San Marco? Ah, but I have a better proposition. We shall take the vaporetto to Rialto, procure appropriate provisions at the market, and I will prepare us dinner at Ca' Ludovici. Surely you cannot refuse such a grand and generous offer, mi amore."

"Oh, Ludo," I answered. "How could I refuse indeed!"

I stood and reached for his hand, helping him with some effort from his chair. He had propped his cane against his chair and it fell to the pavement as he stood. I retrieved it for him and watched him grasp the cane's harlequin head, caressing it gently as he established his balance and held, as had become his custom, the cane in one hand and my arm in the other. We began walking slowly toward the vaporetto stop at Accademia.

"May I read what you have written?" Ludo asked.

The question came suddenly and unexpectedly. I wasn't sure I was ready to share what I had written with anyone.

"What happened to your fear of getting too close to the

scary Blanche Nero?" I asked.

"I still fear closing that space," he said. "But I am also somehow drawn to that fearsome woman. Blame, if you wish, that irresistible shadow that ever falls twixt idea and spasm."

I didn't understand the metaphor but didn't pursue it. I'd become accustomed to Ludo's poetic allusions and enjoyed them perhaps all the more for their opacity. I could relish the lovely words without feeling any need to understand them. Much of my interaction with Ludo was an operatic experience, the orchestration more important than the libretto.

"I'm not sure, Ludo, that the fearsome Blanche Nero is ready quite yet to reveal herself. Perhaps, as you said earlier, it's better to keep a respectable distance from too much honesty. For now, I am your Bianca. I'm enjoying her more than I would have thought."

"As you wish, my dear," he said, leaning heavily on my arm and slowing his pace a little. "As you wish. I must tell you, however, that it has often seemed to me that what one chooses to conceal is more revealing than one intends. We humans are rife with paradox, are we not?"

A deep, succulent cough interrupted his sotto voce chuckle. I didn't like the sound of the cough.

At Rialto, to reach the market from the vaporetto stop, it's necessary to cross the bridge. Crossing the bridge with its unmatched view of the Grand Canal is a marvelous aesthetic experience but the crush of the ever-present mass of gawking tourists, coupled with the physical demands of the climb up the steep row of steps, makes crossing the bridge a fairly demanding feat. By the time Ludo and I departed the vaporetto at Rialto, it was obvious to me that he was in no condition to endure the trek across the bridge to the market. He was leaning heavily on my arm by then and his pace had slowed considerably. He breathed more heavily than usual.

As we walked toward the foot of the bridge, I said, "Ludo, I don't think I'm up to an evening at Ca' Ludovici. I'd prefer another time, if that's all right with you. I suspect we're too late for the market anyway. Come home with me for a prosecco and a little rest. I'll make us a pasta."

I really didn't feel up to an evening at Ludo's. Ca' Ludovici was still a spooky place to me in spite of my growing affection for its owner. And, already a little spooked by the odd afternoon conversation with Ludo at Zaterre, I didn't need any more mystery tonight. For me the approach of night with its predictable visitations was ominous enough. While I could handle Ca' Ludovici on a good night, I had the feeling that this wasn't going to be one of those.

"You are much too kind, mi amore," Ludo replied. "Perhaps a *prosecco* and a little rest will kindle more conversation. I think we have some conversation to complete and we should not leave important business unfinished. But there is no rush."

"Prosecco, rest, and pasta at Ca' Piccolo it is, then," I said, patting his hand clamped on my left arm.

Ludo and I had begun referring to my small flat as Ca' Piccolo, the little house, contrasted to his grander accommodations. My use of that term for my place seemed to trigger something in Ludo's mind.

"Ca' Piccolo and Ca' Ludovici are quite far separated for all their proximity," he mused.

CHAPTER 6: SHOOTING THE
KNOXVILLE RAPIDS

I was wrong to think that there would be no surprises on the road beyond Almsboro. There were many. I even surprised myself.

The seven years beginning that fall at the state university in Knoxville and ending when I strode alone across the dais in the sweltering sun at the graduation ceremony in Nashville to accept my Doctor of Medicine diploma were the most enlightening years of my young life. During those years, I began to learn more about who I was and something of where I came from, more of the bigger world and where I fit in it. And by the time I strode across the dais in Nashville, I thought I knew where I was going.

"Miss Nero." The Dean of Students, a middle-aged tweedy sort who wore a bow tie and a jacket with suede elbow patches, had me in his office the day after I arrived on the campus of the state university in Knoxville. He singled me out.

"I felt it important that we have a chat as you settle into college life here," he continued, sounding like he was repeating a well-rehearsed script. "It is important that you understand the terms of your scholarship."

I've barely arrived and already I'm getting the lecture, I thought. I was certain that Pillowtits had something to do with this. It was naive of me to think that I could so easily escape her antipathy.

"You are very fortunate to have won a highly coveted award," the dean continued, "very fortunate indeed. You should understand, however, that there are some contingencies. From your record it appears that you will have no difficulty with the academic requirements. That's good. However," his brow furrowed as he read from a file opened before him on his desk," there is a somewhat troubling note in your file from your high school principal. She alludes to some behavioral issues, although she is not very specific about what they were."

Thank God for that, I thought,

"At this time I won't inquire further about this," he said, "but you must understand that if you present behavioral issues here at the university, you will lose your scholarship. It's as simple as that," he closed the file emphatically and continued. "The university experience presents many opportunities, Miss Nero. I trust that you will consider those opportunities carefully and make intelligent choices."

He stood and offered his hand. I shook it firmly and said, "Thank you very much for your advice, sir. I won't be a problem for the university. I'm just passing through anyway."

I'm not sure why I added that although it accurately reflected the way I felt. I wanted to get through that part of my education as quickly as possible, shoot those rapids, and get on with the trip down river.

"I suppose we're all just passing through someplace," the

dean responded.

So, as a college freshman, a time when my classmates, freed for the first time in their lives from the constraints of parental supervision, busied themselves discovering the pleasures of sex and hard liquor (that was the drug of choice at the university in those days), I surprised myself by swearing off all of my previous vices. Lack of parental supervision was not a new experience for me. I had already taken full advantage of that situation. So, I buried myself in the pursuit of knowledge. I experienced for the first time the truly exhilarating pleasure of intellectual discovery.

I was well aware that if I was to make it into med school that I would need a stellar undergraduate record, and I set about establishing such a record with a vengeance. Success in the science courses came easily. But I was surprised at how interesting it was to learn about the wider and deeper human experience. In addition to the courses essential for premed, I took extra courses in English and history. I found some of the history courses especially interesting.

I remember one particular course during my junior year that fascinated me. The title of the course, borrowed from Robert Burns, was "Man's Inhumanity to Man." It was taught by Professor Nussbaum. Professor Nussbaum was a short, stooped, round man who must have been in his seventies. He had a rim of unruly gray hair encircling a shiny bald dome and a long, thin face that seemed poorly matched to the rest of his rotund physiognomy. His bright brown eyes darted about the class fixing intermittently on one or another student as he lectured. He paced about the lecture hall as he spoke, gesturing extravagantly.

The course was mainly about the plight of the Jews during the period around the Second World War. Because of my Italian heritage and the vague notion that there was something about the war that was relevant to my father, I was especially interested in whatever had happened in Italy at that time. And a significant amount of the course was spent on the rise and fall of Italian fascism. Professor Nussbaum seemed to have a special interest in and knowledge of that topic.

"Il Duce," the professor intoned on one particularly memorable day, "Benito Amilcare Andrea Mussolini. Mussolini was a large man with a hugely prominent caricature of a lower jaw. He was a ruthless, reckless, and stupid man who did his best to sacrifice his country to his personal lust for power. Even more than Hitler's, his rise to power is difficult to understand. For some unfathomable reason, he attracted a loyal and tenacious following. And he maintained an enigmatic power over his countrymen through repeated failed attempts to expand Italy's world power.

"The human question Il Duce poses for us is, 'What is it about our species that so entrances us by violence against our brothers?' Mussolini was not brilliant. He was no great orator. Il Duce was even devoid of the ideological passion that drove Hitler's evil genius. Benito Mussolini was a stupid, self-centered, violent, misanthropic egomaniac. And yet, he developed for a time enormous power over his countrymen. Rumor has it that there still persist, in the back alleys of Venice and perhaps elsewhere in that beautiful country, pockets of his adherents lurking in his long and dark shadow." He paused, his gaze wandering about the room.

He walked back to the podium and glanced down at the class roll book with its list of students' names that he always placed there at the beginning of class.

"Miss Nero," he said looking directly at me, "what do you suppose there is in us mortals that attracts us so to violence against our fellows?"

For a moment I was paralyzed. I felt some of the same fear that often awoke me from the recurring nightmare, that enduring gift from my father. I could feel cold sweat in my palms. I breathed deeply, trying to get control of myself.

"I think, sir," I said, my voice trembling perceptibly, "that so little distance separates good and evil that we can lose our bearings sometimes. And then we wake up to discover ourselves deep in the wrong territory too late to prevent the consequences of having lost our way. But," I added, "Mussolini's countrymen did wake up. Maybe our salvation is that we won't tolerate evil forever."

"Interesting, Miss Nero, an interesting observation," Nussbaum said, scratching at his chin, "and yet the ignominious fate of Il Duce at the hands of his countrymen was yet another graphic demonstration of our proclivity for violence, was it not?" He paused a moment, letting his statement mature in the silence.

"But let me leave you with that thought," he said, closing his class roll book. "On another day we will address our apparent need for vengeance."

As I left the class, Professor Nussbaum stopped me and said, "You seem to have a special interest in our current topic, Miss Nero. Is it your Italian heritage? I infer from your surname that you have some Italian blood."

The specter of my father's blood rose to haunt me yet again. During those evanescent years at the university, his ghost seemed nearer than I had felt it before. The fact that I was drawn to this particular course was evidence of that.

"Yes sir," I replied, "my father was Italian."

"Was he in the war?"

"I'm not sure about that. It's possible."

I wasn't anxious to get involved in a conversation about my father with Professor Nussbaum or anyone else, and I suppose my impatience with his questioning showed.

"Well," he said, "I appreciate your interest in the class. If you want to pursue the topic further, I can recommend some extra reading. Just let me know."

He turned to gather his things.

"Thank you, sir," I said and quickly left the room.

I thought about the professor's question in class and about my answer. I didn't fully understand the intensity of my emotional reaction to the question. I was usually confident and poised when called on in class. I guessed it was the connection with the very real violence in my personal history that did it. I would have to control that. And I would! But I was starting to realize the enormity of the challenge.

I wrote to my mother the same evening of the disturbing experience in Professor Nussbaum's class. She sent me some money every month after I entered university—she didn't want me to worry about spending money so I could concentrate on my studies, she said. In return, I wrote her a monthly letter.

Dear Mother,

Thanks for the money. It really is a help and I appreciate that. My studies continue to go well. I'm pretty much immersed in my studies although I know that may be hard for you to believe. I don't fit in very well with the other students. Oddly enough, I'm glad. I don't see anybody here that I'd change places with. Although you won't like my saying it, I think being largely neglected for most of my life actually worked out for the better. I can function very well on my own. I guess I should thank you (and dear departed Daddy) for that. You may think I'm being sarcastic, but I'm not. I really mean it.

I had an especially interesting class today. I'm taking this course called "Man's Inhumanity to Man." It was about Mussolini. I didn't know much about him. A scary man, that Italian. A scary man. Did Daddy ever say anything about Mussolini and fascism around the time of the war? I thought of that because it seems like "the nameless dread" you talked about might have some connection to the war. Do you think that's possible? I think you might have said something about that one time.

Thanks again for the money. I hope you are well.

Love,

Blanche

Writing those letters was always painful for me. I decided somewhere early on that I would approach life honestly and my biggest challenge in that regard was dealing with my mother. Writing her a thank-you letter that had any substance but was honest was hard. Maybe I compromised a little. It was especially hard to sign the letter *love*. I don't think I loved my mother and I think she knew that. I don't think she really cared. But she did send money. She didn't come by money easily so I guess that said something. What I really think is that she wanted me to become a doctor as her surrogate. Fine by me.

She never told me that she wanted to be a doctor and settled for second-best. But then she never told me much of anything personal about herself. But I don't think I loved her. In fact, I couldn't think of anybody that I loved. Fine by me.

I kept reviewing that class in my mind. After a decent interval, when I thought I could handle it, I did get some more suggested reading about Italian fascism and the war from Professor Nussbaum. I was drawn to that time and place.

There was a picture in one of the books that etched itself into my brain. It still lives there. It was a piazza in Milan. A large mixed crowd of civilians and uniformed soldiers filled the square. In the center of the square hung the nude corpses of Mussolini and his mistress. They were strung up by their feet on a makeshift gallows, heads dangling awkwardly, their bodies smeared with blood. The people in the crowd were shouting, their faces angrily contorted.

Mussolini and his mistress had been cornered by Italian partisans at Lake Como a few days earlier. They had been executed by a firing squad. Their bodies were then mutilated and brought for display to Milan. I looked at the picture for a long time. I turned back to it frequently as I read about the final days of Il Duce. I was nauseated by the picture but drawn to it. I was mesmerized by the graphic display of vengeance at its most grotesque. Nauseated, mesmerized, attracted, repelled. Violence and death triggered all of those feelings at once.

There have been few days during my six decades of life when I have not felt that conflict. I have tried everything I could think of to resolve it. I used my infatuation with violence and death to some positive ends. I feel good about that. But I am tired of the constant struggle. And I don't feel much closer to resolving my attraction to what repulses me than I did when attracted and repulsed by that picture. Maybe conflict is in my genes. Thank you, Daddy.

Dear Blanche…

My mother didn't usually write a letter when she sent the monthly check, so this one was a surprise. It was near the end of my junior year at the university. I decided from the start that I wanted to finish my bachelor's degree as quickly as possible and so attended classes for the full twelve months every year. From the time I entered university, I hadn't returned to Almsboro. Mother didn't question that. I suspect she was pleased not to have me around, not that she spent much energy on me when I was there. So the letter was unexpected.

I'm sure this letter will surprise you. It surprises me. I'm enclosing the usual check. I hope it helps. I don't know why I decided to write this time but it seemed like the right thing to do.

I guess I (we for as long as there was a we) neglected you. OK. If that turned out better than I deserved, that's great. But it wasn't that I didn't care. At least I don't think so. It's just that I didn't know how to do it. I busied myself doing what I knew how to do. That didn't leave a lot of free time. Maybe I didn't want enough time to have to figure out how to be your parent. I didn't think I had whatever it took to do that. And you seemed perfectly able to figure things out for yourself. And I'm OK with that. So I'm happy to know that you are doing well in school and have an idea of where you are headed. That's good.

There are, however, some other things that give me pause. This infatuation with the war and all of that is not going to help get you where you want to be. It is history. History is over with and done. No need to relive it. And, although I have avoided giving you advice because I had no confidence that whatever advice I gave would be of any real use, I offer this one small piece of advice. Don't ask questions if you aren't sure that you want to know the answers. This stuff about the war and your father? What's the point in pursuing that? I don't know what the truth is and I don't want to know. I'll bet you don't want to know the answers either. Not really. So why ask the question?

OK. I have said what I needed to say. You can take it or leave it. Your choice. Good that you are doing well in your studies. Keep it up. You will be an excellent doctor and if it matters to you at all, I like that thought.

I continue to resonate daily between Almsboro and Haightsville. I wish you a less conflicted life.

Love,

Mother

I was again surprised at my mother's lack of curiosity. What is it about the life unexamined? How could she drift through a life so heavily pregnant with history and experience without at least a little bit of curiosity? Why didn't she care? Did she care about anything or anyone? If so, she was very clever at concealing it.

That letter was the final communication between me and my mother except for a note she left for me to read after she died. A note and a surprising tangible connection with the tenacious memory of my father. On reflection, I wonder about the mixed messages from her about my father. Why bequeath to me his ashes if she wanted me to free myself of that memory? Well, whatever she wanted, that memory and its implications continued to haunt me.

CHAPTER 7: A LAST FAREWELL TO ALMSBORO

"Goodbye, Momma," my whispered words floated on a soft spring breeze out over the Almsboro countryside.

I felt sadder than I would have thought. But then I guess I hadn't thought much about my mother dying. She seemed so durable. When Dr. Edelman, the Haightsville ER doc whom Momma seemed close to, called me in Knoxville to tell me of her death, I cried. Another post-Almsboro surprise.

"She was a good woman, Blanche," Dr. Edelman said. "And she did love you as best she could. She knew you didn't feel that and it troubled her a lot."

There were only three of us: me, Dr. Edelman, and the lawyer, Calibrini. We stood close together watching the gravediggers heft shovelfuls of black Almsboro dirt over my mother's coffin. I was conscious of the rich, fecund smell of the freshly dug earth. I felt the warm spring sun on my face and the breeze riffling through my hair.

Dr. Edelman made all the arrangements according, he said, to very precise directions from Momma—no funeral, no preacher, none of the melodramatic pretense of the usual southern celebration of death. And she was to be buried in the little cemetery behind the Methodist Church in Almsboro, an establishment with which she had no connection as far as I knew.

"If you say so," I answered. "I didn't know her well enough to know whether she was good or bad....or something in between like most of us."

"She had more to deal with than she knew about," Calibrini said. "More, I'd guess, than she wanted to know about."

Calibrini looked very old and feeble. The tremor was still there although it appeared less incongruous than back when he was saddled with the hopeless task of defending my father against his predetermined fate. Now Calibrini just looked like a shaky old man with no need of the "shell-shocked" explanation for his tremor.

"She didn't want to know very much about anything," I said.

"Michelle Nero," Edelman said, "thought it best not to ask too many questions. She thought that the less you knew about yourself and other folks, the less there was to deal with. Just making it through, doing what she thought she had to do, seemed to consume most of her energy. She said that she didn't want to complicate her life with what she thought was likely to be extraneous information."

"The problem with that," Calibrini said, his voice trembling in synchrony with his shaky hands, "is that you don't know what's extraneous and what's relevant until you have the information. Then it's too late to do anything about it. Maybe she was right. Maybe blissful ignorance is the better way."

"Why did she go to so much trouble to arrange all this?" I asked Edelman. "Was she expecting to die?"

"I don't know," he answered. "It just seemed to me that she was intent on putting her affairs in as much order as possible and making sure her posthumous experience was part of it. I guess she knew she'd die like we all do but she surely didn't anticipate the way that happened. Death is a constant companion in the kind of work we do, but most of us don't tend to identify personally with it. Maybe your mom was different that way."

Edelman had recounted to me earlier the events of my mother's last night alive. A crazed gunman burst into the ER and shot the first person he encountered there, fatally wounding my mother before he could be subdued. She died lying in a pool of her own blood on the ER floor. Died right there, ambushed by the Death Angel in the very place where she spent most of the later years of her life battling the constant threat of others' deaths.

The gravediggers finished their task, smoothing down the little mound of black dirt. The three of us turned from the gravesite and started walking toward the family house.

I hadn't been to the house yet. I didn't look forward to that. I took the bus to Nashville and spent the night there, then rented a car for the short trip to experience my final day in Almsboro. I don't remember whether I asked Edelman and Calibrini to join me at the house, but they both seemed intent on doing that.

Edelman had a key and let us in. The place was neater than I remembered it. Everything was in place and neatly arranged— slipcovers smooth on the sofa and chairs, magazines lined up in the rack. Momma was a better housekeeper than I had been. Or did she arrange things especially for this occasion? For me?

For my final visit there?

The three of us sat down in the living room and looked at each other without saying anything for a while. I couldn't think of anything to say at that moment and I guess the others couldn't either. I thought us an odd group: the lawyer who stood by trembling and impotent while my father was sentenced to death, my mother's longtime partner in her lost battle with the Angel of Death. And her biological if not emotional daughter.

"Blanche," Dr. Edelman finally broke the silence. "I agreed to be the executor of your mother's estate. She asked me to do that a while back, and she had Calibrini here draw up a will."

I thought *estate* was a little exaggerated for what my mother left. But I was pleased that she made whatever arrangements for its disposition that she wanted. I never expected anything more from my mother than what she voluntarily gave me. For the past few years, that had amounted to a monthly check sent mostly without comment to my mailbox at the university. Fine by me.

"Of course," Edelman continued, "she left everything she had to you. As I'm sure you can guess, it's not a lot. There's this house and the little farm. She assumed that you would want to sell it since you didn't seem to be drawn very strongly to Almsboro. I can handle that for you if you want. She also had saved some money. I'm not sure how much. I'll see that you get that. And then there is one more thing."

Calibrini, who sat trembling quietly during Edelman's little speech, interrupted, his voice seeming more tremulous than earlier, which also seemed to intensify the tremor of his hands.

"Your father," he said. "I'm not sure what you knew of

him. As best I could tell from the trial and all, there didn't seem to be much of an emotional connection among the three of you. But your mother wanted, and she felt quite strongly about this, to leave something of him with you. She insisted on putting that in her will."

How odd, I thought. Momma had done everything she could think of to discourage me from learning anything significant about my father. And he was long gone. As far as I knew, Momma didn't keep anything of his after he was killed. Shortly after that seminal event, she pretty much purged the house of anything that reminded her of him.

Edelman got up from his chair and walked to the small bureau that sat in the corner of the room. I was struck with how comfortable he seemed in the little Nero house. I began to suspect that he had spent some time there. Fine by me.

Dr. Edelman opened a drawer and removed a terra cotta urn. He brought it to where I sat and handed it to me without speaking. Calibrini produced an envelope from his jacket pocket and handed that to me as well. I sat a little stunned, staring at the urn and the letter that was addressed simply to Blanche in my mother's unmistakable handwriting.

Finally, Calibrini spoke. "After your father's death, your mother had his remains cremated. She said that she didn't tell you that. She said that she wanted you to put that tragic part of your history away, although I don't think she was ever able to do that. But she kept your father's ashes all these years. When she decided to do a will, the ashes seemed to assume a lot of significance to her. I don't know, maybe contemplating one's own death and legacy puts a different slant on history. Anyway, she left your father's cremated remains to you along with the letter, which she wrote privately and in confidence. Neither I nor anyone else that I'm aware of has read the letter."

"I wondered why we didn't have a funeral or something," I said. "But I figured under the circumstances that there wasn't a lot more to say about my father's life and death."

I fondled the urn and felt the ominous cold shroud of terror threatening to engulf me like it often did after the dream. I tried to conceal the feeling, but I guess it showed some.

Dr. Edelman said, "Will you be all right? You look a little shaken."

"I'll be okay," I answered.

"If you need anything, please let me know, Blanche. I did promise your mother that I'd help you in any way I could if she died. Now that I think of it, I actually think she said *when* she died. That seems odd to me now, like she had a premonition. But I didn't think about it at the time."

"Well, anticipating death is hardly a premonition. It's just accepting the inevitable," Calibrini said. "Isn't that so, Doctor? Don't we all have a date with death that we're obliged to keep?"

"Sure," Edelman responded, "but most of us don't have the luxury of anticipating the timing. I envy that." He turned to look at me. "I envied a lot of things about your mother, Blanche. And, although you may not like it, I see some of the things I envied in your mother in you."

"You must have known her better than I did," I answered.

"I suspect that is so," he said. "And you are poorer for it."

"Maybe," I said. Then, "Did you love her?"

I don't know why I asked that. Maybe it was Edelman's apparent familiarity with his memory of my mother and with the house. Maybe I was just curious whether she had allowed herself to be loved.

"Yes, Blanche, I did love her. And I will miss her a lot," he answered.

He turned away I think to hide his tears. But he collected himself quickly and turned back to face me.

"She was a good woman," he said.

"She had more to bear than she wanted to know," Calibrini said.

"What burden do you mean?" I asked.

I was losing patience with Calibrini's vague reference to her burden. She was burdened with an apparently unloving marriage and a distant and difficult daughter. What else?

"You may learn, my dear," Calibrini responded, "if my reading of your curiosity has any validity, that your father brought to their partnership some complicated baggage that she was obliged to share, probably without ever understanding it. She didn't want to understand it, I think. You will probably discover much about your father but I'll not be your source. I promised your mother that."

Consistent with his lawyerly training, Calibrini was breaking his promise to my mother by baiting me to explore my father's history, making it irresistible while technically keeping his promise by not giving me any real information.

"Very well," I responded.

I was unwilling to give Calibrini the satisfaction of realizing the success of his little ploy. I was already haunted by my father's ghost. The events of my final day in Almsboro, bidding farewell to my mother, brought his ghost even closer. Calibrini's statement didn't help.

The two men rose from their chairs obviously preparing to

leave. I was glad. I didn't want to continue the conversation. I had some things to assimilate, a task I had found, over the years, that was better accomplished alone.

"Thank you both," I said, "for being here and for all that you've done."

I did thank them although the tone of my statement didn't sound very much like it.

Dr. Edelman said, "I'll settle the property and everything and be sure that you get the proceeds. It may be a tidy little sum. I'll do the best I can."

"I really do appreciate that," I answered.

"Will you stay the night?" Edelman asked.

"Probably not," I said. "Probably not."

After I saw them out, I located a bottle of cheap Chianti in the kitchen cabinet. I thought it was the same Chianti with which my mother and I celebrated my father's murder. I settled in at the kitchen table. I set the terra cotta urn containing the remains of my father in the center of the table. I opened the letter.

Dear Blanche,

When you read this, you will be an orphan in the real sense. I suppose you've always been an orphan emotionally. Although I regret that, you are probably better off than if we had imposed inept parenting on you. And the only parenting either of us was capable of would have been inept. You've done well in spite of your parents' deficiencies. I'm surprised and gratified at how well you've done. The only really sad thing about dying is losing the chance to see you become whoever you'll become. There is not much else that I regret leaving.

I do regret that I couldn't teach you anything about love. I loved once and then my ability to love in any active way just died. Having another go at it seemed like too big a risk, too much to lose. I don't think I could have stood another broken heart. If there is a lesson in that, I think it's that maybe you only get one chance. If you are lucky enough to find the right person, it is a marvelous chance, but chance is the right word. Loving is an enormous risk and if you lose, you lose something forever. Something dies that, at least for me, couldn't be resuscitated. So I hope that you'll find love sometime in your life but I fear for you the consequences of such a profound experience. Maybe it will be different for you. I hope so.

If all this is happening for you as I planned, you will realize that David Edelman has assumed a special place in my life in the past few years. I asked him to take care of whatever arrangements my death would require including dealing with my meager estate. I trust him. If I could have, I would have loved him. But I couldn't. He wasted a lot of his time trying not to believe that. He is a good man. He thought he loved me and maybe he did. I don't understand why. But then I don't understand that emotion anyway.

You will also have encountered the lawyer Calibrini for the second time in your life. He drew up my will and will deal with any legal matters that need dealing with. Odd that someone so remote from you would be your only real connection between the deaths of your parents. I have always been baffled by Calibrini, his apparent connection to your father. Not baffled enough to ask questions. In fact, I made him swear that if he knew anything about your father's pre-Almsboro history, he wouldn't reveal it to you.

So, why the ashes? Why try so hard to shield you from whatever there was in his history that haunted him (the nameless dread) and then saddle you with the physical evidence? I'm not sure. It just seemed to me that as long as I was alive, there was at least someone that connected you to the human race. At least the potential was there. And when I thought about the situation after I died, I feared that the connection might not hold. I know that doesn't sound very logical. Probably even less logical to think that the ashes of your dead father could be a connection for you. But that's what I hope. As unconnected as our little family seemed, I do believe that there is a biology to family, a blood connection that exists no matter how poorly we deal with it. I hope having your father's ashes will be as pleasant a reminder as possible of that connection. And I hope you will keep them as long as you need to.

Now the hard part. I did love you, Blanche, as much as I could and the only way I knew how. I was also painfully aware of the fact that you didn't feel that either from or for me. That often made me sad. But I also felt good about who you are becoming and proud of the fact that you didn't need me. Lucky you didn't, I suppose.

Goodbye, Blanche.

Love,

Momma

By the time I finished the letter I had finished most of the bottle of Chianti. I folded the letter and returned it to the envelope. I picked up the urn with my father's ashes and held it in front of me. The last remnants of the blood connection that I had yet to resolve. Momma didn't understand that at all. Okay. You tried. Thank you, Mother.

I left the house as it was, drove the rental car back to Nashville, and caught the bus to Knoxville, the urn held firmly in my lap during the trip. Back for my final shot at the Knoxville rapids, newly orphaned and saddled with the only remaining physical evidence of the filial connection that haunted me.

I never returned to Almsboro.

As I write this, I sit at the table in my little Venice flat. It is late at night. The boat traffic on the lagoon has died down leaving only the sounds of the water. I take the terra cotta urn with my father's ashes from its spot on the bookshelf and set it on the table where I write. I open the letter and spread it on the table. The paper is yellow and brittle, showing its age. The ink is fading in places but I can still read it. I copy the letter with careful and deliberate strokes into my writing book.

When I finish copying it, I go to the window. The long, low ghost of San Michele hovers on the dark water. In my mind I hear a faint plaintive moan from the island's grove of spiky cypress trees, troubled from their rest by the rising night wind.

I weep.

CHAPTER 8: DA CADORE

I t was later than usual when Ludo knocked at the door of my flat. It was a gray day and the morning hung long and heavy. Intermittent rain showers pitted the flat surface of the lagoon.

I had been up for a while. I had finished several cups of coffee enriched with more than a little grappa. I had even been up long enough to castigate myself a little for drinking so early in the morning. That was Ludo's fault, I rationalized. I opened the door.

"Buon giorno, Ludo," I said

"Ah, buon giorno, Bianca," he answered. "*Permesso?*"

Ludo always honored the Venetian tradition of asking permission to enter a house.

"*Avanti,*" I answered; he had taught me the appropriate response.

He entered and we sat facing each other in the center of the room. He looked better lately. He had put on a little weight. There was more color in his face. He seemed to have more energy. I noticed that he coughed less often and less ominously. I suspected he had resumed taking the pills. I hoped so. He looked especially bright and energetic that morning.

"Today, Bianca, I wish to introduce you to a truly remarkable Venetian," Ludo said. "You may know some of his work, but you must know something of the man who created such enduring beauty. A wonderful man who was so thoroughly Venetian that to know him is to touch our city's soul. I do want you to touch the Venetian soul. Perhaps that experience will bring you closer to the serenissima you seek. And there is a special reason for introducing you to this particular personage. But I must delay revealing that reason until a bit later, I'm afraid. Am I being too mysterious? I do love mystery, secrets. That is my bond with this beautiful city, the love of mystery, incongruence, coincidence, serendipity. And of course the glorious melodrama that such things feed. As you have no doubt noticed, I am infatuated with melodrama. I absolutely relish it."

"I've noticed," I responded.

"As I suspected," Ludo said, his mouth hinting at its characteristic smile. "But are you not curious to meet this man of whom I speak? No matter. Come, we must be on our way."

Of course I was curious, but I had learned patience with Ludo . He needed no prodding from me to reveal his little mysteries. He would do that in due time. And to interrupt the cadence of his planned experiences would diminish the pleasure for both of us. I retrieved my jacket from the wardrobe and we embarked on whatever day's journey he had in mind.

There is a special intensity to each of Venice's many moods. Devoid of the legendary light that morning, her mood was somber, intimate. Low gray clouds encased her, obscuring the horizon. Ludo and I walked along the fondamenta, his hand gripping my arm. Our gait had developed a special rhythm, time marked by the soft click of his cane on the paving stones.

"We will meet this man of whom I speak in three places. First, at the Gesuiti church just off the fondamenta a little ways down from here. Do you know the church?"

I did know the church. I had walked past it often on my way to the Strada Nova, Cannaregio's main street, to shop. But I had never entered it. It looked like just another church to me.

"Yes," I answered, "I've walked past it several times."

"Good," Ludo answered, "I choose this particular place to introduce you to Da Cadore for good reason."

"Da Cadore?" I queried, "I've not heard of him."

"I am sure that you have heard of him. But I am not surprised that you do not recognize his unfamiliar, what is your American English idiom, nickname. The man is Tiziano Vecellio, our most famous Renaissance painter, known no doubt to you as Titian."

"But of course," I answered. "I know of Titian but I know little of either him or his art. And why Da Cadore?"

"Well," Ludo said, smiling broadly. "You see, I have been less than completely honest with you. Dishonesty is a long-practiced habit that I am not inclined to break although you tempt me in that regard, I confess. The man you know as Titian was indeed Venice's most successful and famous Renaissance painter, but he was not truly Venetian, not a native Venetian, not one of the *cittadini*, not a true citizen of our city. He was, in fact, born and raised to adolescence in a village in the Veneto, Pieve di Cadore. Typical of us egocentric Venetian cittadini, he was known throughout his long life in Venice as Da Cadore to remind him that he was not really one of us. Although he did not seem to mind. He kept the connection with his village even while accumulating our wealth and taking full advantage of our society. So, when I say that to know him is to touch our city's soul, that is true. One could even argue that his work (and his person—it is difficult to separate the two) defined that soul. I have observed that it is not uncommon for outsiders to exhibit more prescience about us than we of ourselves.

"You will discover something in common with Da Cadore before your journey is done, Bianca. But first you must get to know him. Please, bear with me, mi amore. By the end of this gray and somber and intimate day, I assure you, you will have begun to discover something relevant in all of this. I would implore you to trust me except that I know from long experience that I am thoroughly untrustworthy. So I ask only your forbearance. You have shown a great capacity for that already. That is an unusual experience for me and I am inclined to take maximum advantage of it. You may have noticed?"

"I've noticed," I answered.

I did believe that my affection for and appreciation of Ludo's unusual personality must be a large part of his attraction to me. I didn't know what else it would be. Maybe he was just a lonely, dying old man grasping for human connection wherever he could find it. He was right that I was reluctant to trust him. But did that matter? I had decided somewhere along the way that I was going along for the ride at least. And it wasn't going to be a long ride. That much was clear.

We arrived at the church and entered.

"We are to see only one thing here," Ludo said. "It is a late work of Da Cadore and different from most of his paintings. I choose it because I thought it amusing to begin your introduction to him near the end of his life instead of at the beginning. Although the beginning may turn out to be the most significant part for you. It must be clear to you by now that there is little logic to the way my waning mind works. I much prefer being amused to appearing rational.

"But I also choose this painting, *The Martyrdom of Saint Lawrence*, because I am very interested in how you react to it. I am plotting in spite of myself to cause you to reveal something of the real Blanche Nero, that fearsome woman whom I am having an increasingly difficult time avoiding. Of course, I should not reveal to you that the painting is part of my plot...but I seem to be doing that...I prattle on yet again, don't I? Come, the painting is just here to the left."

The large painting seemed dimly lit in spite of the fact that the interior of the church was much lighter than the few other Venetian churches that I had visited. It took a while for my eyes to adjust to the light sufficiently to actually see the painting. The effect was as though the picture were slowly materializing before me. First, the highlighted hand outstretched heavenward, the odd statue in the left foreground, and the bright splash of light in the heavens. Only after a few minutes did the darkly shadowed body of the saint and the other figures appear.

I was stunned. I couldn't speak. The familiar shroud of anxiety that awoke me frequently from the recurring dream of my father's murder threatened to descend. I knew panic intimately, the emotion and the biology, but the feeling still scared me. I grasped Ludo's arm, my hand trembling.

The saint was reclined on a grill, the glowing bed of coals beneath it being tended by a dark-skinned figure. Another figure stood beside the saint, piercing his body with a large fork. He was being roasted alive in the dead of night while reaching toward the lighted heavens that illuminated just his outstretched hand. A depiction of violence at its most grotesque as a magnificent and beautiful work of art. Hideous and mesmerizing beauty; another oxymoron. I also thought I saw in the picture the futility of anticipating redemption. God will let the bastards roast you alive in the night while showing you a light, a way out that you cannot reach.

I felt that I couldn't endure looking at the painting for another instant and yet I couldn't turn away from it. I remembered the picture of the mutilated bodies of Mussolini and his mistress in the book in college. I was at once attracted and repelled as then, but this picture was also beautiful. I had spent most of my life dealing with the consequences of violence and was attracted to that. I had experienced the sexual energy that the commingling of violence and intimacy can stir. I had found some comfort in the small space separating love and hate, pain and pleasure, life and death. But I had never tried to assimilate beauty into that emotional stew. I don't think I had learned to deal with beauty. Beauty had never seemed that important to me. Pretty had always seemed good enough.

Sensing the intensity of my reaction to the painting, Ludo put his bony hand over mine that was clamped on his thin arm. He didn't speak. When finally I turned to look at him, he was watching me with an unusual intensity.

"Shall we have a cappuccino?" he spoke softly, leading me from the scene and out the door into the *campo*.

I didn't answer but followed his lead without thinking. The picture had embedded itself in my brain and commanded my attention even after we left the church. Ludo led me to a small bar just across the campo and we sat at a table outside fronting the square. He ordered two capuccini.

"You must forgive my choice of place for the coffee," Ludo said, obviously attempting to diffuse the intensity of my experience with the painting. "I would not ordinarily frequent a place in Venice named the Tortuga Pub but this is the only place nearby. Tortuga Pub? How could a merchant commit such blasphemy against our city? But I suppose we commit many blasphemies in our quest for the tourists' gold. Perhaps they are necessary. But it is sad to be assaulted by them at every turn. They are not part of *my* Venice. Ah, but I suppose cappuccino is cappuccino, whether Venetian or faux Tortugan may be of little consequence."

A young waiter in jeans and an I ♥ NY tee shirt brought the coffee.

We sipped the cappuccino silently for a while.

"Who was Saint Lawrence, Ludo?" I asked. I had regained some composure but my voice still trembled. "What is his story?"

"The good Saint Lawrence suffered the fate of many who befriend popes and practice generosity toward the less fortunate," Ludo responded. "It was third century, if memory serves. His pope, Sixtus II, was murdered during Emperor Valerian's persecution of the Christians. The pope instructed Lawrence to distribute the church's treasures to the poor. Of course, the pope's motive was not generosity but rather a venal desire to keep the treasures from the emperor. When Valerian's henchmen captured Lawrence, they roasted him alive over an iron grid. The painting is Da Cadore's concept of the scene, set at night and done as chiaroscuro. Perhaps the master's most conspicuous attempt at the technique, I am not sure of that."

"Ludo," I responded. "Is the story true? Did those horrific things really happen?"

"Men have consistently imposed atrocities on their brothers and sisters, Bianca. Whether this story is true or not, the message certainly is. I have found more truth in art than in history, I think. Fiction is often truer than fact because it is not bound by the same constraints. If our race has the potential for salvation (I mean of the race, not the arrogant religious myth of individual salvation), it will spring from our imagination, not our experience. Isn't this city proof of that? So…" he sighed, "you have lured me into vain philosophizing. How naughty of you."

Ludo looked directly into my eyes and smiled his declarative smile of fact and promise. I felt better but I was still confused by my reaction to the painting. I was attracted again to a thing that frightened me nearly to death. And the hideous-beauty oxymoron hid somewhere in my brain. I lost it for the moment, but I was certain it would reappear. I came here seeking my personal serenissima and seemed to be discovering more trouble instead. Things seemed headed in the wrong direction. And gathering momentum. Was it Ludo? Was it me?

"So," Ludo declared, "We will now pay homage to the memory of Nini and visit more beautiful and perhaps less emotionally encumbered works of Da Cadore. Are you prepared for that?"

"I'm not sure what I'm prepared for," I responded.

I paused for a moment, reflecting on the situation.

"Where are you taking me, Ludo?" I asked.

"Only where you wish to go, mi amore," he replied.

"Where you wish me to go," I grumbled.

"Well, yes, that too," he answered, "but I am beginning to hope that our wishes in that regard are similar enough."

"Where you want me to go or where I wish to go, need or want?"

"Where we can go together."

"Nini?" I queried, picking up on his earlier unexplained reference and hoping to lower the gathering temperature of the conversation.

"Nini," Ludo answered with no explanation.

He took my arm and we settled into our practiced walk together toward Rialto. We crossed the bridge and continued through *sestiere* San Polo to the Frari church. Saint Lawrence and the hideous-beauty paradox accompanied me.

'Santa Maria Gloriosa dei Frari, Santa Maria Assunta, the Frari church," Ludo announced as the church came into view.

He made the announcement accompanied by a sweeping gesture imitating the voice and manner of one of those ubiquitous Venetian tour directors (not a very good imitation, I suspected deliberately so). He pointed toward the church as we approached the edifice. As far as I could tell, it was a relatively nondescript beige brick church. Apart from the fact that it was really big, it wasn't clear to me what all the fuss was about.

I said, "What's the big deal, Ludo? This looks like a pretty ordinary church building as Venetian churches go. Explain, please."

"Details, mi amore," he replied, "Look carefully at the details—the sensuous arc of the pediments and the windows, the fine frames and the delicate tracery. Details were substance to the Franciscans. We often pay too little attention to details. Beauty often hides there."

I still didn't get it but I didn't say so.

"You will see, Bianca," Ludo said. "But first we must pay homage to Nini."

He led me to a small coffee bar just across a small *calle* that ran beside the church. We entered and stood at the bar.

The young man behind the bar greeted Ludo. "*Come stai*, Conte Ludovici," he said. "I've missed seeing you of late."

"*Va bene*, Marco," Ludo replied. "Va bene."

"And who is this lovely signora, Ludo?"

"A new friend," Ludo replied. "Bianca, my new friend," he turned to me gesturing, "meet my old friend Marco."

"Buon giorno, Bianca," Marco said.

I replied, "Buon giorno, Marco."

"Marco," Ludo continued, "I wish to introduce Bianca to the ghost of Nini."

"But of course," Marco replied.

He retrieved a dusty package from beneath the espresso machine and laid it on the bar. He brushed off the dust with a sweep of his hand. He seemed to handle the package with the care usually reserved for things of great value. He removed the yellowing paper wrapping to reveal a leather-bound volume. The brown leather was streaked with dark age marks. It could have been a copy of the Bible, a prized heirloom. Marco turned the volume toward Ludo and me. Etched into the leather were the words *Il Libro di Nini*.

"You have probably surmised," Ludo said, "that Nini, may God rest his feline soul, is no longer with us."

"Feline soul?" I queried.

"Nini, mi amore, was a cat. A very special, large, furry, imperious tomcat who lived here until his death over a century ago. As you will see from his book, he captured the imagination of many of the notables who frequented Venice. There was a ritual visit to Nini before going to the church, the visits documented by notes written in this book. When he died, remembrances from many of his distinguished admirers were sent and placed in the book as a memorial."

"Are you serious about this?" I asked. "A cat?"

Ludo opened the book carefully and pointed to several of the signatures there—Pope Leo XIII, Tsar Alexander III, Prince Paul Metternich. There was even the garish scrawl barely recognizable as Giuseppe Verdi decorated with a few notes from Act III of *La Traviata*, at least that's what Ludo said they were. Tributes following the cat's death included a long "Ode on the Death of Nini" and even a poem, Ludo explained, written by Horatio Brown, the English historian of Venice.

I couldn't believe this was serious. I thought it must be some elaborate practical joke.

"A cat," I sighed. "All this over a cat. You are fooling with me, Ludo."

"This is quite serious, Bianca, I assure you," Ludo said. "Nino personifies, if you permit me the anthropomorphic license, an essential part of the Venetian soul. At least a part of the soul of my Venice."

"I don't understand," I said, "and I'm still suspicious that you are fooling me."

"If you are fooled," Ludo declared, "it is not my doing. How do you distinguish the foolish from the wise?"

"I take most things at face value," I replied.

"You miss much of life's beauty, I fear."

"Maybe so, but that approach has worked pretty well for me up to now."

"Really? Then why are you here? Are you not seeking something beyond the obvious?"

I didn't want to continue that conversation.

"You're too hard on me, Ludo," I replied. "Say more about the cat."

"Nini is the marvelous triumph of imagination over logic," Ludo said.

"Are imagination and logic at war? Does there have to be a winner?"

"Only because we make it so," Ludo replied. "There need be no space between the two. We create the dichotomy. Imagination and logic, the head and the heart, are not natural enemies—nor are pain and pleasure, life and death, perhaps even good and evil. But that may be a peculiarly Venetian notion. We see no need to relinquish the pleasure of evil in order to appreciate what is good. An appropriate blend of the two makes for a much more interesting life than choosing between them. One can take the clerical myth of their mutual exclusivity too seriously.

"But you have done your naughty deed again, luring me to vain philosophy. Although I confess that I am more and more easily lured there of late. Perhaps that is your doing. Or perhaps it is in the natural course of things," Ludo sighed.

He closed the book.

"Shall we see what else Da Cadore has in store for us today?" he said, taking my hand and guiding me toward the door.

"Ciao, Marco," Ludo called over his shoulder.

"Ciao, Ludo," Marco replied.

"Ciao, Nini," Ludo mumbled to himself.

The visitors' entrance to the church was around to the left of the main entrance, just across from the coffee bar, former residence and preserver of the memory of the redoubtable Nini. We went in, bought two three Euro admission tickets, and entered the main part of the church.

My impression was of an enormous space hemmed about by soaring walls and ceilings and paintings and sculptures everywhere. In contrast to the Gesuiti's inviting intimacy, the Frari space was cold and forbidding.

"Bianca," Ludo said, lowering his voice in respect. "My advice, and I realize that this may seem strange to you, is to ignore this place. We are here to see two of Da Cadore's most beautiful works. The rest of the Frari defies assimilation. Too big. Too busy. We may have a look at Da Cadore's tomb. But I wouldn't dwell on that. It says more of those who revered him than of the man. It is the man revealed in his works that I wish you to see."

He guided me out into the center of the space and faced me toward the altar. Looking through the corridor that bisected the choir loft, *The Assumption of the Virgin* was framed in perfect symmetry over the main altar. Ludo took my arm and we walked directly through the choir loft to the front of the altar. We stood there looking up at the ascending Virgin.

My impression was of vivid color beautifully composed. I didn't feel anything emotionally. It was a beautiful painting in a way that *The Martyrdom of Saint Lawrence* was not. But its beauty was passive. An object to be observed and admired. I felt like a tourist checking off the required items on an itinerary composed by someone else. This beautiful picture in this cavernous cold building just hung there. If it spoke to me, I didn't hear it.

After a while, Ludo took my arm and guided me back out into the main part of the church and over to the right to the *Pesaro Madonna*—a beatific Madonna holding the Christ Child surrounded by a gaggle of men, women, and children, no doubt, according to Ludo, members of the Pesaro clan who commissioned the work. Vivid colors pleasantly composed. Interesting characters. A painting to be observed and admired. Not felt.

"Well, Bianca," Ludo said, obviously aware of my tepid response to these masterpieces, "let's walk by Da Cadore's tomb across the way and be off."

"Am I disappointing you, Ludo?" I asked. "I think I warned you that I'm no connoisseur of art."

"Oh, no, no," Ludo said, "you do not disappoint, not at all. I find your reactions to Da Cadore's art fascinating. We will discuss at length later. But we have a luncheon date that I do not wish to be late for. Am I hurrying you?"

I think he knew that I wasn't hurried. I'd seen enough art for one morning.

"Perhaps we will save Da Cadore's tomb for another day," Ludo said and we left the church.

During the long walk back to Cannaregio, Ludo was uncharacteristically quiet. He appeared to be relishing the experience. I, too, had learned to lose myself in a walk through Venice. I understood what he was feeling. It was at once intimate and timeless, grand and mundane, breathless and breathtaking. It was possible to isolate one of those sensations as was often done in descriptions of the place. But the real experience was lost by respecting too much the small spaces that separated the myriad sensations. A walk through Venice needed no words.

The numbers 1512 were stenciled in black above the ground-level door centered in a pinkish brick wall. Also etched over the door was an Italian phrase that contained the name *Titian*, the only word I recognized.

"Cannaregio 1512," Ludo announced. "A workshop of Da Cadore, at least that is the legend we perpetuate. I am friends with the current occupant of this historic place and she has been kind enough to invite us for lunch. You will be in the presence of the master's ghost, mi amore."

"I appreciate this, Ludo, I really do," I replied, "but I'm not sure that I need any more ghosts to deal with."

"While you may share something with the ghost of Da Cadore," Ludo said, "he should be a reasonably amiable sort, I should think. And you will surely be amused by Signora Zorzi."

Ludo lifted the large brass lion's head resting in the center of the door and rapped sharply several times.

The door latch buzzed and Ludo opened the door, motioning me into the room ahead of him. I entered the dim interior and beheld the shadowed, decadent magnificence of Signora Zorzi. She sat semireclined on a chaise strategically positioned along the dominant wall of a large and sparsely furnished room. She was an immense woman with burnt orange skin, a color, I thought, that looked like a severe sunburn overlaid on a base of terminal jaundice. Her thinning hair was an alarmingly unnatural deep shade of red. A royal purple shift flowed over her bulk, spilling across the edge of the similarly colored velvet of the chaise. She held aloft a white cigarette holder supporting a thin pink cigarette in her right hand and exhaled a perfectly timed puff of smoke as we entered the room.

"Ludo, Ludo," the signora said. "You are late. Too late for lunch. Where have you been? And who is this? Ludo, mi amore, have your tastes in companionship undergone a change so late in life? You should have let me know!"

"Bianca is a newly found friend, signora. I rescued her from what would surely have been an ignominious fate at the hands of our less scrupulous citizens. Bianca, please meet the infamous Signora Zorzi," he gestured toward her still semi-reclined figure, "notorious aficionado of the pleasures of our fair city and medium to the ghost of Da Cadore."

The signora arose from the chaise with surprising ease and floated across the room to plant a kiss somewhere in the vicinity of either of my cheeks. I returned the gesture. Ludo's use of the word *medium* in his introduction, along with the signora's appearance and the eerie ambience of the room, caused me to wonder what I was in for.

"Vicellio has been less than reliable of late, I fear," Signora Zorzi said, "so I'm not sure whether he'll appear on such a gloomy day. But we shall see if the presence of a lovely signora will attract him from his purgatorial lair."

Ludo had not prepared me for this. Or if he had, I hadn't understood. I had taken his ghost allusion figuratively but it now sounded like we were in for a staging of a literal encounter with the ghost of Da Cadore . I thought this a silly exercise no doubt designed to cater to Ludo's fondness for melodrama. I felt trapped into enduring the experience. I was not amused.

"I mean no offense, signora," I said, "but I'm afraid that you'll find me skeptical of any ghostly communications. I tend to be pretty deeply ensconced in reality."

"Oh, reality for certain!" she replied. "Vicellio's presence when he deigns to grant it is quite real. We'll see if we can lure him out. Come follow me," she said.

Ludo and I followed the signora into a small adjacent room. A round table with a marble top occupied the center of the room. The only light flickered from a group of burning votives arrayed along a narrow table set against a wall. Several sticks of incense also smoldered on the table, their thin smoke plumes shimmering in the reflected light from the votives. Three chairs were arranged around the table, and the signora motioned us to sit.

I would have laughed aloud if I had been in a better mood. The whole scene was a joke. It was a shabby imitation of what I imagined one of those Madame Something-Or-Other fortune telling rip-offs would be like. I looked at Ludo and rolled my eyes. He smiled briefly at me and then focused his attention on Signora Zorzi.

The signora folded her hands in her lap and appeared to be staring intently at the table in front of her. She hummed a soft monotone for a few minutes.

"*Vicellio*," she said, "Vicellio. We have a new visitor."

Silence.

"Will you join us, Vicellio?" she invited. "Our new visitor has been admiring your art this morning."

I assumed that Ludo must have told her in advance of his

plan. It seemed that Ludo had carefully planned and executed the entire day. I felt like he had taken advantage of me. But then, I guess I was a willing victim.

I didn't notice when we entered the room that a small window was open high up on one wall. A gust of wind blew suddenly through the window, extinguishing all but a couple of the candles, deepening the darkness of the room.

I couldn't tell where it came from, but a tremulous, high-pitched voice from somewhere spoke. "You bring one with whom I share something, signora," the voice said.

"Vicellio, this is Blanche Nero," the woman said. "She comes from across the sea seeking serenissima."

What on earth had Ludo told this strange woman?

"Nero," the shaky voice repeated, "from the Neros of my town, Pieve di Cadore, I venture," the voice said. "How delightful to encounter such a lovely descendant of the Neros of my acquaintance. Buon giorno, Signora Nero."

I answered, "Buon giorno, Da Cadore," by reflex before I could stop myself.

"Ah," the voice continued, "you use my other name." A small laugh. "How quaint of you. Signora Zorzi," the voice continued, "I really must not tarry today. Thank you for bringing the lovely signora to my attention. "

Another gust of wind blew through the small window, extinguishing the remaining candles. The room went completely dark.

"He doesn't like the, how do you say, nickname," Signora Zorzi whispered.

Although Ludo invited me to join him at one of the small

restaurants that we frequented for lunch, I wasn't in the mood.

"I want to go home," I said to Ludo. "Some time alone might be just what I need this afternoon."

"Very well, Bianca," he answered, "but we really must talk about today sometime."

"We'll see," I said. "We'll see."

We walked without speaking the short distance back to my flat and I bid Ludo goodbye at the door.

CHAPTER 9: BEFRIENDING PASSION'S CHILDREN

I encountered Violence and Intimacy, Passion's twin children, in that tiny sliver of space between pain and pleasure, life and death. I discovered them in that small space and for a while embraced them. I lived there with them for perhaps too long.

The perineal body. The golden screw. The central tendon that anchors the complex array of muscles of the floor of the female pelvis. The focal point of female human anatomy.

My three male partners in the human dissection lab and I hunched between the spread legs of the formalin-pickled body of a middle-aged African-American woman, peering intently at the most private parts of her anatomy. The assignment of the day was the female pelvis. We had carefully stripped away the skin and subcutaneous fat to reveal the perineal muscles and their convergence at that central tendon. We had exposed her golden screw.

"Amazing," said Seth, one of my partners in the dissection and in some other activities as well. "It's amazing that all that wonderful stuff is held together by a single tendon. Amazing!"

I, too, was amazed at the apparent vulnerability of feminine anatomy seen so close up and personal. I had always felt my body pretty robust, more than a match for its masculine counterpart. That was what experience had taught me. Anatomy might be teaching a different lesson.

I can't explain it even now, but the experience of dissecting a human body—that medical school rite of passage that most students thought was to be endured rather than enjoyed—was an aphrodisiac for me. A total physical and emotional turn-on. Maybe I was rebounding from the three college years of abstinence. But there was also something elemental about the physical sensation of it. The rubbery consistency of pickled skin. The slick clumps of subcutaneous fat clinging to the dissecting forceps and decorating our lab coats with dark yellow spots that reeked of the preservative. And the symmetry of the exposed pelvic muscles intricately arrayed about the central tendon. A lovely anatomy that I shared with our subject. The sensual violence of the dissection, the almost unbearable intimacy with this unknown woman's most private parts. I was exhilarated. I could feel that too-long-ignored lovely ache in my own pelvis. The ache took on a new intensity, enhanced by my newly acquired knowledge of the subject. Head bone and body bone connected! Mind and body engaged!

"I'm going to the john," Beau said, stripping off his latex gloves and shedding the foul lab coat.

Beau's full name was James Beauregard Whinsettle. He was from a wealthy southern family, a long line of doctors. He was trying to do what was expected of him but wasn't very enthusiastic about it. He frequently excused himself during a dissection session for some reason or other, looking a little green around the gills. He probably wanted to be a poet.

Just after Beau left, we heard it. The unmistakable, dreaded, constant low hum of Jungle Jim approached from behind us. The hum was never a discernible tune but rather a monotone like background noise: the professor's idling motor, like a cat's purr. The approach of the hum heralded JJ's appearance at our table and the inevitable merciless grilling on anatomical nuances of the area under study. The three of us looked at each other. Our pupils dilated in unison as the collective tide of adrenalin surged.

Jungle Jim (a.k.a. Dr. James Black, world renowned neuroanatomist , author of the classic textbook on the subject) was the anatomy professor in charge of the course. He was tall and perpetually tanned. His white hair was combed straight back. To us students, he had the appearance and bearing of nobility.

There were no anatomy lectures. We were assigned to cadavers in groups of four. We were told to purchase either *Gray's Anatomy* or Boyd's *Human Anatomy* (Jungle Jim preferred the latter, I think, because it was less familiar to us) to guide the dissections. We spent four hours each day during our first med school semester in the anatomy lab. We were assigned a dissection schedule by areas of the body. Jungle Jim stalked about the lab during those hours, periodically approaching a table, donning gloves, picking up a pair of forceps, and lifting some poorly defined scrap of tissue.

"Miss Nero," he said, carefully grasping a sliver of whitish tissue in the forceps, "can you please identify this structure, tell me where it originates, its anatomical course, and its termination?"

It was sure to be a nerve. I don't think Jungle Jim cared about any other anatomical structures. Since I knew that, I always made sure I knew the neuroanatomy of an area thoroughly. I recognized the general location of what I thought was a nerve and responded with what I thought was the right answer.

"Thank you, Miss Nero," JJ said with no hint of whether I had answered correctly.

He proceeded to lift another sliver of tissue and address questions in turn to the other students.

As Jungle Jim was concluding the interrogations, Beau reappeared. He must not have noticed that JJ was at our table until it was too late to withdraw.

Jungle Jim locked a cowering Beau in the paralyzing glare of his steel-blue eyes and said, "Mr. Whinsettle. Meet me in my office."

JJ strode from the room, throwing his removed gloves into a trashcan with decided emphasis. Beau minced along behind him. I thought I spied the beginning of a slowly expanding wet spot in the back of Beau's crotch as he exited the door. Beau never reappeared at our dissection table. Rumor was that he withdrew from school.

Beau was the only student to enter Vanderbilt Med School at the time I did who didn't finish the four years and receive the degree. But at the time of this episode, the message seemed to be that success was tenuous and could crumble into failure with little warning. Aspiring to join the medical profession was a risky business.

Risk was not new to me. In those days I thrived on risk.

"Move in here close and hold this retractor for me, Blanche," the operating surgeon addressed me, a third-year student, with more familiarity than usually spanned the gulf between our relative positions in the pecking order.

It was the first actual operation for which I had been invited to scrub as I began my clinical surgical rotation. The surgeon was a handsome young assistant professor. I was pretty sure that he had noticed me before. His invitation to participate actively in the procedure confirmed that.

The patient was a fortyish male. The incision site was draped so that all that was visible was a sleek rectangle of rather protuberant abdomen tinted bright orange by the Betadine prep. Although an entire person was buried somewhere beneath the mountain of green drapes, the focus of this activity was an abdomen, not a person. The surgeon called for a scalpel and cut a long incision down the orange abdominal rectangle, neatly skirting the umbilicus with a little half-circle deviation of the otherwise perfectly straight line. A thin line of bright red blood marked the scalpel's path. A resident dabbed at the blood with a sponge.

"Mayos," the surgeon said, extending the open palm of his right hand toward the scrub nurse without looking in her direction.

The subcutaneous muscle layer opened, the surgeon used the snub-nosed Mayo scissors to neatly slit the glistening surface of the parietal peritoneum, the lone remaining membrane separating us from the patient's insides. He took my gloved hand and placed it on the handle of a retractor, carefully positioned so that minimal pressure would hold the side of the wound open.

"He's got an obstruction of some kind," the surgeon said. "We'll need to run the bowel to find it."

Reaching through the incision, the surgeon delivered the tangled mass of pinkish slick small bowel. The mass of intestine writhed about on the outside of the patient's abdomen: unfamiliar territory.

"Help me with this, Blanche," the surgeon said, starting to palpate the bowel just where it attached to the stomach and moving south. "Let your surly friend here," inclining his head toward the resident who had been silent during the procedure, "hold the retractor and just follow my hands along the bowel. If you feel anything unusual, say so."

I felt something unusual all right. The feel of violated pickled human tissue was a turn-on, but living human tissue was another level of sensual experience. The violence too. The sheer bravado of slicing open the body of a living human and the warm, wet feeling of his exposed guts slipping through my hands. I was exhilarated.

"Here we go," the surgeon said when about two thirds of the small intestine had snaked through our hands. "See this, Blanche?"

The two surgical residents who were assisting with the procedure were obviously annoyed that I was getting all of the surgeon's attention. They looked at me over their masks with unfriendly eyes. I loved it. Get used to it, guys.

"See this kink? Like a garden hose. There's an adhesion here, a little harmless-looking strip of scar tissue, probably from some old trauma or infection of some kind. Who knows? But that little strip of scar tissue makes a loop. The bowel slips into the loop and crimps like a garden hose. Obstruction. Traffic jam in the old GI tract. Mayos," he spoke again to the scrub nurse who slapped the scissor handles into his extended palm. "Easy to fix," he said. "That's why I love surgery. Find it. Fix it. Job done."

He snipped the adhesion with the scissors, releasing the kinked bowel. Then he corralled the intestinal mass and stuffed it all back inside.

He turned to the resident who was first assistant on the case and said, "You can close. Let me know when you're done. I'll be in the lounge. Blanche, come with me."

We both broke scrub and I followed him to the surgeons' lounge at the end of the row of operating suites.

The surgeon obviously liked me. I thought at the time that the attraction was sexual, which was no doubt true to a degree, but he also seemed interested in helping me with a career direction. The conversation we had that day in the surgeons' lounge was mostly his discourse on the beauty and unambiguity of surgery as a career. I liked that. I wasn't that sure about the beauty part but I certainly got the sensual part. And I was determined to avoid as much ambiguity as possible in my life. Find it. Fix it. Job done. Next case.

So, medical school was dominated for me by a coupling of violence and intimacy. The intellectual part came really easily and didn't require that much of my energy. Reflecting on those years, most of what I remember is that coupling of Passion's children and my physical coupling with several of my fellow med students. And a few others. During those years I discovered that little niche between pain and pleasure and set up shop there. They were exhilarating years.

In my few quiet times during med school, I often marveled at the unlikely convergence of events that made it possible for me to enroll as a medical student at Vanderbilt. True, my college grades were more than adequate. But the tuition was far beyond my means and in those days, there were no medical school scholarships. The final stroke, the enabling event, was my mother's death. The proceeds from selling the Almsboro place, a life insurance policy for which I was the beneficiary, and a lot more in Mother's savings account than either I or Dr. Edelman expected provided me with plenty of money for the tuition. So the experience of my father's death (thank you, Daddy) motivated me to write the essay that won the scholarship that got me through college and my mother's premature death (thank you, Momma) gave me the resources for med school. Was the Angel of Death running interference for me? Did I really want to follow his lead? It could have been that the Death Angel was taking charge of my fate. But I had never felt more alive.

CHAPTER 10: FALLING IN LOVE WITH THE ANGEL OF DEATH

"Hey, Sweet Cheeks, can you lend me a hand here?" a chief surgical resident yelled at me over the deafening cacophony of the emergency room.

I was doing a six-week externship in Baltimore in the Johns Hopkins Accident Room as a special adjunct to my medical education at Vanderbilt. The Accident Room (the idiosyncratic designation for what every other medical institution called the Emergency Room) was cleanly split in two, creating a medical side and a surgical side. A triage nurse at the front desk gave each new customer a quick once-over and announced on the PA system, "Patient to the medical side" or "Patient to the surgical side," or, if an obviously emergent trauma case, "Patient to the trauma room." The latter customer didn't need even a superficial once-over by the triage nurse since life-threatening trauma is pretty conspicuous to even the most casual and untrained observer. When "patient to the trauma room" was announced, everyone on the surgical side dropped whatever they were doing and converged on the trauma victim. If the victim didn't bleed to death on the spot or succumb to irreversible shock (which he or she often did—the Death Angel was always in the vicinity), the team initiated resuscitation, got an IV going, sent a blood specimen for type and cross-match, and hustled the victim to the OR or the Surgical ICU or wherever was appropriate.

On that Saturday night, all twelve of the Accident Room cubicles were occupied: a young man vomiting blood; a teenager with a red rubber tube in her stomach getting an activated charcoal gavage in an effort to retrieve the active ingredients of the handful of unidentified pills she had swallowed for some stupid adolescent reason; a young man in the throes of a grand mal seizure, teeth clenched over a bite block, lying in a puddle of his own urine; and several other of the usual Saturday night suspects. It was still early for the Knife and Gun Club—bearers of the really interesting gashes and craters that were the bread and butter of the budding surgeons on a Saturday night. They would arrive later. They always did.

"Move that perky ass of yours over here and hold this compress while I get scrubbed," the resident continued.

I hurried over to the gurney where the resident pressed a wad of gauze sponges against a six-inch gash in the right cheek of a grizzled old man. At least he looked grizzled and old to me. But then everyone there looked old and grizzled to me. You didn't wind up in the Johns Hopkins Accident Room with a six-inch gash in your right cheek clean-shaven and well dressed, fresh from attending a formal dinner at the Center Club. They were all grizzled and old-looking when they arrived. The kind of violence that got you there wasn't a respectable activity and it didn't look like it.

The bright blood gushing from the wound had soaked

through the sponges and oozed between my fingers, dripping down the man's face and making red rivulets across his bare chest. I put all the pressure I could on the compress while the resident went to scrub and a nurse brought a fresh sterile suture pack and set it up on a bedside stand. The stitching must be done here and now, no time for the niceties of a gleaming, sterile OR. You take risks in emergencies.

I liked taking risks and even as a junior medical student had already taken more than my share. Life in general seemed like a risky business to me. I was in my element in the emergency room, enthralled by the violence and the urgency. I also liked competing in what was then almost exclusively a man's world. I was used to the guys' comments about my anatomy, of which I was, I thought, justifiably proud. I actually wore the Sweet Cheeks moniker they hung on me as a merit badge. I was more than pretty and learned way earlier to use that to my advantage. And I enjoyed delivering on the promise as well as long as it didn't get in my way. Nothing was going to get in my way. Nothing and nobody.

"You're an angel," said the grizzled old man with the lacerated cheek, looking up at me, his articulation distorted by my pressure on his bleeding face.

His eyes sought something in my unlacerated face that wasn't there.

He'd been well dosed with morphine earlier and wasn't feeling much pain. At least not physical pain. Who knows what other kind of pain lurked behind the deep cut in his face.

"I'm a doctor, not an angel," I said, quite confident that I wasn't an angel and knowing that I wasn't really a doctor yet— in those days, "young doctor" was the common designation for medical students when introduced to patients. Everyone understood that.

I wanted to call him by his name but couldn't remember it, couldn't even remember if I had read it on his ER admission sheet. Truth is, it didn't really matter what his name was. Who he was and whatever else his needs for personal recognition were, they weren't my concern and weren't relevant to the current situation. We needed to fix the big gash in his face. What else needed fixing was not within the area of responsibility of the emergency room, certainly not the surgical side of the Accident Room of the venerable and distinguished Johns Hopkins Hospital. I could handle that.

"Can you fix it?" he asked.

"You'll be fine," I said. "We have some work to do to put you back together, but no big deal. You'll be fine."

"She did it, you know," he said.

I didn't honestly care who did it. I didn't care and didn't want to know. Whatever lay behind his need to talk about the history of this incident would only distract us from the problem at hand. He had a deep gash in his cheek that was bleeding a lot and we needed to get that fixed.

"OK, sir," I said. "Just try to relax as much as you can. The surgeon will be here in a second to sew it up. You'll be fine."

"My face may be fine if you guys know what you're doing, but you may be oversimplifying the situation."

"Our situation is your face. If you've got another situation, you'll have a fixed face to confront it with," I said.

The resident returned holding his scrubbed hands and forearms aloft. The nurse, who had scrubbed already and donned sterile gloves from the surgical pack, extracted the additional pair of gloves from the pack and held them for the surgical resident.

"OK, Sweet Cheeks, I've got it now, thanks," he said.

The PA blared, "Patient to the trauma room."

The collective reaction to that announcement was so immediate that by the time I got to the trauma room, the hapless subject was surrounded by a bevy of health professionals spanning the ranks from chief surgical resident through trauma nurse to nurse's aide (there may even have been a janitor there, I wouldn't be surprised—"patient to the trauma room" was a communal event in the venerable and reputed Accident Room of the Johns Hopkins Hospital) and me, a lowly medical student solidly ensconced at the bottom of the pecking order. But the avalanche of adrenalin triggered by "Patient to the trauma room" easily reached the bottom of the pecking order. It may even have gained momentum as it raced down the black diamond slope of the surgical hierarchy. I was immediately and profoundly pumped.

"Sweet Cheeks," the resident spied me on the periphery of the action—I was accustomed to being singled out by the male residents. "Could you possibly," he continued, "deign to involve your remarkable persona in our collective effort to prevent this unfortunate soul from joining his maker in the Great Beyond? In other words, get your lovely ass over here and PUMP THIS GUY'S CHEST LIKE YOU MEAN IT!!!"

I had pumped this resident a couple of times and it was a mediocre experience, at least for me. Maybe I hadn't meant it.

I was not a large woman and effective cardiac compression required exerting substantial pressure on the patient's chest. In the few cardiac resuscitations in which I had participated as a student, I learned that the only way I could generate enough pressure to be effective was to actually mount the patient, straddle his or her midsection, and use all of my modest weight to periodically press against my hands positioned palm on hand on the patient's sternum. In that position, I could rock up on my knees to shift my weight to the patient's chest for systole and rock back on my ass, releasing the pressure for the simulated diastole. There was a rhythm, like the lub-dub sound of the beating heart through a stethoscope. Lub-dub, lub-dub. You could imagine that sound like a metronome setting the pace. You could really get into the rhythm of it. I honestly did not imagine what my approach to cardiac resuscitation must look like to anyone watching. I blush to think about it now.

I forced my way to the exam table and grasped its edge, hoisting myself up onto the table. I hiked my skirt up over my thighs to give my legs sufficient room to maneuver and straddled the patient, positioning my hands appropriately on his sternum, and started the pumping motion, getting into the rhythm of it—up on my knees, back on my ass... Lub-dub, lub-dub.

I vaguely remember hearing the resident remark sotto voce to a trauma nurse, "Can we charge extra for that?" nodding toward me, straddling and pumping like I meant it.

I was pumping this guy's chest like I meant it, bare thighs gripping his torso...and I did mean it. I was focused. My immediate job was to pump this guy's chest and by God, I was doing that with all the energy and concentration that I could muster. I was completely focused. I paid no attention to the action around me—medication orders called out by the resident, hemodynamic numbers called out by the trauma nurse, EKG status called out by the anesthesia resident who had responded to the STAT page, intubated the patient, and stood at his head, periodically compressing the black rubber Ambu bag attached to the endotracheal tube and watching the EKG monitor. Everybody had a job and I was focused on mine.

I was unaware that the resuscitation was stopped until the resident in charge tapped my shoulder and said, "Sweet Cheeks, if you are enjoying what you're doing, feel free to continue, but the resuscitation has been cancelled. The guy's been flatlined for the last half hour...dead as a doornail."

Damn, I thought, settling my ass back into the diastolic position and wiping beads of sweat from my forehead with the back of my hand.

Score another one for the Angel of Death.

So my first serious and only enduring love affair was with the Angel of Death, a passion fueled by the antipathy that often haunts affairs of the heart (too little space between love and hate, pain and pleasure, life and death). It was probably the experiences of that night and others like it in the Accident Room of the Johns Hopkins Hospital and elsewhere that sealed my professional fate. I was mesmerized by the handiwork of the Death Angel and determined to engage him in a lifelong match of wits and fortitude. I kept that commitment but I was to learn that old A.D. was "one tough motherfucker," as a denizen of the East Baltimore Knife and Gun Club might have said. One tough motherfucker indeed.

"So why in the world would you choose surgery?" the resident who had run the unsuccessful resuscitation earlier asked. "Don't women do pediatrics mostly...or internal medicine if they're really smart? You could do that. Surgery is a demanding mistress, Blanche...or I guess master in your case. Why put yourself through that?"

"The other specialties are OK," I answered, "but surgery, especially acute trauma...that's what gives me a rush, excites me. My brain is fine, but the purely intellectual stuff just doesn't excite me that much. I love the blood and guts. And I crave the excitement of working at the edge. I like the risks."

The resident and I were having a friendly beer at Arturo's after we finished our Accident Room shift. Arturo's was a little bar and modest restaurant that straddled the northern border of Little Italy a couple of blocks up Wolfe Street behind the hospital. Arturo's was a regular haunt of Hopkins medical students and house officers when they could safely disappear for an hour or two. You could even sign out there with the hospital operator in case anyone really needed you and you didn't answer a page. The proprietor, Arturo Renzetti himself, would locate you and send you on your way back to the world of the sick and injured in response to a call from the operator.

This conversation with the resident was the price of a beer as far as I was concerned. I didn't really like him very much and he seemed to place a different value on the couple of times I had bedded him than I did. I felt no need to give him any real insight into my career plans and so was just making conversation, letting him play the role of the advisor to the poor naive third-year student. I learned somewhere along the somewhat tortured path to where I was that if you just played along with this kind of man, gave him sufficient room to play the masculine role, he would sooner or later either run out of gas and slink away or entangle himself in a web of testosterone-driven conflicts that rendered him ludicrous. The latter ones just really wanted to get into your pants, and it was confusing for them to discover that the mating ritual was superfluous—at least in my case. A spade is a spade, I believed, and I didn't see the point of pretending otherwise. I thought that attitude would serve me well as a surgeon and it did.

"I really should be going," I said. "Early day tomorrow."

"Can I walk you home?" A hopeful note in the resident's tone.

"No, thanks," I answered and got up from the table and left.

"Goodnight, Sweet Cheeks," he called after me.

The half dozen other students and residents there echoed in a chorus, "Goodnight, Sweet Cheeks."

I'm not sure who they all were, but I was accustomed to being recognized even by people I didn't know, so I wasn't surprised. I waved back at the room over my shoulder as I left. I may even have added a little something extra to the sway of the anatomical feature that was the source of the moniker. I didn't mind playing the role of Sweet Cheeks at all when it suited me. But that was just a passing distraction. I was headed in another direction and gaining momentum.

As Arturo's door closed behind me, I heard a faint sound of applause floating from the bar out into the chilled night air. I felt good.

On my way to the small apartment I rented for my six weeks in Baltimore in the high-rise across North Broadway, in the front of the hospital, I cut through the ground floor of the oldest part of the hospital. I entered the unpretentious back door just across from the School of Public Health (affectionately known among students as the School of Pubic Health because of the faculty's preoccupation with sexually transmitted diseases) and walked along the corridors to the "rotunda." My footsteps echoed from the terrazzo floor in the eerily vacant early morning space.

The epicenter of the original hospital building was "the dome, an icon of the scientific revolution that ushered in modern medicine. Under the dome were two symbols, the juxtaposition of which never ceased to amaze me. A gigantic statue of Jesus Christ was centered under the dome; on the wall behind the statue hung the original painting of the godfathers of modern medicine (I thought of them as the Four Horsemen of the Apocalypse sans horses)—Osler, Welch, Kelly, and Halsted, founders of the new era of science-based medicine in each of their fields: medicine, pathology, obstetrics, and surgery. The Godfathers of the Great John. To view the painting, one had necessarily to turn one's back on Jesus, which I thought was appropriate. The godfathers did their best to rid the medical profession of the magic that had been its dominant feature for centuries, and while they may have given lip service to religion of some sort, they would not have entrusted whomever they perceived their God to be with the welfare of the sick and injured.

I stood in front of the painting for a while, focusing my attention on the surgeon, Halsted. Were he still in control of surgery at Johns Hopkins, I wouldn't have a chance to enter such training. In fact, all of the godfathers of The John excluded women from their training programs; they even excluded married men. Residents in training must live in the hospital and take at least implicit vows of chastity and poverty. These guys were probably turning over in their graves at the fact that there was a Sweet Cheeks haunting these hallowed halls.

I said aloud, "Get used to it, guys. You started something special and a generation of people like me is what you've got to depend on to keep it going. You can count on it, though. But then, I guess you no longer have a choice."

Looking at the picture, I thought Halsted was kind of cute in a fatherly sort of way.

When I turned to leave, I didn't speak to Jesus, although the enormity of his presence demanded some sort of recognition. I had never been inclined to speak to Jesus under any circumstances and saw no reason to make an exception then. But He was so damn big and His location centered under the iconic dome—a place carefully chosen to occupy the epicenter of the medical scientific revolution that emanated from Hopkins in the early twentieth century—made it hard to ignore Him.

"Okay, Big Guy," I said, "Okay. I see you."

I'm not sure now what I was thinking, but I remember flipping a middle finger at the statue as I walked toward the hospital entrance that fronted my apartment building.

I exited the front door and jogged across the two oppositely directed thoroughfares and the median that comprised that section of North Broadway, the official street address of the Johns Hopkins Hospital. Jonesie, the Pinkerton guard who served as our tenuous late-night protection from the East Baltimore Knife and Gun Club, was dozing in front of my building, propped upright in a corner beside the entrance. He snorted awake as I walked by and nodded, lifting a hand halfheartedly.

In my apartment, I took off my clothes and showered. I put on a robe and poured myself a glass of the cheap Chianti that I always kept for occasions when I was alone and needed alcohol. I sat by the front window that overlooked North Broadway and across the way to the red brick façade and the greenish oxidized copper dome of the hospital. I reflected on the unlikely path that had led me to this place and time. I thought about the anonymous man in the Accident Room whose dying torso I grasped with my naked thighs, pumping his chest with abandon. How little difference my effort made. But I did my best. You win some you lose some. A.D. was a tough motherfucker but he didn't win them all.

I remembered the sensation of straddling the dying man and rocking back and forth on him—lub-dub lub-dub. The systolic thrust alternating with the diastolic pause. Lub-dub lub-dub. I put my hand between my legs and pressed against my pubis, letting my hand rest there for a minute, relishing the sensation.

So little space between life and death.

Later, exhausted, I lay in bed. On that night as on many nights when drifting off to sleep, I thought about my name. Blanche Nero. White-black. I liked that. White-black. That made everything easier, simplified the situation. I felt totally capable of dealing with life as a dichotomy. White or black. Spare me the shades of gray.

CHAPTER 11: WATER AND FLOWERS

Ludo stood ankle-deep in the morning *acqua alta*, steadying himself with the harlequin cane in his left hand. The water lapped against his green rubber knee boots. He had arrived at my door on a cold November day earlier than was his habit.

The incoming tide routinely flooded the city that time of year. The high water was less of an issue in Cannaregio than in San Marco or Dorsodoro where dealing with the flooding of the ground-level shops and restaurants was a routine part of doing business. Although my flat was on ground level, the floor had been raised during its renovation a good eighteen inches above the level of the street. Fortunately, acqua alta didn't seem to get that alta.

Virtually everyone who lived in Venice owned a pair of the green rubber boots—the English would call them "Wellies." Venetians relished the opportunity to don the boots and slosh about the city for the couple of hours of high water that receded with the outgoing tide.

Ludo seemed especially exhilarated by the high water. In anticipation of it, he had escorted me a month earlier to a special shop on the Strada Nova where I bought a pair of the classic boots, badge of the Venetian cognoscenti. So I expected, maybe even anticipated, acqua alta. But I was surprised to see the water level within an inch or two of my threshold when I opened the door. I was also surprised to see a green-booted Ludo standing in the water in a thigh-length yellow rain slicker from the unbuttoned neck of which peeked out the orange and black and white face of a cat, its wide green eyes staring at me.

"Buon giorno, Blanche," Ludo said.

Since the day of Ludo's elaborate orchestration of my introduction to Da Cadore, there had been a palpable change in our relationship. I avoided him for a while after that on one or another transparent excuse. I wasn't sure why. There was something profoundly troubling about that day. I couldn't put my finger on it but I didn't want to discuss it with Ludo. I'd sort it out. I always had sorted out whatever needed sorting by myself. The few times Ludo and I had talked since the Day of Da Cadore, the tone of the conversations was different, more guarded, less frivolous. And Ludo had abandoned his name games and reverted to addressing me as Blanche Nero without even the signora. Ludo was beginning to look frail again.

Sounding uncharacteristically timid, Ludo asked, "*Permesso?*" then added, "and *permesso il gato* as well?"

I hesitated for a moment, registering the tableau. Count Lorenzo Ludovici, sole occupant of the terminal position in a long line of Venetian nobles, standing at the door of my modest flat up to his knees in acqua alta, nestling a cat in his bosom and timidly asking permission to enter my house and probably to reenter my life. I couldn't suppress a smile that Ludo immediately returned.

"Avanti," I sighed, stepping aside to allow him into the small foyer.

Ludo entered and removed his boots and slicker, hanging the slicker on the hook in the foyer. He handed me the cat while he took off his slicker. I had a lifelong aversion to animals occupying any phylogenetic niche lower than Homo sapiens. But, unable to see a graceful way to decline, I accepted the cat and held it awkwardly. Although I held the animal around its midsection, which couldn't have been comfortable, it wriggled against me emitting a loud purr.

"Here," Ludo said, "let me take Violetta."

He gently nestled the cat in the crook of his arm where she seemed serenely content.

"What's with the cat, Ludo?" I asked.

I wasn't pleased that he'd brought the animal into my house. But I'd permitted it, so I couldn't be too upset.

"This is Violetta, Blanche," he answered, "Actually she and I just met and I have given her that name. She seems quite pleased with it. You see," Ludo continued, "I was enjoying a lovely walk in the high water and passing by the Gran Teatro La Fenice,"—unlike most people, Ludo always used the theater's full title when referring to it, never just the too-familiar La Fenice—"this beautiful kitten was stranded at the top of the steps to the theater barely escaping the acqua alta and no doubt alarmed at her predicament. She called to me as I passed, pleaded with me actually. I could not resist such a plaintive cry. And so I rescued her. Is she not charming?"

He put the cat down onto the floor and she immediately began to rub herself around my ankles, stretching languidly and continuing the loud contented purr.

"And," Ludo said, "I named her Violetta after the beautiful courtesan in *La Traviata* in honor of her escape to the opera house steps. Do you not think that she is a lovely Violetta?"

The animal began to wander about the flat, rubbing her face against every piece of furniture she could reach. I was to learn later that this was a feline gesture that claimed territory, marked domain. I had no idea at the time how totally helpless I was to prevent the invasion of this animal into my space.

I invited Ludo to sit. We sat facing each other in the two chairs in the center of the small room. The animal, Violetta or whatever, completed her rounds of the flat and returned to rub herself around my ankles, finally resting at my feet and leaning heavily against my lower leg.

"I have missed our little times together, Blanche," Ludo began.

"Yes," I responded. "We had some delightful times together. Maybe we used up whatever there was to share."

"Oh, Blanche," Ludo answered, "I certainly do not believe that. What I really believe is that we were approaching the reality of what we share and that frightened both of us. I suspect we should indeed have been frightened."

"I am *not* frightened," I said with as much emphasis as I could muster. "I'm not sure what I'm feeling but it isn't fright. I'm certain of that."

I wasn't telling the whole truth. I wasn't sure what I was feeling, but fright was part of it.

"I come this morning to propose a truce, Blanche," Ludo said. "Will you join me this evening for dinner? I have reserved us the table on the canal at Da Fiore for nine. Will you join me? A conversation over dinner surely can do no harm."

I thought. Da Fiore (The Flowers), a jewel of an *osteria* nestled by a small canal in a quiet corner of San Polo, was the best restaurant in Venice. I had eaten there only once and the experience still resonated somewhere deep inside my viscera. And I was beginning to feel that I had been a little unfair to Ludo. I did feel that he had taken advantage of me, apparently for some ends of his own that were still unclear. But I bought into it. Maybe I owed it to Ludo and to myself to find out more about what he intended. And I couldn't imagine a more pleasant setting to explore the situation than over dinner at Da Fiore.

"Okay, Ludo," I replied, "I'll join you for dinner. We do need to talk."

"Excellent, excellent, Blanche," he replied.

The cat had curled into an orange and black and white ball at my feet, apparently sleeping.

"Thank you so much, Blanche," Ludo said, "Now I must be going. I have an appointment at Banco San Marco in a quarter hour."

We both got up and started toward the door. The cat didn't move.

Ludo donned his slicker and was pulling on his boots when he said, "Blanche, may I leave Violetta in your charge for now? I really must get to the bank. I will pick her up later if that's all right?"

I looked back at the cat sleeping peacefully at the foot of the chair where I'd been sitting.

"I suppose," I answered, "but do retrieve her. I don't do subhuman animals."

"Of course, of course," Ludo answered. "And we'll leave

around eight-thirty for our walk to San Polo."

He launched himself with a deliberately loud splash back out into the acqua alta. The water was beginning to recede.

A little past eight-thirty that evening, Ludo knocked at the door of my flat. I was dressed for dinner and sat on the sofa waiting for him. The cat, Violetta, joined me on the sofa and was curled up asleep against my thigh. I was annoyed that Ludo hadn't come back to claim the animal after his appointment at the bank as he promised. I was aware of the warm spot where the cat touched my leg. It wasn't an unpleasant feeling.

I got up to answer the door. The cat awoke, slipped gracefully to the floor, and followed me.

"Buona sera, Blanche," Ludo said, "I apologize for being somewhat late. I suppose we really should be on our way. I'll wait here for you to get our coat."

"What about the cat, Ludo?" I said. "You didn't come back to get her."

"Oh," Ludo affected surprise, "Oh dear. I forgot Violetta. Can she wait until after dinner? I would take her up now, but we really are running a bit late."

I stood in the foyer with the door open, and Violetta was rubbing about my ankles again, purring. When Ludo asked the question, she looked up expectantly.

"Okay," I said, "but you're taking her home with you tonight!"

"Of course, Blanche, of course," Ludo answered. "Now, get your coat and let's be on our way to San Polo."

"You have been avoiding me, Blanche," Ludo said. "I am sad

about that. I thought that we were just becoming real friends, whatever that means. I haven't put much stock in real friends before. But anyway, I have missed you. What did I do to offend you so?"

We sat in the window overlooking the small porch and the canal at the rear of the restaurant. This was the prime spot for dinner at Da Fiore, the best seat in the best restaurant in Venice. The owner, Mauricio, greeted us warmly when we arrived. It was obvious that Mauricio knew Ludo, but then Mauricio greeted everyone who entered with the same courteous and elegant familiarity.

Mauricio had served us each a glass of *prosecco* when we were seated and we finished about half of it in silence, relishing the ambience, before Ludo opened the conversation. He looked tired. He had lost weight. There were dark circles under his eyes. The amusing lilt in his voice had faded. The cough was back although not as ominous as it had been at its worst.

"Look, Ludo," I said, sounding a little harsher than I intended. "Although you may have reason to believe otherwise, I'm actually a very independent woman....some have said fiercely independent. I'm not sure why I seemed to give you a lot of control of my life for a while. Maybe the charade with my name fooled me into thinking that it would be harmless enough to pretend to be someone else for a while. But it was a mistake, my mistake.

"Ludo, I've made something of myself against some pretty stiff odds. I've even done some good for some unfortunate people. I did those things by depending on myself. By making damn sure that I called the shots. I didn't get where I am by trusting my fate to other people. I don't trust people. I never have. I see no reason to start now. If I led you to believe something else, I'm sorry."

Ludo didn't respond for a few minutes but looked absently out through the open doors to the porch at a gondola slipping silently along the canal. A waiter came to our table.

"Conte Ludovici," the waiter said, "and signora. Good evening and welcome to Da Fiore. Have you been able to review the menu? Do you have any questions?"

Ludo turned to me. "With your permission, Blanche," he said, "could we have the chef prepare a few tastings for us to share?"

I answered, "Of course," without thinking, relinquishing control again to Ludo.

Ludo turned to the waiter. "Damiano," he said, obviously familiar with the young man, "Do you think Mara would be willing to prepare some tastings of her choosing for the signora and me to share?"

"I'm sure that she would be delighted," the waiter answered.

"Will you order wine?" the waiter asked as he collected the menus.

Without asking my permission this time, Ludo replied, "There is a *ripasso* from the Veneto that Mauricio has recommended several times. It is especially delightful. He will remember."

"Certainly," the waiter replied.

After the waiter had gone, Ludo leaned across the table toward me and said, "There is a story to this beautiful little restaurant that I'll tell you sometime. Mara, the chef, is Mauricio's wife. She is self-taught and very creative. They are an excellent team."

Ludo exhaled a barely perceptible, raspy thin cough. He frowned.

"Well, Blanche," he said, leaning back into his chair and responding at last to my little speech. "I think I told you that I am habitually both dishonest and untrustworthy. So, I am not surprised by your concern that you may have given me too much liberty to decide the course of our...shall we call it relationship? You are wise to be concerned."

"You've been playing with me, Ludo," I said. "I'm not sure why or exactly what you're up to, but it feels to me now like I've been lured into a trap that's threatening to spring. A trap set by you."

"Yes," he sighed. "Yes, there is truth in what you fear. But you give me far too much credit. I think it is history and circumstance that set the trap for both of us, not I. And I have not been toying with you, Blanche. I confess to having been less than completely candid. I warned you of that. Of course, you had no way to know how serious the warning was. In spite of my apparently flippant approach to life, and I do find flippancy an often effective defense against the boring gravity of truth, but despite that carefully cultivated affect, I am very serious about Blanche Nero. I only fear that harm may come of it. I fear that more for you than for myself. I am beyond any lasting harm but you have much time left. I desperately want to know Blanche Nero revealed, to share in whatever there is for you to discover, but I am afraid for both of us, especially for you."

"Don't protect me, Ludo, I don't need a protector. You needn't be afraid for me. I'm responsible for myself. I always have been. I won't share that responsibility with you or anyone else."

"I have generally observed," Ludo responded, leaning again across the table toward me, "that relinquishing control but retaining responsibility is not a particularly wise thing to do, mi amore."

The tuxedoed sommelier arrived with the wine. He was a thick man with horn-rimmed glasses and a major overbite that distorted his faux grin. He uncorked the bottle, sniffed the cork, and placed it on the table in front of Ludo. Ludo moved the cork across the table, placing it in front of me. Absorbing the message intended by the gesture somewhat belatedly, the sommelier, his Jerry Lewis caricature grin unaffected, interrupted his move toward Ludo's glass and poured a small amount of the deep red wine into mine. I swirled the glass, smelled the rich bouquet and tasted it, nodding my approval. I was not a wine aficionado, but I liked the full taste of the wine. It didn't remind me at all of the cheap Chianti that was my introduction to red Italian wine when I was fifteen. I was pleased at that.

"Ludo, what happened that day that you so carefully orchestrated my introduction to Da Cadore?" I asked. "What were you trying to accomplish? I confess I felt like I was taken advantage of. What was the point?"

He swirled the wine in his glass and drank what appeared to be a rather large swallow. He held the glass up to the light, admiring the deep color. He set the glass down, placed his elbows carefully on the table, and leaned again toward me, looking directly into my eyes. I felt uncomfortable in a way I had not felt with Ludo before.

"Blanche," he said, "There is a very long story here and I

suppose I have delayed telling it for as long as I can. I do not relish this, Blanche. But let me at least begin."

He leaned back in his chair again and took another large drink of the wine. I also drank. I couldn't imagine what he was leading up to. Another Ludo melodrama?

"I wished to introduce you to Da Cadore because of your familial connection to his place of birth."

"Assuming that connection is in fact true, and I'm not sure of that, how did you know anything about my family connections?" I interrupted him, intent on getting as near to the bottom of the Ludo enigma as possible.

"I will explain that and much more, perhaps more than you wish, in due time," he replied, "and I did wish you to see Da Cadore's work. Especially the dark piece in the Gesuiti. Especially that work exactly because of its dark marriage of beauty and ghastly violence." He paused and took another sip of wine, then continued. "You spoke when we first met of watching the murder of your father. You chose a career as a trauma surgeon, constantly immersed in human violence. You allude occasionally to your dark side, your *nero*. I suppose I wanted to see if you were inured to human violence, desensitized by lifelong exposure. Had that been true, had you not reacted to the *Il Martirio di San Lorenzo*, I would have been much less interested in finishing the task I had set for myself."

"The task you had set for yourself?" I asked.

"Yes," he said, "Yes." Then, "Blanche, it is not news to you that I am dying. Not entirely a fault of mine; I have much in my too-brief life to atone for. Atone. Such a strange word. I am not religious but somehow feel a need to atone. When I learned that you, a woman from America with the surname Nero, would be leasing the *apartamento Americano.* You see the flat is often rented by Americans and so we call it that. When I learned you were coming, I thought that perhaps I was being given my opportunity to atone. I am learning that even a reprobate cynic such as I, when faced with an imminent encounter with the Grim Reaper, is inclined to reflect critically on his life."

"Ludo," I said, "level with me for once. There is no way you could have known who I am even if you somehow discovered my name and that I had rented the flat. And what is it about the Nero name, Ludo? Is this story yet another expression of your penchant for melodrama?"

"Signore e signora," Damiano said, arriving at our table carrying two plates and ignoring the fact that we were engaged in serious conversation.

Damiano placed before each of us an oval white plate on one side of which was a pool of soft polenta; adjacent to that was a small mound of tiny shrimp the soft orange-brown color of an exquisite fall leaf, glistening with a thin sauce and speckled with green flakes of parsley.

"Your first course is our *schie con polenta,*" Damiano announced. "As you know, Conte Ludovici, the *schie* are only found in our lagoon and only at this time of year. This is a very special dish, signora, uniquely Venetian."

"Grazie, Damiano," Ludo replied.

When the waiter left, I tried to return to our conversation.

"Come clean with me, Ludo," I said.

Ludo gazed at the plate before him, took another drink of the wine, and said, "Blanche, mi amore, I will come completely clean with you as you ask. But it would be obscene to distract us from the enjoyment of this wonderful dish. The shrimp, the *schie*, are like nothing you will ever taste anywhere else in the world. And Mara's polenta is like no other. She is a magician. There is time enough for me to tell you my story. My time is not without limits, but there is time enough for me to come clean with you. I will do that. But for now, buon appetito."

Ludo was right, at least for the moment. We ate for a while without talking.

The shrimp and polenta more than delivered on the promise. The shrimp were especially tender with a sweetness unlike I had ever associated with shrimp. There was an herbal-garlic taste to the sauce, distinct but subtle. The tastes of the nutty, salty polenta and the shrimp complemented each other. It was truly an exquisite dish.

And so the evening went. When we had finished the *schie con polenta* and half of the next course (*gnocchi di zucca* garnished with a generous heap of translucent flakes of white truffle shaved at our table by Mauricio himself), Ludo ordered another bottle of wine, this time a ruby red Barbera d'Asti. I had eaten truffles only once before but they were black truffles without the intense earthiness of the white variety. Maybe it was the wine, the incredible food, or the , fecund truffle smell and taste that made me forget about continuing the earlier conversation.

We ate the truffled gnocchi, the steamed *branzino* with stewed apples flavored with dollops of an intense syrupy balsamic vinegar, and the merlot-poached pears. Sated, we sat staring out at the canal, munching from a plate of meringues with sliced almonds and sipping a second glass of grappa before we spoke of anything beyond the elegance of the meal, the restaurant, and the evening.

It was well past midnight. Ludo smiled to himself. I noticed what I thought were new lines etched deeply into his forehead and radiating from the corners of his mouth. In the dim light he looked old and fragile. He coughed, covering his mouth with a spindly hand. It was obvious that our partner in this dance hovered in the wings, awaiting his imminent cue to join us for the finale.

Ludo turned to me and said, "Thank you for joining me for dinner, Blanche. Although it may seem to you that I am avoiding your request to, as you say, come clean, I am not really. I will do that. In fact, it may be more important to me than to you to do that, given our relative locations in our respective chronologies. If I have disappointed you this evening by not responding more directly to you, I apologize. But please be patient with me. You will not need much patience for time is not my friend."

We left the restaurant and walked slowly in the early morning chill back to Cannaregio. At the door to my flat, Ludo put his arms around me and held me close to his thin body for a few minutes. I returned the embrace.

"Tomorrow," Ludo said, "tomorrow afternoon, could we go over to San Michele and walk among the tombs?"

"How morbid of you, Ludo," I answered.

"Not really," he responded. "The cemetery is a lovely place and there is strength in contemplating those who have preceded us into the Great Unknown. And perhaps it is an appropriate setting to begin to introduce you to the very strange and serendipitous story that links us. Perhaps I can even initiate the process of my atonement. What more appropriate place than among the buried dead to bury my guilt as best I can."

"This really does sound morbid, Ludo."

"I honestly...there I go again breaking my cardinal rule. Well, it is time the silly rule was put to rest. I honestly don't mean my invitation to be morbid. Please agree to join me tomorrow."

"Very well, but don't come early," I said.

"Afternoon. I'll come by around two. Buona notte."

"Buona notte."

I watched Ludo walk slowly away toward the fondamente, leaning heavily on his cane. I unlocked my door and turned on the light.

Violetta sat facing the door staring at me. She emitted a loud howl and sauntered over to rub against my legs.

"Violetta, your master has deserted you again," I said, speaking aloud to a cat that I hardly knew and didn't like appearing so comfortable in my space. "Very well. You can stay the night. But tomorrow you're moving to Ludo's place if I have to carry you there myself."

Violetta said, "Meow."

CHAPTER 12: AN AFTERNOON IN THE DEATH ANGEL'S VICTORY GARDEN

When Violetta's resonant purr awakened me, it was broad daylight. Bright sunshine backlit the window curtains. The clock read eleven. I couldn't remember ever sleeping that late. It was a long, sound, dreamless sleep. If I'd ever slept that peacefully, it was a very long time ago, beyond the wall in my memory where everything relevant to my adult life started.

Violetta lay on my pillow, nestled against my head. I remembered her lying beside me when I went to bed but I was unaware of her through the night. Now I felt her softness against my hair and the contented vibrations of her purr. Without thinking, I reached a hand up and stroked her head. I stretched lazily and rolled over on my back. Violetta stood, mimicking my lazy stretch. She crawled gingerly onto my stomach where she lay, her white-tipped paws extended toward my face. She looked at me for a long time.

"What will I do with you, Violetta?" I asked, looking into the black slits in her emerald green eyes. "Is that rascal Ludo trying to trick me into feeling something I've spent my whole life trying to avoid?"

I didn't remember ever having had a pet of any kind. Pets seemed to me a waste of human energy and affection. Squandered resources. At least in my adult life I had made a serious effort to husband my resources carefully, all of them. There was no room in my life for a pet.

Violetta gently massaged my stomach, still purring. She got up, stretched again, leapt from the bed, and wandered about the room meowing. She disappeared into the bathroom for a few minutes, then returned and continued pacing about.

"Are you hungry, Violetta?" I asked. "You must be hungry. Let's see what I can find for you."

I got out of bed and put on a robe. I opened the window curtains. Bright sunlight spilled into the room, flooding it with magic Venice light. Violetta lay on the floor in a swath of sunlight. She rolled onto her back, splaying her legs to let the warm rays bathe her white belly. She writhed about pawing occasionally at something invisible floating in the shaft of light.

I put on a pot of coffee and rummaged through the cabinet looking for something for Violetta to eat. I found my last jar of tuna, the wonderful oil-packed Sicilian tuna that I had discovered recently in the little grocery where I picked up odds and ends. The tuna was really delicious. Like nothing StarKist ever imagined. I had been saving this last jar for a snack. I opened it and immediately Violetta smelled the rich aroma and sauntered over to rub against my ankles. I forked some of the tuna into a small bowl and set it on the floor. Violetta dove in like it was her final meal. She wolfed it down, occasionally pausing to look up at me.

I poured a cup of coffee and drank it *sans* grappa sitting at the kitchen table. Violetta finished the bowl of tuna and leapt into my lap where she settled in, kneading my thigh and purring. I decided to wait for Ludo to come for our outing to San Michele to return his cat.

I looked out the window at the elegant horizontal wall that fronted the cemetery island. My only visit to any cemetery had been to the little graveyard behind the Almsboro Methodist Church when my mother was buried. My fascination with the knife-edge margin that separated the living from the dead caused me to choose a profession that operated in that small territory. But I had little interest in what if anything lay beyond that margin. I didn't look forward to our afternoon outing. I suspected that Ludo, advancing ever closer to the other side, was looking for something among the dead souls on San Michele that he was unlikely to find. But I guessed it wouldn't hurt me to grant him that small indulgence. I thought, however, that I was still granting him more control over my life than I was comfortable with. I didn't know why.

Ludo knocked on my door precisely as the clock on my kitchen wall read two p.m. I noticed that because my experience had been that Ludo was anything but reliably punctual. I thought that he was deliberately late, that tardiness was a calculated expression of his personality. I didn't understand that. I'd always been compulsively punctual. Maybe Ludo was becoming more conscious of how important time was as his allotment of it drained away.

"Buon giorno, Ludo," I greeted him at the door.

"Buon giorno, Blanche. Permesso?"

"Avanti."

He entered and sat in his usual spot at the room's center. I took my place opposite him. Violetta sat at my feet, leaning hard against my leg and eyeing Ludo.

"So," he began, "are you anxiously awaiting our stroll among the deceased? When I spoke of it last evening, you sounded less than overwhelmed by the thought. But I am sure you will find the *cimitero* an interesting place."

"Perhaps," I responded, "perhaps. It's just that I haven't found it necessary to seek out experiences with the dead. Those experiences seem to have sought me out without much effort on my part."

"I suppose that is true of most of us." Ludo spoke the words more to himself than to me; he paused for a moment gazing out the window and then said "Shall we go?"

Violetta leapt onto my chair as I got up. She took a few turns screwing herself into a tight ball. She appeared to be settling in for the afternoon.

"The cat, Ludo," I said. "You must take the cat."

"Of course, of course," he responded absently.

The day was cool and Ludo and I sat below on the vaporetto, out of the wind, for the short ride on the number forty-two from the Fondamente Nova stop to the landing at San Michele, around to the side of the island. Ludo launched into a short history lecture during the ride.

"When our fair city fell to Napoleon in the late eighteenth century," he began, sounding very much the professor, "the occupiers decreed that our dead were to be interred on this island, in the grounds beyond the lovely fifteenth-century Codussi church. You see, not overly concerned with sanitation—Venetians have never been compulsively hygienic—we had traditionally buried the departed in the city's churchyards or beneath the paving stones in the *campi*. It is not difficult to imagine the consequences of the city's frequent floods for the remains of our loved ones, not to mention the aesthetic senses of the living. Such a practice appalled even the less-than-fastidious French invaders and thus the decree that located the *cimitero* here. Everyone was to be buried on San Michele...well, not the Jews, of course. They have their own place on Lido. And even we Venetians were frightened enough of the plague that we had always buried the remains of its many victims on the out islands."

Impressed at the ease with which he spoke of the historical segregation of Jews even post mortem, I asked, "Are you anti-Semitic, Ludo?"

"Oh no, Blanche," he answered, "Of course I am not. Ca' Ludovici is even located in the historic Jewish ghetto. But I am Venetian and our city has a complicated historical relationship with Jews. I do have some familial baggage in that regard. I do not carry those passions in my heart, but there is a connection with history that has some hold on me still."

Ludo and I were the only passengers who got off at San Michele. There were a few German-speaking tourists on board, bound for the next stop, Murano, and the glass shops. They weren't pleased that we interrupted their trip by causing the vaporetto to stop at the cemetery island.

"The church," Ludo said as we passed by the building and the cloisters of the old monastery proceeding toward the entrance to the green expanse of the cemetery, "is dedicated to the archangel Michael, lending the angel's name to the island. Michael is such a peaceful name, don't you think?"

"I suppose so," I answered.

Although I placed considerable value on the significance of names, especially my own, I couldn't recall any emotional attachment to the name Michael.

"It seems appropriate that the dead should be watched over by the peaceful gaze of Saint Michael," he mused.

"I will be buried here," Ludo continued. "We will visit my future home, the Ludovici mausoleum, this afternoon. If there is any pleasure in contemplating my demise, and I do not often ponder that, it is that my final rest will be in this beautiful and peaceful place."

I didn't know how to respond. Of course I knew that I would watch Ludo die, but I didn't like thinking about it.

We walked as usual: Ludo grasping my arm with one hand, holding his ebony harlequin cane in the other, and alternating his support between the two. He stopped and turned to look directly at me.

"I have a favor to ask, Blanche," he said. "I have delayed asking the favor of you for I think as long as I dare. The time has come to ask."

"Of course, Ludo," I answered.

He continued, still looking directly into my eyes. "Blanche, I have watched friends, yes and lovers, I can say that to you openly now. You cannot understand the relief you grant me with that freedom. You are from another generation and another place and cannot understand the burden of my sexual preference.

"You may recall that I told you on that first morning over coffee and grappa that my secret that I am dying of AIDS was coupled with another secret. That secret was my promise to my father on his deathbed that I would not, how do you say, come out. I promised him that I would never reveal publicly what surely has been an open secret for my entire adult life. It was a silly promise to a dying old man but I have kept it until now with you.

"I made another promise to my father that I will reveal to you as well...but the favor, the favor I wish to ask of you. As I started to say, I have watched the virus ravage the bodies and minds of people whom I loved. I have watched the agony and the dementia, helpless to respond in any way that could make a difference. I wish to avoid that fate, Blanche. I wish to declare defeat before then, to cheat the virus of its most sinister work. But I fear that I will lack the will, the physical strength, or the means to do it. I am asking, pleading, with you to assure me that you will see that I am spared the terminal pain and indignity. Can you grant me that?"

I was aghast. I was a doctor. In spite of my fascination with death, I had dedicated myself to doing everything in my power to preserve life. I was honor-bound to do that. Ludo had lured me into this fatal ménage à trois and I was doing that dance with him. But I didn't see how I could promise to put him out of his misery even when the misery became too great to bear.

I could understand. In the same situation, I'm quite sure that I'd have the same wish. In fact, I thought the wish entirely rational. I'd wrestled with that issue some at the Big Free when the fury of Katrina hit. Human misery is not a pretty sight, especially hopeless misery that presses against the boundaries of human tolerance. I was very fond of Ludo, more fond than I would have chosen to be. Or maybe I did choose to be without weighing the consequences. I didn't look forward to watching him die the wretched death that I knew all too well awaited him. I dreaded that. I dreaded that for both of us.

I took Ludo's hand and started us walking along the gravel path that meandered among the gravestones. I didn't say anything for a while and Ludo didn't press.

At last I said, "I don't know how to answer you, Ludo. While it would be difficult to see you miserable, I'm sworn to work with the forces on the other side."

Ludo answered, not looking at me this time, but letting the words waft out over the graves of the dead, "Whether by choice or circumstance, Blanche, you are in league with the Death Angel. And you are giving him the upper hand."

"How can you say that, Ludo?" I was surprised and hurt by his statement, "I've spent my life working on the side of the living."

"As you are well aware, mi amore," Ludo answered, "life is a fatal condition. Our date with the grim reaper is inevitable. But must it be on his terms? Is it not possible that your dogged commitment to prolonging life is doing his bidding, enabling the worst of his arsenal of tortures?"

So little space between life and death.

I gripped Ludo's hand, squeezing his bony fingers.

"I will do everything I can to see that you do not suffer too much, mi amore," I said the words without fully appreciating their meaning.

It was the first time I had spoken to Ludo of love. The two words that he used so casually burned my lips as I spoke them.

A broad smile opened on Ludo's face. "Thank you Blanche," he said, "I am forever in your debt…well the limits on my forever may permit less repayment for your kindness than it deserves."

He laughed quietly to himself and the laugh degenerated into a deep wet cough that interrupted our walk for what seemed like several minutes.

When the cough subsided, Ludo put his arms around me and held me tightly to him for a while. When we separated there were tears on both our faces. I remembered crying several decades earlier when Dr. Edelman told me of my mother's death. As then, these tears surprised me.

Ludo took hold of my arm and we resumed our stroll without speaking. It seemed as though he was guiding us along a particular path. After a while we arrived at a grave with a flat stone marker. It was the grave of Ezra Pound. He released my arm and with ceremonial precision, placed the cane in front of him and leaned on it with both hands, standing erect and staring at the gravestone. After a long pause he spoke.

"Ezra Pound," he said, "one of the few notables buried here," he paused again, shifting his weight on the cane. "Ezra Pound was not a good man," he continued, "Like many others he was seduced by Mussolini and his fascist notions. It is odd how notoriety attracts us, is it not? Notoriety seems to take on an unexamined life of its own. Someone once spoke of the tyranny of the prevailing paradigm. I suppose there is truth in that. I met Mr. Pound once, in my father's house. He seemed such a benign man when I met him."

"You met him in your father's house?" I asked, surprised.

I knew little of Ezra Pound except that he had been a poet of some note. I didn't know that he was a fascist and wondered about the connection with Ludo's family.

"Yes," Ludo sighed.

He continued, "I wanted us to visit Pound's grave. And the Ludovici mausoleum. It is nearby. He and my father were friends."

We walked the few yards to the mausoleum. It was a large marble structure, with garish carved angels guarding the entrance. The experience was beginning to feel like something from a horror movie. I half expected ghosts to float from the tomb and moans of the dead to rise from their graves. A dark cloud drifted across the distant western sun sinking toward the Venice skyline beyond the lagoon.

"My final resting place," Ludo said. "I will be buried here next to a father with whom I shared too little and to whom I promised too much."

I wanted to ask a thousand questions. But Ludo seemed in no mood for questions. They would have to wait.

"I wished you to accompany me here for good reason, Blanche. If I am to come clean with you as you wish, you need to know some of the story that is buried in this gaudy tomb a stone's throw from the grave of the fascist poet. I will recount that story to you. But I am very tired this afternoon and if you will permit some delay, I would prefer to save the story for another time."

"Of course, Ludo," I said.

He did look very tired. I hadn't noticed that until now. He took my arm and leaned heavily against me.

"Shall we return home?" he said.

We made our way slowly back to the vaporetto stop, bobbing together from side to side along the gravel paths. A chill sharpened the edges of the breeze freshening in the late afternoon dusk. The evergreens rustled in the wind. A wave of incredible sadness washed over me as we walked. I fought back those unfamiliar tears again. I didn't like the feeling.

Safely seated aboard the vaporetto, I said, "This really was a morbid idea, Ludo. Shouldn't we try to enjoy what time we have? Why prolong the agony?"

"We will do that," he responded with apparent resolution, "But there are some unpleasantries that we need to get out of the way. I seem to be having a great deal of trouble addressing those unpleasantries directly. Bear with me a bit. Unburdened....if we can relieve ourselves of the burden we have been given, there could yet be more pleasure for us. I confess to being a practiced procrastinator, but I will get to it. Maybe tomorrow."

When we arrived back at my door, I invited Ludo in for a drink and he accepted with some reluctance. He looked exhausted and had said little on the walk from the vaporetto stop up the fondamenta. He took the steps of the single bridge we had to cross with difficulty, pulling himself up with the handrail and placing his feet with great care as we descended the other side. We sat nursing a grappa. Violetta came to rest at my feet.

Ludo stared at Violetta and said, "I must take Violetta home with me, Blanche. She is beginning to look much too comfortable here with you. You seem to hold a special attraction for her."

"I fed her tuna earlier," I responded, "Maybe that's the attraction."

"Perhaps," Ludo answered.

He got up from the chair with some difficulty and said, "Come, Violetta, we must retire to the lonely confines of our palazzo."

I retrieved Ludo's coat from the foyer and helped him on with it. It was the green cashmere topcoat that he wore on our first meeting in the piazza and it hung even more loosely on him than it did then. Ludo was wasting away. I picked up the cat and placed her in the crook of his arm where she rested but continued to stare at me. I handed Ludo his cane and ushered him gently out into the *corte*.

"Buona notte," I said.

"Buona notte."

Violetta strained to peer at me looking back over Ludo's shoulder.

The knock on my door didn't awaken me. I had tossed and turned through the night, unable to free my mind of the experience of the day. When I did doze off sometime long past midnight, the dream descended on me in all its terrible glory. I awakened from the dream and sat up in bed trying to compose myself. I looked at the clock and it read four a.m. The knock persisted.

I got out of bed, put on a robe and opened the door. Ludo stood there holding the cat who glared at me for a moment, then leapt from his arms and ran into the flat.

"Do pardon me for the intrusion, Blanche," Ludo said, "but Violetta has been impossible. Since I took her upstairs, she has not ceased to howl throughout the night sitting at the front door. I could not sleep for her noisemaking. Violetta is not at all happy in Ca' Ludovici. She seemed so content here. So I return with a plea that you at least allow me a bit of sleep by keeping Violetta for a few hours."

"Did you try tuna?" I asked.

"Yes, of course," Ludo replied. "She steadfastly refused to eat a single bite."

"Very well," I answered, "It's too early in the morning to debate this and I haven't slept much either. Leave her and we can talk about what to do with her tomorrow."

"I am forever in your debt, mi amore," Ludo replied. "Buona notte once again."

"Buona notte."

When I closed the door and reentered the apartment, Violetta was curled up on the bed carefully positioned just next to the impression I'd left in the bedclothes. I took off my robe and lay back down. The cat nestled beside me, touching my thigh. That sensation is the last thing I remembered until the sun and Violetta's resonant purr awoke me at noon.

CHAPTER 13: MOUNTING THE SHOULDERS OF GIANTS

When I crossed the dais on the Vanderbilt University lawn in the searing late spring sun and received my doctor of medicine degree, I knew exactly where I was going next. I also thought I knew where I was going with my career. But there would be more surprises.

I had spent a harrowing day in the ER, an elective rotation for especially masochistic senior med students; most students considered the end of their senior year a time for doing something much less demanding, such as a stint in the psychiatry clinic or a research elective. When I arrived at my apartment house well past ten in the evening and removed the beige envelope from my mailbox, it didn't strike me at first as anything special. That is, not until I read the return address: Office of the Chair, Department of Surgery, The Johns Hopkins Hospital, 600 North Wolfe Street, Baltimore, Maryland 21287.

I sat down on the floor in front of the panel of mailboxes and carefully slit open the envelope with a forefinger. This letter was to chart the course of my professional life, one way or the other. Either I was accepted into the most prestigious, oldest, and most competitive surgical residency training program in the country or not. If so, the doors to my future career were opened. If not, I would have to devise a plan B. I hadn't thought about a plan B. Against the advice of peers and mentors, I had only applied to Hopkins, no backup. I'm not sure if that was arrogance or just naïve single-mindedness, but since my externship there, I couldn't imagine another comparable training experience. I was determined to be the best trauma surgeon possible and that meant getting the best possible training. It had to be Hopkins. I wouldn't settle for less.

The letter, signed by the legendary William Robert Fathergill, MD, PhD, Chair, Department of Surgery, welcomed me to the incoming class of Hopkins surgical interns. While I was elated at the news, as I recall that seminal moment in my life, I wasn't surprised. I had expected it, counted on it even. I can't explain the arrogance of that even now.

In addition to the necessary formalities, Dr. Fathergill's letter read:

You have been singled out from among your peers to benefit from the rich legacy of surgical discovery and practice that built the Johns Hopkins program. From your privileged vantage point on the shoulders of the giants of American surgery who preceded you, you will view new horizons. You are given a rare opportunity and with it the responsibility to perpetuate our unique tradition. As an introduction, you will shortly receive my biography of William Stewart Halsted, the founder of modern surgery and the father of the Hopkins program. I look forward to working with you.

I remembered being struck with the appearance of William Halsted in the famous painting of the institution's four founders that hung opposite the statue of Jesus beneath the dome of the Hopkins Hospital. Dr. Fathergill's biography of the famous surgeon piqued my interest in the man. I spent some time during the month between med school graduation and the start of my internship learning more about the famous Dr. Halsted.

Fathergill's book was a disappointment. It was a rambling tribute to someone the author imagined, a cardboard saint of a character unencumbered by humanity. But some additional research was revealing. It turned out that this giant from whose shoulders I was supposed to view new horizons was less saintly than Dr. Fathergill's hagiography suggested.

Halsted was a genius. He was an early champion of sterile surgical technique (asepsis); he removed the first gallbladder from a living human (his sister, the pioneering cholecystectomy done on the kitchen table); he invented the radical mastectomy for the previously uniformly fatal disease of breast cancer; he invented local anesthesia; and, at Hopkins, started the first formal science-based training program for future surgeons. But he was a cocaine and morphine addict, a victim of the very chemicals that he discovered could modulate human suffering. William Welch, another of the four Hopkins founding fathers, brought Halsted to Hopkins from New York where his stellar reputation was suffering from his addictions and deteriorating skills. Welch banished Halsted to a pathology laboratory for a couple of years to sober up. He sobered up at least enough to regain sufficient surgical prowess to be named chief surgeon when Hopkins Hospital opened in 1889, and American medicine was changed forever. Halsted helped to make that happen. He was a giant, but he was no saint. I was pleased to learn that saintliness was not a requirement for success in my chosen career. To discover otherwise would have been more than a little disconcerting.

It was ungodly hot in Baltimore that summer. My internship started at the stroke of midnight on the hottest June thirtieth in the city's recorded history. The air-conditioning in my apartment in the 550 North Broadway building, just across from the hospital, wasn't working for reasons that were never explained. I was to learn that this was a recurring malfunction that defied explanation by the best minds that Johns Hopkins University could call upon to address the problem.

When my phone rang at approximately twelve fifteen a.m. on July 1, I lay in bed naked, sweat-soaked, and wide-awake. The resident on the phone informed me that we had an emergency case and that I was to be in the OR scrubbed in fifteen minutes. He was on his way there from the Accident Room with the patient. I was second call, but the intern who was first call was tied up with another case. Apparently it was a busy night in Baltimore.

This was the reason I was there: my first case as a real doctor. As a surgical intern I occupied a place in the hierarchy only slightly higher than that of a medical student, but it felt different. I was part of the team now. The fun and games were over. This was the real deal.

"This is a forty-year-old veteran of the East Baltimore Knife and Gun Club," the resident described the case to me as we were scrubbing. "He took a couple of shots to the abdomen and he's got some serious internal bleeding. We've pumped in seven or eight units of packed cells, maybe more, I'm not sure. His liver chemistries are a mess but his platelet count is OK. He was in shock for who knows how long when he arrived but we've at least got a blood pressure now. We'll need to work fast."

The resident's name was Donald Little, a name at odds with his well-over-six-foot frame. He was a senior assistant surgical resident, three years into his postgraduate training. I learned later that he was a Mormon. I don't know why I remember that or why it seems important.

"You'll be first assistant on the case," he continued. "We're short-staffed so we'll have an anesthesiology resident, a scrub nurse, and a circulator but the surgery is up to me and you. Think you can handle it, Dr. Nero?"

"I can handle it," I replied, thrilled at having the title attached to my name for the first time that I remember.

The patient was intubated and anesthetized when we entered the OR. He lay naked on his back on the operating table, his chest oscillating in time with the sigh of the respirator. A bored-looking anesthesiology resident sat at his head, glancing periodically at the vital signs monitor. The patient's abdomen had been shaved in the Accident Room or someplace on his way to the OR.

"Prep and drape his belly," the resident instructed.

I put on a pair of gloves and dipped a square of gauze sponges held in a long clamp into a stainless steel bowl of Betadine, slathering the bright-orange solution over the patient's stomach. I clamped the green drapes in place around the perimeter of the operating field. I changed gloves with the help of the scrub nurse and rested my hands on the patient's now technically sterile stomach. A healed surgical scar ran down the middle of the field, exactly where the new incision should be made. The resident donned a fresh pair of gloves and joined me on the opposite side of the table.

"As you can see," he said, "this gentleman's abdomen is not exactly virgin territory. That means he'll probably have adhesions. Adhesions tend to bleed a lot and what with his liver function and the fact that most of his blood is of the stored variety, lacking essential clotting factors, it'll probably be a bloody mess in there. I called for some fresh frozen plasma but I'm not sure how much is available. It's been a busy night."

"Scalpel," he said; the scrub nurse slapped the scalpel handle into his palm.

He made a long incision parallel to the healed one. Blood oozed from a thousand spots along the surface of the incision.

"Clamp those bleeders," he said.

I took a stack of mosquito clamps from the scrub nurse and threaded them on the little finger of my right hand, swiveling them one at a time into my palm as I located and clamped the source of as many of the bleeders as possible along the incision. I dabbed at the blood with a gauze sponge with one hand and snapped the small clamps on the bleeding spots with the other. The result was a linear array of mosquito clamps neatly aligned along either side of the incision.

"Cautery," Little said.

I grasped the cautery handle and zapped each of the clamps as Little held them up. There was a rhythm to the procedure. Zap click, zap click, zap click as I touched the cautery to each of the clamps and he removed them.

Inside, this gentleman's belly was indeed a bloody mess.

"Suction," Little said, impatience creeping into his voice.

There was a sea of fresh-looking blood in which floated islands of livery, dark, slimy magenta semi-clot. The suction tip clogged intermittently with the clots. Gradually, the field began to clear a bit but fresh blood was welling up almost as fast as the suction could remove it.

"Got to find the source," Little said, then to the anesthesia resident sitting mute at the patient's head, "How's he doing?"

"EKG looks OK," the anesthesiologist replied, "but his blood pressure looks a little iffy."

"Let me know if it starts falling," Little responded.

"Can't fall much further," was the halfhearted answer.

"Keep suctioning," Little commanded me.

He rummaged around among the abdominal organs with his hands.

"Looks like he's got a small laceration of the left lobe of his liver, see that?" he lifted the edge of the liver to expose the tear. "But not enough bleeding to explain all of this."

The suction was still struggling to keep up with the accumulating blood.

He moved his exploration to the left side of the abdomen, exposing the surface of the spleen.

"Here's the problem," he said. "Look at this!"

The spleen was almost bisected across the middle and blood was pouring from the wound.

"Kelly," Little called to the scrub nurse, requesting an instrument that bore the name of one of Hopkins Founding Fathers.

The shoulders of giants.

He lifted the wounded spleen, guiding my hands to support

the organ in a position that exposed the splenic blood vessels. He applied a Kelly clamp to each of the vessels. The bleeding slowed and then stopped. I suctioned the field, which slowly cleared of blood.

"Okay," he said, "Now we can catch our breath."

I noticed the beads of sweat on Little's broad forehead.

The pace of the procedure slowed, absent the life and death urgency of rapidly accumulating blood. We proceeded to tie off the splenic vessels and remove the spleen.

After suturing the small laceration in the liver, Little said, "We better have a look at his bowel. We don't know how long he was in shock. He could have infarcted his bowel. We wouldn't want to miss that while we're in the neighborhood."

Running the bowel was tedious. Progress was often obstructed by numerous adhesions between loops of bowel and more adhesions tethering parts of the bowel to the abdominal wall. It took a while.

"Here," Little said, fondling a segment of small intestine, "see how pale this looks? It's not infarcted but probably ischemic. Not much blood getting to that spot."

"How's his blood pressure?" he asked the anesthesiologist.

"Holding steady."

"Should you resect it?" I asked, referring to the segment of pale bowel.

"Nah," he answered, "not just for ischemia. Maybe it will get enough blood supply to keep the tissue alive if we can keep his pressure up. You'll have to watch him closely post-op though."

It dawned on me that the post-op care was going to be my job. Forget about any sleep tonight.

"Why don't you close?" Little said.

I was ecstatic. I had practiced tying knots with silk suture material wrapped around a bedpost for hours and had mastered that. I had done the lab-animal surgery sessions and done them well. I had watched several operations as a student. So I knew exactly how to close the incision. But this was my first chance to actually do it, to suture with my own hands the warm, supple tissue of a living, breathing human being.

"Thanks," I said, then to the scrub nurse, "4-0 chromic."

I fixed the curved needle with its attached length of chromic suture in the needle holder and began layer by layer, closing the wound, the resident serving as my assistant. It felt good. The whole experience felt better than good.

After we finished closing, removed the drapes, and made sure the patient's vital signs were stable, we went for a cup of coffee. I would catch up with the patient in the recovery room.

"Good job, Nero," the resident said as we sat in a deserted break room drinking terrible vending machine coffee.

"Thanks," I said.

I was still feeling the aftereffects of the hormonal surge that the experience of the evening triggered. I didn't really feel like talking. But Dr. Donald Little had been gracious to me, letting me do some of the procedure that a new intern would probably not ordinarily be permitted to do. I appreciated that.

"You okay?" he asked.

"Better than that," I answered and smiled.

He returned an understanding smile, maybe recalling his own similar experience a few years earlier.

"This'll be a tough few years, Nero," he said. "But I bet you'll be just fine. Incidentally," he continued, "I'm not sure if you've seen tomorrow's OR schedule, but you're scrubbing in with Billy Bob at seven."

I knew that when he was not present, William Robert Fathergill was known with varying degrees of affection as Billy Bob.

"As in a.m.?" I responded.

"Yep," he said, "Welcome to the major leagues, Dr. Nero. Call me if this guy's vital signs start to slip."

He got up and left me to enjoy my hormonal afterglow and to come down from that high to the hard prospect of a sleepless night and an early surgery with the chairman of the department.

I spent the night at the patient's bedside, checking his blood pressure and pulse every quarter hour. A recovery room nurse offered to spell me a couple of times, but I refused the offer. I wanted to be there personally. This guy was my responsibility. I had a personal investment in him and wasn't about to delegate the responsibility that went with it.

Sometime about four in the morning, I noticed that the patient's blood pressure was drifting ever so slowly downward. Just as I was about to call the resident, the patient expelled into the bed a massive liquid dark-red, particularly foul-smelling stool. While an orderly was cleaning up the mess, I called Little, obviously waking him up.

"Damn," he said, a sleepy slur to the word. "He's infarcted his bowel. We'll have to go back in, like immediately. Be sure we've got enough blood typed and cross-matched, check again on that fresh frozen plasma, and get him to the OR. I'll meet you there."

The segment of small intestine that had been pale when we last saw it was now a deep magenta color, obviously infarcted...dead tissue. The resection was rocky; the patient's vital signs kept fluctuating. After four more units of packed red cells and a couple of units of fresh frozen plasma that appeared miraculously in the middle of the procedure, things stabilized. By the time we were through and the patient was in the recovery room and stable, it was six a.m. Little dropped by around six-thirty to tell me that I should go ahead and scrub in with Billy Bob. He would see that I was covered here.

"Thanks," I said with considerably less enthusiasm than when I thanked him earlier.

OR number one was an operating theater at its most theatrical. The large theater was the Sanctum Sanctorum, the private domain of the self-proclaimed high priest of American surgery, Professor William Robert Fathergill. His handpicked team of assistants—an aging but elegant blonde scrub nurse, two circulators, and Harvey Blankenship, the chief's major collaborator in the surgical laboratory who, legend had it, was the actual inventor of some significant surgical advances— stood at attention in their designated places. When I arrived, the patient was asleep, prepped, and draped. The chief surgical resident stood at the patient's left side flanked by two senior assistant residents. There was a vacant space at the patient's right side, awaiting the arrival of the Great Man. Two more senior residents lined up next to the reserved space toward the patient's feet. Each of the residents' gloved hands rested in the sterile field. Four medical students stood on a bank of steel risers a few feet from the operating table. They looked uneasy in their unfamiliar scrubs, surgical masks, and caps. They jostled about trying to assure themselves the best view of the imminent proceedings.

My place was at the end of the line of residents at the patient's left side (the lesser of the two options). From that spot I could barely reach the prepped "sterile" area. No one spoke. The silence was broken only by the occasional metallic clink as the scrub nurse arranged Dr. Fathergill's personal collection of instruments on the green-draped table. Music played softly in the background. Opera. I learned later that Dr. Fathergill owned a rare collection of recordings of arias sung by Maria Callas and insisted that they be played when he operated, conducted his surgical master classes.

Dr. Fathergill burst through the swinging doors and strode to his reserved spot, freshly scrubbed hands held aloft before him. He was an imposing figure. Although it had been several years since he was an All-ACC linebacker at Wake Forest, those years had been kind to him. He would still have looked more at home on the football sidelines than in this role presiding over a bunch of exhausted, pasty-faced doctors in training gathered there to bask in the reflected glory of American surgery's favorite son.

The scrub nurse held the latex gloves for him, spreading the cuff of each as he shoved his long fingers into them with a single deft thrust of the skilled hands whose dexterity would shortly dazzle his audience.

"This patient is a sixty-year-old male with a carcinoma of his esophagus," he intoned. "The procedure is an elaborate one, involving resection of a substantial portion of his esophagus and mobilization of abdominal tissue grafts to the resected area in order to restore esophageal structure and function. This is a major operation that requires entering both the thoracic and the abdominal cavities. This man is fortunate in that we discovered his malignancy early, before it was large enough to interfere with his swallowing. He is especially fortunate to be at this institution. Our results with this difficult cancer are the best in the world."

That was a true statement but the Hopkins results were still pretty miserable. I later learned that there were several reasons for Hopkins's slightly better outcomes with this disease. They included Dr. Fathergill's technical skill for sure, but they also included insights from Harvey Blankenship, and the contributions of a world-class radiology department where novel approaches to early diagnosis had been perfected.

Dr. Fathergill was meticulous—and very slow—at his work. He frequently interrupted the operation to make one or another teaching point to the audience, waving a scalpel or a Halsted clamp in the air for emphasis. Sometime after he was well into this case, he instructed the chief resident to proceed with the next step, broke scrub, removed his gloves, walked over to a blackboard mounted at the side of the room, and gave the group a short lecture on the technical aspects of the procedure, illustrated by an impressively detailed drawing using several different colors of chalk. The medical students were enthralled. The residents were deferential, an essential trait for surgical residents. They grow out of it later.

I was dead on my feet, only vaguely aware of the spectacle. I leaned against the OR table and dozed horse-like, standing up. I heard very little of Billy Bob's lecture.

The operation lasted five hours. My only role was to hold

the handle of a retractor that was positioned by the chief resident who placed my hand on the handle of the instrument and adjusted it just right, instructing me to hold it in that precise location. I couldn't see the operating field from my place at the end of the line of assistants. I had to just hold the thing and stare at the drapes or at the back of assistant resident number nth who was in front of me. I held the retractor for however many hours the procedure required the abdominal cavity to be exposed. My hand cramped a couple of times and I let the instrument slip. When that happened, the chief resident repositioned the retractor, glared at me over his mask, and replaced my hand.

"Hold it exactly there," he repeated.

And so it went, as they say. From that first day at Hopkins, I was thoroughly convinced that trauma surgery was what I wanted to do. While the heady theater of elective surgery in the setting of a preeminent academic institution had its appeal, I had no desire to emulate Dr. Fathergill. It was the blood-and-guts urgency that attracted me.

During those years I learned to both tolerate the idiosyncratic egos of the senior faculty and to respect them for their truly incredible accomplishments. I learned more of the earlier giants whose ghosts still haunted the place—Halsted, of course, and Alfred Blalock who, with his pediatric colleague Helen Taussig, devised the blue-baby operation that saved countless infants born with the heart abnormality called Tetralogy of Fallot from certain death...and many others. I was privileged to live and work those years in the land of giants, present and past. And, yes, I think I saw further from their shoulders than would have been otherwise possible.

What I think now is that the view from that lofty perch was in one direction, a tunnel vision look at the possibilities. I didn't see further into myself for that experience. Too busy. And too tired most of the time.

CHAPTER 14: LUDO'S HISTORY LESSON: AN INTRODUCTORY COURSE

"It was not a felicitous time for children," Ludo said, "at least not in the Ludovici household. But, I suppose it would be unrealistic to expect war to be child's play."

Although there was a bright sun, it was a cool day, cool enough that both Ludo and I wore coats. He insisted that we sit outside. We sat together in the bright midafternoon sunshine on a slatted bench near the cistern at the center of the Campo Ghetto Nuovo. A sharp breeze stirred a scattering of brown leaves about the square. Three small boys, bundled up against the cold, kicked a ball against a wall and raced each other to retrieve it. From where we sat I could see the portion of the wall where Arbit Blatas's "Memorial to the Holocaust" was mounted. The seven bronze bas-relief plaques were shadowed from the sun so that I couldn't make out the details of the hideous scenes of suffering Jews.

Before we sat down, Ludo had insisted that we observe the memorial close up while he told me something of the artist. Blatas was a Lithuanian Jew who escaped successfully to America but lost his mother to the Holocaust. The memorial plaques—Deportation, The Final Solution, Execution in the Ghetto, Punishment, Crystal Night, The Revolt of the Warsaw Ghetto, and The Quarry—were dedicated to the night in December 1943 when the first two hundred Venetian Jews were deported, only seven to escape death in the concentration camps and gas chambers. It was ghastly art, maybe a work fitting for the ghastly history that it commemorated.

I was sure that Ludo selected this particular place to recount his own experience with the war for effect. His penchant for melodrama. It worked. I was still depressed by the sight of the memorial as Ludo began to recount, with obvious difficulty, that part of his personal history. I was reminded of those excruciating afternoons with my mother years earlier, extracting from her as much of the family history as I could. But it was Ludo, not I, who seemed intent on forcing himself to dredge up something from his distant history that he needed me to know.

I didn't feel the need. He was dying. What difference did his history make? He spoke of atonement earlier. For what? And why did I have to be his confessor? Why couldn't we just enjoy whatever time there was as much as possible? Serenity for me was proving an elusive and complicated goal.

"I was thirteen years old," Ludo said, "when those two hundred Jews, my countrymen, my fellow Venetians, were sent to the death chambers."

His gaze was fixed on the memorial wall in the distance and his voice was dreamy, unattached.

"It must have been a frightening time," I said. "Being here during the war."

"It felt so wrong," Ludo answered. "Everything about the

situation was wrong, incongruent. It is not that my city is innocent of evils. No, no. Quite the opposite. My city is no stranger to the often grotesque violence of evil men with dark motives. But this war was different. So much was unspoken. A menacing silence descended upon us from the time that Il Duce cast our lot with the Germans. I was ten years old then. From then until Venice was liberated by the Italian partisans and the Allies almost a decade later, there was an ominous silence broken only by the occasional nocturnal shock of blaring air raid sirens set off to hide the screams of the Jews being rounded up in the ghetto. We spoke in hushed whispers when we spoke. The soldiers branded anyone daring to oppose them with dry, hissed epithets—Jews, homosexuals.

"My father opened his palazzo to those people. You see, the original Ca'Ludovici was a palazzo on the Grand Canal. My father was a very pretentious person. He relished the attention of those bigots. And he was determined that I would carry that torch. He forced me to join the Ballila Youths. I joined. I wore the red-banded black Ballila fez. I did the marches, such as they were. You see, we Venetians, probably Italian youths in general, did not share the passions of the Hitler Youths. The Ballila were a performing troupe. It was an adolescent show. And I admit now after so many years, this will not surprise you, that I enjoyed the performance. I held no malice in my heart. I was a child, just coming of age. Trying to discover myself. The marches, the performances, were a blessed respite from the pervading and ominous silence.

"There were signs, written evils that went unspoken. I recall a handwritten sign on the door to Harry's Bar—No Jews Allowed. The occupiers spread a rumor that Giuseppe Cipriani, the bar's owner, was sympathetic to Jews and homosexuals. Whispered rumors, innuendo, were their stock in trade. The soldiers no doubt forced Cipriani to display the sign. I thought the sign a symbol. So many things were forced, unnatural. Il Duce and his people were not leaders. They force-marched us toward perdition. Venetians! We who had honed the art of compromise to a fine edge, at least some of us, joined blindly in the march. I think now that we were more driven by fear than led by ideology."

Ludo's words slowly registered with me.

"You were a fascist, Ludo," I said.

"A fascist," he repeated the accusation. "Yes, I played their games."

"Games?" I said. "Murderous games."

"Yes. I was not a murderer, though. Nor was my father, I think, although he may have been. He certainly did nothing to prevent their crimes. He shared our elegant life with them. And, at least near the end of that black ordeal, I was old enough to know. I knew. It was more cowardice than villainy that let me lend the silence of my own voice to the terrible silent chorus that was Venice's dubious contribution to the war."

He exhaled a long sigh and coughed, covering his mouth with a handkerchief. When he took the handkerchief from his mouth, I saw that it was stained bright red with blood the cough had produced. He quickly folded the handkerchief and returned it to his coat pocket, staring absently off into the distance.

"Do you really want to keep on with this, Ludo?" I asked.

"Yes," he said.

We sat quietly for a while. Evening was descending and the fading sunlight left the square dim and cold. The playing children disappeared into one or another of the stone facades bordering the space. I buttoned my coat snug at the neck and folded my arms tightly, trying to keep warm. Ludo must have been cold, but he sat still and quiet, his breathing audible.

"So," he finally broke the silence. "Now you know. I was a fascist in the elegant and comfortable home of a fascist family while the Jews here were being rounded up and sent to their awful death. Like many others, I raised no voice of protest. My sin of silence has haunted me all these years, Bianca. When my father died and I inherited the Grand Canal palazzo, I sold it and bought the more modest place in Cannaregio. I suppose I wished to force myself to live where my silent assent to evil was played out. You understand now why I speak of my need for atonement."

I felt a tear tracking down my cheek and brushed it away. Ludo and I sat a bit apart, not touching. We were in different places.

"Of course, my life then was complicated by my discovering my sexual orientation as I grew into young manhood. I thought at first that the feelings must be a passive rebellion against the fascists. They hated homosexuals. Had I been found out then, probably even by my father, I might well have been turned over to them. I do not know when my sexual preference for men dawned on my father but it must have been much later. He never spoke to me of it until he was dying and then only to extract the promise that I would not, as you say, come out. There was no love in that deathbed exchange between us."

"So why did you make the promise?" I asked.

"Bianca," he said, his voice strained, "I have never been a brave man. I have been content to enjoy what pleasures I could find and have avoided the unpleasantness of confrontation whenever possible. In that regard I am not unlike my city. I personify Venice's preference for compromise over principle. Look about you if you think that an unwise philosophy. What other city set in the midst of the geography of war escaped so wonderfully intact. Venice was spared the physical destruction of war because of her moral, shall we say. plasticity. Perhaps the same is true for me...until the virus. The virus appears to thrive on moral compromise."

"I doubt that," I responded. "You surely don't buy disease as punishment."

"Well, I suppose not. How unsophisticated that would be." He was drifting off now, his mind lost in the fog of history.

My mind, too, drifted into a fog of history. A history dominated by death. I couldn't remember anything about my life before that bleak afternoon when I sat by my mother on a discarded Methodist church pew and watched my father's electrogenic grand mal exit from the world of the living. An exit that he seemed to have arranged, orchestrated for private reasons that he chose not to share. My life was anchored at its nether end by that violent death and the mystery that also died there. If my mother was party to more understanding of the mystery, she kept it to herself, or at least kept it from me. Then she died prematurely, another victim of apparently random violence. More mystery. And why did I choose, was drawn to, a profession that kept me in constant struggle with the Death Angel, up to my elbows most of the time in human gore, the handiwork of man's inhumanity to man? Mystery compounded.

I didn't understand any of the seminal events in my history, who I was and how I got there.

And what drew me to Ludo, another person full of mystery whom I was watching die? I had grown very fond of him but was it him I grew to love or was it another infatuation with that other member of our ménage à trois? As I sat that afternoon a little ways apart from Ludo in the center of the Campo del Ghetto Nuovo, surrounded by ghosts of another time, Ludo's ghosts and perhaps some of my own, I felt quite certain that I could keep my promise to end Ludo's misery once it became intolerable. It wouldn't be long now. I began to cry.

Darkness had overtaken the campo and with it a damp chill. Ludo looked off into space, unmoving. I began to shake with the cold and the sobs that I was desperately trying to suppress. I don't know why it mattered, but I didn't want Ludo to see me cry. I don't think I was crying for him so much as for myself. Maybe some of both.

After a few minutes, I got control of myself and said, "Ludo, I'm getting chilled. Can we go home?"

He seemed startled by my question. He jerked around to face me. His face was flushed. His eyes were red but if there were tears I didn't see them. He cleared his throat with a slight cough.

"Of course, mi amore," he said, "of course. It is always cold in the evenings here. We should go."

We stood. Ludo grasped my arm with his right hand and fixed his harlequin cane in the other. We began the walk back up the Fondamenta Misericordia and across to Fondamenta Nove. A strong wind blew in from the lagoon raising whitecaps that sloshed up onto the walkway. Ludo leaned against me, steadying his gaunt frame against the wind.

"Do you go often to the Ghetto Nuovo?" I asked.

We had not spoken since leaving the campo and I asked the question lightly, an effort to pull us away some from the somber place where we had been.

"Yes," he replied, "I go there often."

When we parted at the door to my flat, Ludo said, "There is a great deal more to the story, Blanche. A great deal more that I need you to know. But it is difficult."

"I'm not sure about that, Ludo," I said. "This seems so hard for both of us. I'm not sure I want to know any more. Does it really matter that much?"

"It matters," he answered. "It matters. You came here to learn about your father and I can help you do that. I need to help you do that. I admit that it is selfish. I tend rather much to selfishness. But have you lost your curiosity about your roots? Do you not wish to complete your journey?"

I remembered criticizing my mother for her lack of curiosity. I didn't want to be like that. I didn't want to be anything like my mother. But this thing with Ludo was just so damned difficult. And he was dying, for God's sake!

"I'm not sure anymore," I answered.

We stood for a while looking at each other, the wind whistling through the Corte Berlindis from the lagoon.

"How is your writing coming along?" Ludo asked.

"I'm writing," I answered, "but I'm not sure that was such a good idea."

"You have embarked on a difficult journey, Blanche," Ludo said, "but you are past the point of no return, now. *Il punto di non ritorno*, we would say. The point of no return. You must complete the journey. You will not be happy otherwise. You are not one, I gather, to give up easily."

"I guess we'll see," I said. "I don't give up easily, that's true, but I don't think I ever undertook anything this difficult before. Maybe I've finally overdone it, bitten off more than I can chew."

"If I thought I would be around long enough to collect, I'd make you a sizeable wager that you will finish the task," he said. "It is not an altogether pleasant task, but you must finish it."

"We'll see," I said.

I hadn't thought about Violetta during the afternoon. When I entered the apartment, I didn't see her. The bowl of tuna that I had left for her was empty. She was not in her usual spot in the living room chair. I called for her but there was no response. I looked around, under the sofa, in the corners. It was a small room and there weren't many places where she could hide. Finally I went into the bathroom. I had left the top of the commode open and Violetta crouched on the edge of the bowl, relieving herself. She looked at me, a wide-eyed expression of accomplishment. I smiled. I had vaguely wondered about her bodily functions. I hadn't let her outside for fear that she would get lost. She hadn't soiled the house that I had seen. So, Violetta had learned to use the facilities. How civilized.

She leapt from her perch and came to rub against my legs, meowing loudly. I picked her up and held her tightly against my breast.

"What a smart girl," I said.

She made a soft guttural sound that I hadn't heard from her before.

I walked to the living room and sat down, still holding the cat. The tears started up again and I let them run down my cheeks and drip onto Violetta, making a dark wet spot on the orange part of her fur. She didn't seem to mind. She nestled against me, switching her long tail in slow deliberate oscillations and purring.

Violetta slept with me that night and many more after that. It was a long, deep, dreamless sleep. I felt refreshed when I awoke late the next morning.

CHAPTER 15: BODY AND SOUL: LIFE AND DEATH AT THE BIG FREE

There were two events in my life of such cataclysmic proportions that they either obliterated prior memory (my father's murder) or altered my perception of what went before so that I am no longer sure if what I remember is as it was at the time. That is how I now feel about antediluvian New Orleans. But anyway here is how I remember it.

I remember the Big Easy before the flood as an overindulged adolescent of a city, contemptuous of mortality and blissfully unconcerned about (mostly unaware of) her precarious and unnatural position below the level of the surrounding water, the flimsiest of barriers separating wet and dry. I fell in love with the place. The Big Easy was there to be had. She was the whore with a heart of gold. There were no rules or where there were, they were not rules in the non-New Orleans sense. Most folks there considered rules the baseline from which you began negotiations rather than any substantive societal structure. Since I had often thrived by flouting rules, this was my kind of place. I was drawn to risk, and this city epitomized the risky life.

The initial attraction was the job at Charity Hospital,

affectionately known as the Big Free in those days. And it was the Big Free. A freewheeling, blood-and-guts acute approach to the practice of medicine and the major provider of free medical care to the area's indigent. There were a substantial number of indigent in the area, many of whom were fond of inflicting significant injury of one sort or another on their peers with predictable frequency. It was exactly the opportunity I was looking for when I finished surgical training at Hopkins. I thought it a perfect fit. The Big Easy, the Big Free, and Blanche Nero. Even my name was a good fit. Had I believed in such things, I might have sensed on my shoulder the encouraging urge of Fate's not-so-gentle hand.

It was the only job that I seriously considered when I finished training. The Hopkins people wanted me to stay there, but I was ready to move on. Billy Bob, after his serious heart-to-heart talk with me about my opportunity to participate in the perpetuation of the noble history of Hopkins surgery, was shocked at my refusal of the offer and didn't speak to me after that meeting. It took only a single visit to the Big Easy to feel that I had found my place. The opportunity to perpetuate the noble history of Hopkins surgery seemed pale and sterile next to what New Orleans offered.

As I remember it, the epiphany overcame me in the bar at the back of Muriel's, an old New Orleans restaurant on the corner of Chartres and St. Ann in the Quarter. I was milling about the Quarter relishing the decaying elegance of the place, breathing the wet air redolent of salty musk and spices I didn't recognize. As I passed Muriel's, I was drawn to a large framed photograph on the wall just outside the entrance. Although it was an iconic picture, it was the first time I had seen it. The scene was Jackson Square engulfed in the mist that steals from the river across the square in the emerging daylight. The arrogant form of Andrew Jackson, poker-spined Old Hickory, astride his mount straining at the reins, appeared in the fog to be perched atop a gray cloud, the horse's hooves floating on the flimsy gray blanket. It struck me as a lovely photograph that captured something special about the place. New Orleans was an unlikely city sprung from the marsh, substance resting precariously on ephemera, arrogantly flaunting its tenuous existence with ribaldry and excess, decidedly oblivious to others' realities. And blithely oblivious to the distant gathering forces of nature.

The front part of Muriel's was up-market New Orleans dining—pretentious crisp linen and gleaming crystal table settings, hovering tuxedoed waiters (there were no waitresses in up-market New Orleans dining establishments). But the bar, way in the back of the place, was where the real action was. It was a smallish bar with lighting dark enough to obscure the cracked leather of deteriorating barstools and the accumulated effacements of the bar. Compensating for the dubious aesthetics was an intimidating array of spirits confronting the thirsty patron with limitless opportunities for arriving at the state of advanced inebriation that seemed to be a common goal of patrons of French Quarter bars.

Even though it was early afternoon, I indulged my taste for dry gin martinis, acquired in Baltimore. Very unlike in Baltimore, I sensed that there was nothing unusual about drinking dry gin martinis in the early afternoon in this city. I was sipping slowly at my second drink and making small talk with Scott, the prematurely puffy bartender who had drifted from Breckenridge to New Orleans when he tired of the snow or of the Colorado scene or for some other equally flimsy reason (a girlfriend, a boyfriend, who knew). Sitting there relishing the warmth of slowly sipped cold gin, I became aware of the feeling that I had found a place that could feel like home. It was an unfamiliar feeling. I had found pleasure and success in several places, but not a home. Home was not a concept with which I was familiar in any usual sense of the term.

I decided to buy a house. It had to be in the Quarter. The first place I was shown by a realtor suggested by what passed for an HR department of my future employer was a one-flight walkup on Bienville with a street-level one-car garage. The front was some sort of stucco-like material painted a dark red, and there was a good-sized balcony off the main room overlooking the street. The kitchen had been renovated and equipped with excellent appliances. The one bedroom was large and overlooked a garden at the back of the place. I loved it. Using my potential worth as a gainfully employed surgeon as collateral for a mortgage, I bought it and set about creating the first real home that I had ever known. In the couple of weeks before my duties at the Big Free actually started, I bought the kind of modern European furniture that I liked, furnished the kitchen with the best cookware and other paraphernalia essential to serious cooking, and generally got everything I needed to make the place homey, all chosen by me, according to my tastes. Homey by my inexperienced definition. It was a heady couple of weeks.

"Well, well, well, what have we here?" Dr. Edwin Zimmerman Petty, the chief trauma surgeon at Charity chose to personally conduct my "orientation" one-on-one and opened his monologue in an unpromising tone.

"Dr. Blanche Nero, it is my duty, I will not say pleasure as that remains to be determined, to welcome you to Charity Hospital, beacon of modern medicine illuminating however briefly the dark lives of the poor and dissolute of Orleans Parish."

Dr. Petty was a small man with a prominent paunch. His head was shaved slick and he wore designer glasses with aqua-colored frames and perfectly round lenses that magnified his eyes, giving his squarish face a distinctly froglike appearance. One could imagine his dangling wattle capable of inflating into a reddish balloon-like structure typical of the species. His skin was not green but it was sallow enough to give credence to the frog simile. He stood in front of me and paced back and forth in a mincing, penguinlike gait. His black shirt (silk, I think) and white knit tie under an open white lab coat also enhanced the penguin simile. Trying very hard not to react to his arrogant and condescending manner, I amused myself by imagining him as a chimera, an actual penguin with a frog head. I must have smiled.

"My intent here, Dr. Nero," he said, "is not to amuse you. There is little amusing about the duties you have chosen to assume. My intent is to impress you with the challenge you will face and to assure you that you will be given no quarter for your gender. I am not here to make your job easy. I am here to be certain that you do your job according to Charity standards. There is a way of doing things here that is not optional.

"You are the first woman trauma surgeon to be employed at Charity. In fact, you may be the first woman trauma surgeon in the world; one would hope that is the case. Having chosen such a career as a woman, you have committed an unnatural act; trauma surgery is a thoroughly masculine endeavor. I did not favor employing you. But nonetheless, you are here at least for the time being. You may find your elite training something of a disadvantage as well as your gender. I suppose we will see."

I later learned a bit more of Dr. Petty. Edwin Zimmerman Petty was born and raised in New York. He held an undergraduate degree in art history from Princeton. Deciding somewhat late on a career path, he returned to New York after graduating from Princeton and obtained an M.D. degree from Cornell. He did his training in general and subsequently trauma surgery at Bellevue. He was a veteran of the Korean War, headed a MASH unit there, allegedly with some distinction. His middle name was the maiden name of his mother. The origin of Edwin and Petty apparently needed no explanation; at least I never heard one. He was saddled with the insecurities common to small men (there may have been other explanations for his insecurities as well), and as a result, he was arrogant, pretentious, and often ungracious to his coworkers, especially those beneath him in the pecking order and especially women. Years earlier, shortly after he joined the Charity faculty, surgical residents and medical students, ever creative with faculty names, evolved Dr. Petty's name first to EZ Petty, then (apropos of the local French influence) to EZ Petite, and inevitably translated at last to Little Easy, the moniker by which he was known ever since by virtually everyone at Charity, sometimes even to his face by a superior. In spite of his best efforts, I was not intimidated by Little Easy.

I was, however, more than a little intimidated by the Big

Free. Charity Hospital was one of the oldest hospitals in the country and one of the biggest. It was a huge barn of a place, featuring soaring, darkly stained ceilings with mostly missing retrofitted acoustic tiles browned by steady drips of unknown fluids from a maze of pipes that crisscrossed the ceiling above the tiles. The floors were terrazzo from an earlier era, worn slick more from eons of foot traffic than from any excessive attempts to maintain sanitary conditions. The hospital had over two thousand inpatient beds and the busiest emergency room in the country. And the clients in the ER made the denizens of the East Baltimore Knife and Gun Club look like rank amateurs. Little Easy was fond of saying that if you had the misfortune of being the recipient of a gunshot wound, New Orleans was the best place in the world to receive it since Charity Hospital had more experience with such trauma than anywhere else in America, probably in the entire universe. Although Little Easy was often given to rather florid hyperbole, in this case he was probably accurate.

My professional introduction to the Big Free was a baptism by fire. Little Easy assigned me first call on the first day of my employment. It began on a Saturday. For almost forty-eight hours, my beeper did not cease to beep. Most of that time I was scrubbed in the OR and had to get a scrub nurse to answer it. It was always a call from the attending ER doc to arrange surgery for the next trauma victim. I spend those hours up to my elbows in the bloody viscera of indigent residents of Orleans Parish, attempting to fix the anatomical distortions inflicted upon them by other indigent residents of Orleans Parish. While I was no stranger to the consequences of violence, in fact was attracted to addressing the consequences of violence as a chosen profession, the sheer volume and diversity of the consequences of violence that I confronted during those hours was a new experience. The experience was to trauma surgery what pornography is to sex. By the time the orgy was over, or at least my assigned participation in the orgy was over, I was overwhelmed and physically and emotionally exhausted. As I staggered to bed still dressed and collapsed into sleep, I wondered briefly whether I had taken on more than I had bargained for.

"Dr. Nero." Awakened from a deep sleep, I grabbed the phone after who knows how many rings and only vaguely associated the voice responding to my gruff hello with that of Little Easy. "Did you plan to join us in our review of your weekend handiwork or have you made more interesting plans for your morning?"

Rounds on Mondays started at eight. These rounds were especially important because they were an opportunity for the entire team to review the cases from the weekend, critique the handling of the cases, learn what there was to learn, and make plans for follow-up. I looked at my bedside clock. It read eight-thirty. For the first time in my professional life, I had overslept and missed the start of rounds.

"I'll be there in fifteen minutes," I answered and hung up the phone.

Still dressed in scrubs, I got out of bed and went directly downstairs and drove as fast as I could to the hospital. I must have looked awful but I didn't care.

When I caught up with the team, they were arrayed around the bed of a young black man whom I didn't recognize.

"I am so pleased you could join us," Little Easy intoned as I tried to hide inconspicuously at the margins of the group. "Dr. Nero, perhaps you could fill us in on the history and course of this patient."

I did not recognize the patient and had no recollection of his injury or what I had to do with the case. I didn't respond.

"Dr. Nero," Little Easy continued, "I am given to understand that you entered the thoracic cavity of Mr. Easton and effected some anatomical intrusions intended to reengage his injured lung in its normal process of respiration. Am I correct?"

I remembered something of the case although I didn't recognize the name.

"He had a contusion of his left lung and a hemothorax," I answered. "I did a thoracotomy, evacuated the pleural space, and sutured the tear in his lung."

"Thank you, Dr. Nero." He turned to the patient and sat down side-saddle on the edge of the bed, resting a hand on the man's arm and engaging his eyes as he spoke. "Dr. Nero here seems to have done you a favor, Mr. Easton," he said, gesturing in my general direction with a sweep of his hand.

"You know Dr. Nero, of course, do you not, Mr. Easton?"

The patient's eyes wandered about the group of white coats hovering over his bed.

"Which one is him?" he asked.

"Dr. Nero," Little Easy continued, "come here and let me introduce you to your patient, Mr. Easton."

Little Easy took me by the arm and drew me to the bedside.

"Mr. Easton," he said, "this is Dr. Nero, your surgeon. I should have thought that the two of you might have met earlier, perhaps prior to Dr. Nero's surgical assault on your person. But I suppose it is better late than never. Would you not agree, Dr. Nero?"

I was furious. I could feel the pulsing heat in my flushed face. Little Easy was obviously intent on embarrassing me in front of not only the cluster of residents, medical students, and the head sister (as the charge nurse was called), but in front of the patient as well. I had just spent nearly forty-eight goddamned hours saving the lives of this guy, Easton or whatever, and his ilk. I did not need a personal relationship with him. Easton or whatever didn't need that either. He needed the blood removed from his chest and his lung repaired and, God damn it, I did that as well as any trauma surgeon in the world could have done it. I saved his life. What was Little Easy's problem?

I extended my hand to the patient and said, "I am pleased to meet you, Mr. Easton," my voice laced with a slight adrenalin tremor. "When we first met, I'm afraid the urgency of your condition kept us from a proper introduction. How are you this morning?"

"Thanks, doc," he said, "I'm good this morning. Breathing good. Hurting a little, but breathing good."

As the group moved to the bedside of the next patient, Little Easy whispered in my ear, "See me in my office after rounds, Dr. Nero."

I got the message. I was a problem for Little Easy. It would be interesting to see how he chose to deal with Dr. Blanche Nero.

As I came to learn over the next few years, a calm demeanor was Little Easy's fiercest affect. When I went into his office, he sat at his desk, arms folded across his chest, staring without apparent emotion out the small window that looked onto a blank brick wall. He did not acknowledge me when I entered his office without knocking, marched in ready for battle. I stood in front of his desk for what seemed like several minutes. I was still angry but less tremulous than earlier; the adrenalin surge had subsided some.

Refusing to tolerate the embarrassment of being ignored, I launched into what can only be described as a tirade, the adrenalin-stoked fury returning with a vengeance.

"Just what the hell are you trying to prove, Dr. Petty," I said, sarcastically emphasizing the doctor title. "If you have a problem with my surgical judgment or technique, let's hear it. I just spent forty-eight hours up to my ears in blood and guts, and if you've got a problem with how I handled the situation, let's get the cards on the table. You have no right—I don't care what your position is—to deliberately attempt to embarrass me in front of colleagues and patients. That is unprofessional conduct. I have worked with surgeons who wouldn't give you the time of day and I've never been treated so shabbily. What is your problem?"

I was breathing a little heavily by the time I concluded my little speech and was fully prepared for however Little Easy responded. Ready for battle. He had not changed his position, still sat arms folded staring out the window. If my outburst had any effect on him, his body language didn't betray it.

Little Easy slowly turned to face me, arms still folded across his thin chest. He engaged my eyes and held them for a long moment. He was stonily calm.

"Dr. Nero," he said, the words measured and without

inflection, "if while in my area of responsibility, you ever operate on another person without the courtesy of introducing yourself and connecting with them as a fellow human being, I will fire you on the spot without ceremony or explanation."

He turned his gaze back to the window and, after a pregnant pause, said, "You may go."

Little Easy was not a great surgeon. He wasn't a great person in any way that I could tell. He did his job, a difficult job, with stamina and wit in spite of the arrogance with which he treated many of his colleagues. And I came to understand that he genuinely cared for the people unfortunate enough to need his surgical expertise. Cared for them as fellow humans in ways that I had neither learned nor considered important. I still had no great store of empathy for the great unwashed of Orleans Parish. But I did not once after that encounter with Little Easy operate on anyone without introducing myself in advance and explaining the procedure. It didn't come naturally at first, but it grew on me.

I don't think I ever told him so, but somewhere along the way I came grudgingly to appreciate Little Easy's admonition. I don't think that it made me a better surgeon. But it may have made me a better person.

CHAPTER 16: LOVE AS BLOODSPORT

I don't know why but I'm compelled to write about this now-remote episode in my history that I would rather forget but am unable to. I still don't understand the significance of it and also don't understand why, even after all this time and at almost sixty years of age, well into the postmenopausal hormonal desert, the memory still stirs something primal, organic in me.

It is a story of sex and violence. I was always attracted to both but hadn't personally commingled the two before I encountered Brad Palance and for a brief time lost my grip on that small space between pain and pleasure. It's difficult to write about this because neither sex nor violence translates easily into words. And the feelings that the memory stirs still disturb me. But, trying hard to be true to my decision to write about how I got to this place and time with as much truth and clarity as I can, I will write what I remember as true to the experience as words permit, hoping that I'll discover something new in putting it into words and writing them down. Even as I write this, I am haunted by the suspicion that it may be a story that would be better left untold.

Although lust is obviously a contact sport, I didn't think that should be true of love. But then, I had no reason to understand much about love at all. I had had precious few role models and little experience with it. In my mind, love was something vague and ill-defined that didn't seem very relevant to what I was about. (Was it Tina Turner who said that love has nothing to do with it?) That was before I met Brad Palance. Brad taught me that love was more than a contact sport. With Brad Palance, love was a martial art.

As adolescent as it now sounds, I can only describe what I felt upon first viewing Brad's truly magnificent body and feeling the heat of his hollow black gaze as falling in love. The feeling was unlike any I had felt before. I was overwhelmed and I was not used to being overwhelmed. At the time I had no idea what it meant. But even had I known what was to come of it, I wouldn't have done anything differently. In retrospect, I wish I had been wiser. But then maybe my brief encounter with Brad Palance made me wiser. It's also possible that neither love nor wisdom had anything to do with it.

I should preface the description of this irrational episode in what I think was my otherwise pretty rational history by recounting my pre-Palance attitude toward the human body. You could think of it as an architectural attitude—function trumped form.

I was not particularly attracted to the proverbial hunk. From a purely aesthetic point of view, I thought the female body was much superior to that of the male. Obviously, the real aesthetes and artists have generally favored that view. I genuinely enjoyed the experience of sexual intercourse. It was the function of my partner that interested and excited me.

It is obvious by now that I had many partners. I didn't keep either a mental or an actual catalogue of those experiences, annotated or not. When I recall them, it's the feelings that I remember, not how the naked male body looked. Looking at the outsides and insides of naked bodies of both sexes is part of my chosen profession. (As I reflect, it is interesting that I chose a subspecialty that is predominantly focused on males since that is the gender most prone to violence and other risky behaviors.) But looking at naked human bodies is really just part of the job. I have never understood the market for nude pictures. Maybe movies—pornographic movies were one of ways that Brad expanded my sexual experiences—but still photographs of beautiful men's bodies? I see, would be my response, what they look like, but let's see what they can do!

Nor did I believe in anything like chemistry between two people unless you mean sexual desire. I certainly believed in that. But to me that was biology, not chemistry. And it was a generic male-female (or sometimes same sex, which I recognized but didn't identify with) response, not individual chemistry between a specific pair of Homo sapiens. Man (the generic man) is not by nature, I had often stated with thorough conviction to myself and others, a monogamous animal!

Given all that (and I was very comfortable with myself sexually and otherwise), my initial encounter with Brad Palance was a disorienting emotional cataclysm. This was more than chemistry. This was nuclear physics.

Late on a Friday night, shortly before I was to go off duty, I got a call from the ER that we had a VIP with a gunshot wound, and the resident wanted an attending to put in an appearance, cover his backside in case there were any PR or legal issues that emerged. We hated VIP patients. They were generally intolerable prima donnas and often excessively concerned about preventing any leaks to the press and about any possible legal implications of their care at Charity. Fortunately, we didn't get many VIPs. If you had money, you generally went elsewhere if you had a choice.

But, for some reason that was never explained to me, a star running back for the New Orleans Saints, his well-muscled abdomen having been the unfortunate recipient of a stray gunshot from a drunk and unhappy customer of a French Quarter bar, was picked up by an ambulance and transported without his consent or knowledge to the closest emergency medical facility, the Charity ER. His arrival created a buzz among the staff. Most of them were rabid Saints fans. Virtually everyone who could get free of their legitimate duties for a few minutes converged on the ER to catch a glimpse of their hero, the man dubbed, I learned later, Saint Brad by the local media.

I was never much of a sports fan. I had only a vague notion of whatever was the point of the game of football. I certainly didn't understand the passions it seemed to stir in a lot of otherwise reasonably stable and intelligent people. When the breathless ER resident told me on the phone that the VIP was a star running back for the Saints, my first thought was to wonder why there was such a position as a running back on a football team when I thought the point of the game was to run (or pass or whatever) forward.

I was unprepared for the scene I encountered in the ER. A horde of medical staff jostled about the curtained cubicle that housed the gurney where lay Saint Brad, each one maneuvering to get as close to him as possible. The spectacle made me mad.

It was unprofessional behavior by people who generally prided themselves on their professionalism. I pushed my way through the crowd, trying to make it clear from my body language that I was very unhappy with the situation. I apparently succeeded since the crowd first parted, then slowly withdrew, hopefully returning to caring for the needs of the non-VIP, non-running backs who were our primary responsibility.

So the crowd parted and withdrew, creating a direct path for me to the reclining Saint Brad. Harry Slocum, the pudgy, red-faced senior resident in charge of the case, ran toward me and trotted alongside jabbering something in my ear as we approached the patient…gunshot wound to the abdomen…appears stable…not sure about internal injuries. Still annoyed at the scene, I wasn't paying much attention to Slocum. Although Saint Brad reclined on the ER gurney directly ahead of me, I didn't really look at him until we were at the bedside.

Saint Brad lay on his back. The head of the gurney had been cranked up so that he was semirecumbent. A sheet covered the lower part of his body but his abdomen and upper body were naked and exposed. I couldn't help but stare at the field of moguls spilling down from the base of his sternum toward his nether parts, a topography of rippled abdominal muscles straining at their covering of flawless café-au-lait skin. When my gaze eventually reached his face, he was smiling. He looked directly into my eyes. He had the blackest eyes I had ever seen. The irises were so black that they merged imperceptibly with the pupils. They looked like big black holes in the middle of pristine white sclerae. His eyes were at once laser-hot instruments boring into my being and big dark portholes inviting a view of something remote, exotic, new. For what seemed like a long time, I stood there relishing the heat of the moment, the shiver of passion frolicking along my vertebral column, the heavy wet spasm in my pelvis.

My voice was a bit unsteady by the time I got enough control of the situation to say, "Mr. Palance, I'm Dr. Nero, the attending surgeon. Are you in pain?"

He broke into a broad smile and said, "Not really."

I deliberately avoided his eyes, attempting to regain some modicum of composure. I had a job to do. I had always studiously avoided getting personal feelings mixed up with my job. Brad Palance threatened that resolve.

"Where were you shot?" I asked.

"The Quarter."

"I mean where in your body, Mr. Palance."

"Stomach, lower part," he said.

Was he playing with me? He said the words in a matter-of-fact tone. No evidence that he was feeling anything.

"May I have a look, please?" I said.

"Of course."

I moved the sheet down to reveal the lower part of his stomach. There was a small entry wound a few centimeters below his navel. I palpated the area. If it hurt, he didn't show it. I could feel the bullet under the skin just in the superficial part of the muscle beneath. It was a small-caliber slug that hadn't had sufficient force to penetrate the steely muscles of Brad Palance's remarkable abdomen.

I pulled the sheet back up and said, "The bullet is just in the tissue under the skin. It didn't penetrate into your abdomen. We'll need to remove it, but it's a minor operation. We can do it under local anesthesia if that's okay with you.

"That's fine," he said. "Will I need to stay in the hospital?"

"Probably a good idea to keep you overnight just to be safe," I said.

"Will you do it?" he asked.

"No, Dr. Petty, the head trauma surgeon, is just coming on duty and he'll be your surgeon. He'll introduce himself and explain everything to you. It's a minor procedure."

He caught my eyes again and said, "Will I see you before I'm discharged?"

There was something in the tone of his voice and that hollow black gaze that triggered the hormonal surge again. I paused a few moments, taking control of the surge with some difficulty. I was not unfamiliar with sexual attraction, desire, but this feeling had a new intensity and it felt like something more than physical desire. The feeling was scary as hell. No way was I going to stoke that flame.

I responded, "I'll probably see you on rounds in the morning. You'll be fine."

"Thanks, Dr. Nero," were his soft parting words.

But his eyes said something else.

So much is still unexplained. How did he get my home telephone number? Why did I invite this total stranger to my apartment the very first time he called? And what, in God's name, was I thinking when we made violent love that first night without any of the conventional niceties, sans even the politeness of formal introductions. I do not understand, didn't understand then, the urgency of it. But there was urgency, a delicious, ecstatic, and unguarded urgency.

"Dr. Blanche Nero." The voice on the phone said my name as a statement, a declaration, not a question. "This is Brad Palance."

It was after nine on a Friday evening and I was off duty for the rest of the weekend. When the phone rang, I wondered who could be calling me at this hour on a Friday night when I was off call. While I had spent more than one night wrestling with erotic fantasies involving Saint Brad and myself, the dream competing successfully for a few nights with the more familiar and less pleasant one, I didn't expect to hear from him. There was no reason to expect it. It had been almost a month since our first meeting. But the sound of his voice on the phone, the intensity of how he said my name, and the memory of our first encounter set off an anamnestic hormonal surge that took my breath away. I couldn't answer for a few seconds and when I did my voice was breathy. I sounded unfamiliar even to myself.

"How are you, Brad?" I finally managed to respond, deliberately using his first name, again for God only knows what reason.

"I want to see you," he stated simply.

I answered immediately, a hormonal reflex. "Can you come to my place?"

No thought of a different, more rational answer.

"Yes," he said. "You live in the Quarter, on Bienville, right?"

"That's right."

I didn't wonder how he knew where I lived. I should have wondered about that and a lot of other things. This was uncharted territory for me but I was anxious to explore it. To hell with the niceties. To hell with caution. Since when did I concern myself with rules of engagement?

When Brad arrived at my apartment, we barely spoke. We immediately fell into a hard embrace, locking our bodies together, clashing together as though drawn by the power of a suddenly activated electromagnetic field, some mystical force seizing control of us. We kissed hard and deep enough to bruise my lips. I felt the sweet taste of the bruise. I could feel the beginning of swelling in my lips by the time we were naked and writhing about on the living room rug.

Brad was a savage, even brutal lover. It was as though he could push beyond the margins of what I had considered normal sex, push far beyond that but still stop short, just barely short of completely losing control. For the next several hours—I have no idea how long—Saint Brad and I explored each other, explored every square centimeter of each other's bodies, violated every orifice, tasted and felt it all with an almost unbearable intensity that came in waves, one after another. My mouth hurt and my pelvis ached, a pain so exquisite that just its intensity was enough to bring me near to orgasm. My anus hurt, my previously virginal anus, violated repeatedly by Saint Brad's fingers and penis. I relished the pain, wanted to feel him in me again. In me everywhere, all at once. I could not get enough of this incredible man. Orgasmic waves washed over us again and again.

At some point we fell asleep together on my bed. It was for me a profound dreamless sleep. The late morning sun, a slash of bright light across the bedroom, awakened me. I was alone. My body ached everywhere, a delicious surreal aching. For a drowsy few minutes, I thought the memory of the previous evening was a dream, that it had not actually happened. When I looked in the bathroom mirror, surveyed the damage, I knew it was no dream. My lower lip was swollen and blue. There were large, hand-shaped bruises on both my breasts and teeth marks around the nipples. There was a large angry bruise visible through the dark hair that covered my mons pubis, a recurrent injury that I came to think of later as The Mark of the Saint. The muscles of my legs ached. There was a heavy pain deep in my pelvis. My anus burned. I stood for a long time relishing the intensity of what I was feeling. I wished Saint Brad was still on the premises. Bloody but unbowed, I was ready for round two.

Brad's note on the kitchen table said simply, "Sorry, I had to leave. You were sleeping so peacefully that I dared not wake you. I'll call. We have some unfinished business to take care of, you and I."

Later, Brad told me that he had been a landscape architecture major as an undergraduate at Michigan State. He said that he was serious about that as a profession and that football was just a way to get there. It came easy for him and paid well. Of course, I learned a great deal more about Saint Brad. I also finally learned that he was not an impeccable source of information about himself.

For several months, Brad and I saw a lot of each other. The sexual attraction was so intense that we didn't do much else during those months. And the sex got more and more, shall we say, adventurous. There were the porn movies. He was aroused by them and that was contagious. I was so turned on by this man that I was ready for him when, however, and as often as he wanted. There were many long nights and some afternoons that lasted into the wee hours. During those months, I felt pain and pleasure as I had never felt them and could not, for the life of me, separate the two.

I can't bring myself even now to recount in words, to write down, a description of the event that brought me to my senses. It involved Brad and one of his teammates appearing unexpectedly at my apartment, apparently high on something and ready for action. The action they sought caused me pain of a kind and intensity that was well beyond any connection with pleasure. They were not concerned with my pleasure, seemed in fact to be excited by my repeated expressions of displeasure with the situation. I can't write any more about that night. It hurts too much.

If there was anything positive about this episode in my history, it was that it revealed to me something unfamiliar and scary about myself. For one thing, I learned that I had no idea what love was and that I was capable of deluding myself to a dangerous degree. I thought I was in love with Brad Palance and it wasn't love at all. Or if it was, then I didn't want anything more to do with it. And it caused me to regain my grasp of the critical nature of that space, however small, that separates pain and pleasure.

I am unable to sleep tonight. I get up and go for a walk, through the narrow *calle* of *sestiere* Castello and up to Piazza San Marco, deserted at this hour. There is a full moon that reflects from the paving stones' sheen of early morning damp. The black ghosts of gondolas bob about in their moorings at the edge of the *bacino*. The lion of the patron saint, wings rigid at his sides, keeps his vigil, surveying Serenissima from his lofty perch. I try to drown the relived past pain with present living and durable beauty.

This story is better left untold. I'll burn those pages tomorrow.

CHAPTER 17: A DAY TRIP INTO TIME

In the center of the town square in the village of Pieve di Cadore, an easy Trenitalia day trip from Venice's Santa Lucia station, is a bronze statue of Titian. I suspect that Ludo was remembering the statue as we trudged the few short blocks from the train station to the square. As we walked, he set about preparing me for the experience he had planned for the day.

"Blanche," he said, leaning heavily on my arm and gesturing elaborately with his harlequin cane, "I wanted us to come here to meet someone with whom you have a special, if somewhat remote, connection. Bear with me. Do not protest," he said, raising a flattened palm toward me. "The story wanes. We near the final chapter."

There were several inches of snow on the ground and there had been no apparent attempt to clear the streets and sidewalks. We walked very slowly, our boots imprinting the snow blanket with a rhythmic soft crunch, a slow rhythm, adagio. Ludo was unsteady on his feet, a sailor used to the pitch and roll of a different voyage searching for his land legs, trying hard to settle into our practiced synchronous bob and weave.

His waning strength was obvious to both of us. He made no

effort to hide it anymore. And the cough. The cough was regular now, predictable. And the blood, sometimes a tinge, sometimes a bright red stain on his handkerchief, regularly accompanied the predictable cough.

"You see, mi amore," he continued, "this is Da Cadore's town of origin and, you will see, where you have roots as well. It is a lovely village. And the statue of Da Cadore in the square is exquisite."

He said those words just as we rounded a corner into the square and were confronted by the statue.

It would not be accurate to say that the statue dominated the square. It was more as though it presided over the square, perhaps over the entire village, perhaps its past as well as its present. Maybe its future as well. The presence of Titian, one had the impression, was the essence of the place. The hovering spirit of the Master may even be the town's reason for being, its *ragion d'essere*.

My view as we entered the square was of the statue, a proud but somehow gentle persona, head and extended arms white with a generous coating of fresh snow, and in the distance beyond the snow-covered Dolomiti, alpine peaks that were the winter playground of the rich and famous. A multicolored array of shop façades enclosed the square. Near to Christmas, there were strands of colored lights, manger scenes, Santa Clauses, and holly wreaths scattered about. But my eyes were drawn to the statue. I recalled the painting in the Gesuiti church in Venice. I recalled Signora Zorzi's bizarre séance in Titian's former workshop in Cannaregio, the high pitch of the conjured voice and the familiarity with which that strange voice addressed me.

"So, Ludo," I said, "I hope this isn't another one of your magic tricks. The thing with Signora Zorzi pretty much exhausted my patience with such stunts. I'm not sure how much time we have left, but can we just level with each other for however long that is? Can we drop the melodrama and just try to relate as real people in a real if not so pretty world?"

"Ah, reality," Ludo responded. "Reality indeed. Surely I am the very personification of reality. Do you need words? Do you need to wallow in the ugly reality of encroaching death? Is not imagination, even pretense, a more potent deterrent of the inevitable, a more robust position from which to engage the Death Angel in the final struggle? And what of your quest for your roots? Are we to abandon that to relish my ignominious demise? Surely not, mi amore, surely not."

I was tempted to reply, "Don't call me Shirley," to try to lessen the tension that was clear in Ludo's voice but resisted since I doubted that he would understand the humor. Ludo would have been a very unlikely fan of Leslie Nielsen.

We continued our walk around the square without speaking for a few minutes. Ludo coughed up some more blood. It was a prolonged, meaty cough that appeared to produce a substantial quantity of the stuff. Ludo tried valiantly to hide the blood from me, shielding the cough with a handkerchief already dyed blood-red. I was worried about the blood. He had assured me that his doctor had ruled out TB. Still determined not to interfere in his medical care, I hadn't inquired further. I didn't want to be Ludo's doctor.

"Ludo," I said, "I don't like the reality any more than you do. It's just that I can't make a game of it. I can accept difficult realities. But they have to be dealt with as realities, not obscured behind veils of denials and distractions."

"All right, Blanche," Ludo replied, a tone of grim determination coloring the words. "You want reality? Be careful what you ask for. The realities you wish for may be more difficult for you to accept than you think."

I pondered his words. I didn't want to provoke Ludo. Quite the opposite. I wanted to be a comfort to him. But I seemed to have trouble getting that message across. Often the words I said to him sounded provocative even to me. That frustrated me as much as it frustrated him. Why couldn't I just let him behave however he wished at this point? Why couldn't I just relish that? Why couldn't I admit that I loved this man and that the anger I felt was not at him but at the Fates for taking him away from me?

A strange thought. I, Blanche Nero, wrestling with an emotion I had felt only once before when I ran from it like a frightened child. The love I had once abandoned come back to take its revenge, to introduce me to the pain of being the abandoned one. And why Ludo? He was such an unlikely person for me to love. I was again drawn to the small space that separates opposites, this time love and death. It was a small space and the opposite forces bounding it inched ever closer, threatening to crush me as they came together. They would come together. It was inevitable.

We didn't speak for a while. I held Ludo's arm tightly against my side, trying to send a physical message, hoping he would feel something more than the words we exchanged seemed to indicate. If he did, I couldn't tell it. I desperately wanted to find some different words but could not. Words are a pathetic substitute for feelings, even careful, perceptive words. Why am I writing this, trying to translate a life pieced together of senses, feelings, into words? It may well be futile. We will see. But for sure words for Ludo at that moment failed me.

We stood together for a few moments in front of the Titian statue. Ludo freed his hand from where I gripped it with my arm hard against my side. He removed his glove and began to rummage through a coat pocket, eventually extracting a small crumpled piece of paper.

"Ah," he said, carefully straightening the paper and peering at it. "Here it is. The address we seek, mi amore," he waved the piece of paper in the air. "We come to this charming village to visit the resident of this address. I take you there at some risk that I will not be well received by the resident. However, you will be welcomed, I am sure."

He took my arm again and started us walking off to the left side of the square, trudging noisily through the snow, doing the oddly synchronous Blanche-Ludo dance, bobbing to and fro.

"Why would they not welcome you?" I asked.

"They have good reasons for that," Ludo answered. "There is history lurking here. History seems to lurk everywhere in my life these days. Odd. I have spent much time and effort trying to avoid the most difficult parts of my history. I say odd, meaning that it is odd at this late hour of my brief life to be motivated to confront long-avoided history by you, a stranger, a woman, an American...an American, *per l'amor di Dio!*" waving his cane in the air and almost losing his balance. "I mean no offense, Blanche; it is just an incongruity that I do not understand. The incongruity of you and me together rooting around in our pasts like truffling pigs, hoping to uncover an earthy nugget that will bring some resolution to this grand dilemma that is life.

"Ah…." he sighed. "Once again I am led by your lovely presence to the barren land of philosophy. But do you not see the incongruity?"

"Oh yes," I answered. "Yes. I'm haunted by the incongruity of late. The incongruity of you and me together more than the quest, wherever that's headed. I'm frustrated by the space the incongruity puts between us. You probably see that I have trouble finding words strong and true enough to carry across that space, no matter how loudly I shout them. And I get really angry about your failing health."

I added the last comment without thinking. Ludo's health was looming very large in my heart and mind. It would trump all the other stuff before long. The vise was screwing methodically closed.

"You need not shout, mi amore," he said. "The distance may be smaller than you think. And your words carry well. Words! My fondness for them must be obvious to you. But…they can be mercurial things, even for the most articulate of us. Fortunately, I think that words sometimes do not mean what they say, or mean much less than their speaker intends. I perhaps understand more of your words, what you intend with them, than you fear. We are connecting, I believe, in some way that does not translate well into either of our native languages, or any other for that matter. Another oddity. The invention of language, words, by our species separates us from the lower animals but impedes discovery of the deeper passions that we desperately seek, passions that are second nature to the lower species. There is no Language of Love," he sighed. "The very concept is an oxymoron."

"Love?"

We stopped walking and turned to face each other, our eyes meeting.

"I love you, Blanche," he said.

"I love you, Ludo."

"I do not wish to die, not now."

"Oh, Ludo.," I fought back a giant sob that began as a nidus deep within my breast and gradually expanded, threatening to overwhelm me. "If only wishing it so were enough."

We trudged on in silence but for the adagio crunch of our snow tread. Glancing occasionally at the piece of paper that he held in his hand, Ludo guided us through several turns until we stopped in front of a wooden door that opened directly onto a narrow street. Beside the door were several brightly polished brass plaques with names engraved. Beside each plaque was a tiny brass lion head, a brass button protruding from its yawning mouth. I glanced at the names. I especially noticed one plaque etched with the name Nero-Corsini.

"I think I recall a small bar, just near here," Ludo said, "Perhaps we could have a coffee and talk a bit there."

"But," I protested, "isn't this the place we came to visit?"

"Yes, it is. But we need to take a small time to plot a strategy," he said.

"Okay," I answered, determined to resign myself to Ludo's plan, whatever it was.

"Some background," Ludo said.

We sat at a small table in the bar, each nursing a cappuccino. There were no other patrons in the place. Ludo ordered the coffees and brought them to the table. When he sat down, he was wheezing audibly. He frowned. The ravines traversing his elegant face were deepening by the day. He sighed. He cleared his throat. I thought I sensed that he was suppressing a cough with considerable effort.

"I must give you some background for this little visit. I am not yet ready to reveal the entire story, but some background may be in order."

"Please, Ludo," I begged, "tell me what this is about."

It took considerable effort for me to conceal the frustration I felt at Ludo's determined opacity. Why? Why the mystery?

"Yes, yes," he answered, "So, we are to visit Signora Nero-Corsini. She is rather old now and I suspect that age has taken some toll, although I have not seen her in a very long time. I am not sure what to expect. I am quite sure that she will not recognize me from that distant past. But she would surely recognize my name. That would not make for a felicitous visit. I think it best that we avoid that. The visit is for you, not for raising old animosities."

"Perhaps you can explain?"

"The old animosities, you mean. Suffice it for now to say that our families had, how do you say in your American divorces, irreconcilable differences. But what is important is that the signora is the sister of your father. She was married to a Signor Corsini who I am told died many years ago and that she has since remained alone."

"My father's sister, my aunt?" I said.

I was shocked. I had no idea that my father had a sister. But then I knew next to nothing about my father's Italian family.

"That is correct, mi amore. A younger sister, I believe. She is probably in her eighties now. The signora is probably your only living source of direct information about your father. The only eyewitness, as you might say."

"And you knew Signora Nero? Were you friends?"

"No, no. That would not have been possible. But I did meet her a time or two in my youth."

"And my father? Did you know him?"

"No, no, mi amore. I never met your father. I was younger and he was off fighting with the partisans when I met Signora Nero. It was a chance meeting. It was not pleasant."

"My father fought with the Italian partisans in the war? I suspected that he was in the war but didn't know anything about the details. Can you tell me more about that?"

"Oh, yes. I can tell you much more about that than you may wish to know. But not now. I will do that later. Now we must decide how to approach Signora Nero-Corsini."

I started to insist but Ludo interrupted me, shushing me with a pointing finger.

"As I said, she would recognize my name. I suggest that I masquerade as your interpreter. She probably speaks little English. I will introduce myself as your interpreter, Antonio Palmestrina. She will recognize the name as Venetian. I will introduce you as Giovanni Nero's only child, come from America in search of your roots and leave the conversation entirely to you and the signora. I will only interpret for each of you."

My heart raced as Ludo pushed the button in the lion's mouth beside the shiny brass Nero-Corsini plaque.

There was a long pause before a gravelly "Si?" emanated from a small speaker next to the door.

"Signora Nero-Corsini?" Ludo said to the speaker box.

"Si," the voice repeated.

Ludo spoke some words in Italian that I didn't understand except for my name and his recently invented pseudonym, Antonio Palmestrina. The speaker box went silent. He cast a quizzical look at me. We stood there for a few minutes before the door opened.

Signora Nero-Corsini was a slim woman, obviously of some years; how many was not immediately apparent. She wore a dark green dress that looked expensive, probably cashmere, and brown leather boots that reached above her slim ankles. A beige shawl lay across her narrow shoulders and her longish gray hair fell across the back of the shawl. I searched her face for something of my father but couldn't find it. Maybe there was something of him in her dark brown eyes, but I wasn't sure.

"Buon giorno," she said, holding the door open and moving aside as an implied invitation for us to enter.

"Permesso?" Ludo asked.

"Avanti," she answered, gesturing with her free hand.

She led us up a flight of stairs and into a large room furnished with two sofas and several upholstered chairs, all of indeterminate age and genre. It appeared to be a comfortable, lived-in room without pretense or affected elegance. She motioned us to sit.

"Caffe?" she asked.

"No, grazie," Ludo answered.

The signora sat down opposite where Ludo and I sat on one of the sofas. No one spoke for a few minutes and Signora Nero-Corsini looked intently at me, studying my face. Looking directly at me, she said something in Italian.

Ludo said, "The signora says that you are very beautiful."

"Grazie, signora," I replied looking into her dark eyes.

We both smiled.

The conversation that ensued over the next two hours was of necessity made of words. But there was a great deal more, it seemed to me, that was exchanged that afternoon. My questions about my father as she knew him were answered with both words and gestures, vivid expressions in her face and eyes and body language that several times I thought did not fit the words that Ludo translated to me. A few times I questioned the accuracy of his interpretation of her response and he elaborated in an effort to better convey her meaning.

"I will translate the words as true to the Italian as I can, mi amore," Ludo said. "But alas, Italian is spoken with much more than words. As is true of another language we have spoken of."

"But even if the words don't carry the full meaning, they should at least be consistent with it. Shouldn't they? Shouldn't the words at least fit the music?" I said.

Ludo said, "Perhaps," and turned his attention back to the signora.

I learned that my father had an identical twin who died at the age of twelve. The two of them, virtually inseparable, were swimming together in a local lake on a hot summer day and something happened; the signora purported not to know what. Some kind of accident and Giovanni's twin, Paolo, was drowned. There were no witnesses to the accident and Giovanni steadfastly refused to talk about it.

After the incident, Giovanni's personality changed. A formerly joyous, gregarious child, he became introverted and morose. He avoided human contact. He refused to make friends. He alienated himself from the family. And when the war came, he volunteered as soon as he could to fight with the Italian partisans. Signora Nero-Corsini did not believe that he did that for any reason of ideology. He never seemed to be taken with political or social causes. She thought he was trying desperately to escape from something deep inside that threatened to destroy him. She suspected that he half hoped to die in the war. When he disappeared to America after the war, his family was not surprised. They had long since given up trying to connect with him. She was the only remaining member of his immediate family, and she never tried to contact him after he left Italy. She saw no point in it. As she told that story, tears wet her eyes and fell down her cheeks onto the breast of her elegant dress. I too struggled with threatening tears.

When I told her that my father was dead these many years, she was not surprised and didn't show much emotion. She asked nothing about the circumstances of his death and I told her nothing. She said something to the effect that he was long dead to his family. She had preserved the happy young Giovanni in her trove of memories and resigned herself to his death at the same time she was forced to accept the death of his identical twin, his other self. Perhaps Giovanni had done that as well. Perhaps he lost interest in becoming half a man. How does one learn to live half a life with full enthusiasm?

The signora said that my father became enamored of violence after the tragedy. He fought with boys his age at school and almost anywhere else there was opportunity. The time or two he came home after joining the war he talked incessantly of the violence of the war. He seemed to relish it.

As the conversation wore on into the late afternoon, the signora seemed to withdraw from me. Recounting the story that brought her tears changed something. Her expression hardened. Her answers to my questions became terse. She stopped elaborating. Lines appeared beneath her eyes and her forehead wrinkled. When Ludo and I stood to leave, she made no move to embrace me, the traditional embrace and kisses to either cheek that I had come to expect. Rather she shook my hand briefly. Her hand was cold and hard. She saw us to the door and we parted, exchanging only an emotionless *arrivederci*.

Ludo and I walked back through the square toward the train station, reflecting on our encounter with Signora Nero-Corsini.

"Did you know all this about my father, Ludo?" I asked.

"I had heard the story. It was widely circulated at the time. I know little of the details and nothing firsthand. I was not an eyewitness to your father's youth."

"I might have expected a warmer response from the signora on discovering her previously unknown niece. Especially near the end of our conversation, she seemed less than jubilant about my existence."

"Yes," Ludo replied. "Perhaps too many history-burdened words exchanged among strangers. You are after all strangers, are you not?"

"Doesn't blood kinship count for something?"

"What is your saying? Blood runs stronger than water, something like that? Perhaps the two of you share too little blood to overcome the distance that separates you. And discovering you did not kindle fond memories, only long-avoided painful ones. We humans are not generally fond of pain."

We came to rest again in front of the statue of Titian in the town square. Ludo released my arm and addressed himself to the statue, feet spread, cane positioned in front of him with both hands clasping the heavenward-gazing harlequin. He rocked back and forth ever so slightly, alternately approaching toward and retreating from the likeness of Da Cadore gazing off into the distance.

Without turning away from the statue, he said, "There is an arcane myth of Da Cadore, you know. Well.…he, or his legend, has spawned many myths, both popular and arcane. But there is one that may especially interest you. You may suspect that this story is my invention but I assure you that is not the case. While I cannot attest to its verity, the story has persisted for several centuries. As with my city, perhaps persistence is a test of verity. Do you think that is possible?"

It seemed to me that Ludo was losing the train of conversation more easily than had been true earlier. He seemed more easily distracted by a stray thought. But I was determined to just let happen what happened. A meandering conversation was likely to be a trivial aberration compared to what was coming.

I answered, "You mean that if myths are repeated long enough they become real? I don't believe that. I tend to think of reality as pretty much fixed, all or none. Perceptions of reality can change, if that's what you mean. And perceptions are influenced by myth. Otherwise there wouldn't be religion. But not reality. What do you think?"

"Yes, that is true. But I suspect that my view of what is real is considerably more fluid than yours."

He turned from the statue toward me and took my arm. As we bobbed and wove our way toward the train station, Ludo recounted the story.

"The story is that Da Cadore was actually one of a pair of identical twins, born and spending their early years here in this village, much as did your father and his twin. And the coincidence enlarges. The story goes that at the age of twelve years, a terrible accident took the life of Da Cadore's twin brother."

"Ludo," I smiled. "It's very difficult for me to believe that you haven't invented this story."

"I assure you, that is not the case," Ludo said. "But let me finish the tale. Before the death of his twin, it is said that Da Cadore had shown no special artistic talent. But after the tragedy, the young man blossomed. He rapidly developed into an artistic prodigy and of course grew to become perhaps the greatest and most influential artist of his day, living a luxurious life in Venice to a ripe old age. The legend has it that the death of Da Cadore's twin made him twice the man, the fullness of his being no longer divided into two but completely his."

The story ended, we walked along for a bit without speaking.

"How odd," I finally said, "that the two stories—this one and my father's—could be so alike, that the experience was the same, but the results were completely different. If I'm to believe Signora Nero-Corsini, the death of my father's twin was his ruination while your myth of Da Cadore has the same experience: an epiphany of sorts for the surviving twin, a salvation story."

Ludo mumbled to himself something that sounded like

"Yes, odd," then more audibly to me. "That is why I recount the story to you. I suppose there is a lesson that the same tragedy may eventuate in good or ill and that may depend on how events are perceived by those remaining. Is it possible, mi amore, that good or ill is determined by perception more than reality?"

"Oh, Ludo," I sighed, "You're determined to point out flaws in how I see life, aren't you?"

"There is truth in what you say. But it is not malicious. It is that I wish for you the pleasure of experiencing beauty, and I have found that beauty is rarely painted in the stark geometry of a black-and-white, all-or-none dichotomy. I am certain that such a paradigm serves you well in your professional pursuits. But you have come to the most beautiful city in the world, taken up with...dare I say *loved*," he engaged my eyes with his and smiled, "a dying old man who is intent on enduring that experience with as much grace, elegance, and dignity as possible. You have come so far in search of something. Knowledge, of course, of your roots. But surely beauty as well. The truth you seek will be a partial truth if made of facts alone."

We arrived at the station with half an hour before the next train. We sat close together on a bench in the crisp air of the platform. We said little more before boarding the train and returning to the most beautiful city in the world.

CHAPTER 18: THE OLD CURIOSITY SHOP

Out the door of my small flat, turn left on the Fondamenta Nove, cross a single bridge, and stop at a small storefront on a corner facing the *laguna* just before D'Alvise, the small trattoria that Ludo and I favored for lunch or an early dinner when we didn't want to walk too far. I passed this shop almost every day and usually stopped to look in through the windows. The shop was never open as far as I could tell. The door was always locked. The place was chock-a-block with all sorts of strange objects. To the right at floor level was a large cast concrete sculpture that appeared to be a likeness of Mussolini (the telltale protuberant mandible). An enormous chandelier dominated the ceiling. There were all sorts of old signs, miniature gondolas, glass pieces of various designs, and old pieces of furniture covered with numerous little knick-knacks filling the room. The chandelier was always lighted during the day and turned off at night and the objects appeared cleanly dusted, indicating that someone was attending to the shop although I had never seen such a person. There were old photographs, some of which appeared to have been taken in a wartime Venice. To the rear, visible only by pressing my face to the window and cupping my hands about my face to shield out the daylight, was a red flag with a large black swastika mounted on the back wall. There was something more than faintly sinister about the shop. That seemed to be its attraction to me. I asked Ludo about it a couple of times and each time he responded with some uninformative, dismissive comment. That only deepened the mystery and the attraction for me. There was no identifying sign on the storefront. Dredged from some remote Dickensian memory, I thought of the place as The Old Curiosity Shop.

I was very surprised when late one sunny December morning after coffee (*corretto* as usual) in Ludo's palazzo, as the sun struggled upward toward its apogee, spilling its uniquely Venetian rays into the room, Ludo raised the subject of the mystery shop.

"Today, mi amore," he said, "I will introduce you, if you wish, to the proprietress of that shop down the way that so intrigues you. I have avoided doing that for all this time because such an introduction may require a degree of deception and you have made it clear that you are not fond of deception. But, alas, it is an inevitable experience sooner or later and perhaps this is as later as is likely to provide the occasion."

As if to emphasize the increasingly obvious brevity of our remaining time, he coughed the deep, wet cough that periodically wracked his waning frame and produced again the crimson evidence of the looming specter of our partner in this dance.

"Deception?" I asked, doing my best to ignore the cough and what it signified. "What deception? Whom are we supposed to deceive?"

"The signora, the shop's proprietress, Blanche. She must not know your name, who you are. There is more history here and of darker hue that we have so far addressed."

Again, Ludo's frustrating opacity.

"Can you explain a little more?" I asked.

I was making every effort to be gentle with Ludo. My concern for his comfort was becoming more important than the reason that brought me to Venice in the first place. My reason for being there had evolved in a different direction from what I had anticipated.

"There is a connection with your father. The signora would recognize your surname and surely make a connection. Her sympathies, and those of her late husband, were and are very different from those that motivated your father. I can assure that she would not be pleased to discover that Giovanni Nero had a daughter who suddenly appeared from out of the ether to haunt her with unpleasant memories."

"Is there more to this story?" I asked.

"Yes, mi amore," he answered, "There is more...But I must tell it at considerable personal risk and I am not yet ready to take that risk. Please indulge me for a bit longer. You will discover part of the remaining story upon meeting the signora. The rest will come later."

"Did the signora know my father?" I queried.

"Not personally as far as I know," Ludo answered, wrinkling his brow, deepening the furrows already there. "But she certainly knew of him. That is for certain. And he had a special significance to her. That is also for certain. She knows the name. No doubt she does not associate the name with pleasant memories."

It took a great deal of self-discipline to tolerate Ludo's melodramatically paced unfolding of my father's story, whatever it was. But I did that. I focused on Ludo, his rapidly approaching fate, and my feelings for him that were very much in the here and now. The history had become more important to him than to me. I would just let him tell the story in whatever way and at whatever pace he chose. Why was I doing that? I didn't have a clue. I really didn't like feeling clueless. I had never thought of myself as that sort of person.

It was later in the day, sometime after lunch, when Ludo and I walked along the fondamenta toward the shop. The afternoon was cold. A hard, sharp wind sliced at us from somewhere across the lagoon.

Sometimes I would stare at the lagoon from my window and wonder what was on the other side, beyond Murano, Burano, out across the bristle of the Aegean. Of course I could look at a map and learn the names of the places on the other side. But I didn't like the cold two-dimensionality of maps. I had never understood how one could read a map. What was there to read? Names of places? Yes, but names, as important as they can be, only paint the surface. What was it really like out there beyond the islands and across the bristling sea? What lived in those distant places? What would it feel like to open them up and feel their wet pink pulsing viscera slither through your hands? What exotic smells radiate from their innards? What sounds drift from their sacred places? Can you, as in New Orleans before the flood, taste their air?

My mind wandered. Ludo walked even slower than usual that afternoon. He hadn't spoken for a while.

"So, Blanche, mi amore," he finally said. "Let me tell you a bit about the signora, mistress of your curious shop."

His voice was hoarse, a soft rasp that struggled to be heard above the whine and rustle of the cold laguna wind. He leaned close to me breathing the words into my ear.

"I'm afraid the Signora Petacci-Flaherty is very old now," he continued. "And more than a bit infirm as well. She must use a chair to get about. Oh, how do you say it…a wheelchair. Such a literal word I should have no trouble remembering it."

He coughed again, that damnable wet cough. He covered his mouth with a fresh handkerchief, soiling its pristine laundered whiteness with a deep magenta morsel of the accumulating evidence of his impending fate.

I looked at him. His practiced elegance was decaying. A life winding down. Entropy getting the upper hand.

The signora's name didn't register with me at the time. Possibly his pronunciation, the hard *a* and truncated *y*. A moment of potential recognition lost in the fragility of spoken words.

"I do not see the signora often," Ludo continued, "but in recent years she has seemed to live more and more in the distant past. The shop reflects that. A relic suspended in a time of difficulty that is relevant now only in the minds of those who are suspended in that time. I fear that the signora is herself a relic. Perhaps it is best to think of her that way. She can be difficult, Blanche. You should try to see her as the relic that she is and to suppress any inclination to react to her idiosyncrasies."

"Idiosyncrasies?"

"Whatever you choose to call them. Fixations? A bit of her

history may help. She was married to a soldier during the war. He was not Venetian, not even Italian. He was infatuated with Il Duce and the cause and came from his home country to fight with Il Duce's army. They were apparently very much in love and the signora adopted his passion for the cause."

"So what happened to him? Was he killed in the war?"

"In a manner of speaking. He fell victim to the irrational passions for their cause that consumed many of the fascists. Unchecked passions are often fatal, you know."

"You evade my question, Ludo. Was he killed in the war?"

"I apologize, but the story of his death has some significance that must wait a time before revealing itself. To address more directly your question—and I am aware of your need for dealing with more directness than is my habit—he was not killed in the war. He was, however, in a very real sense killed by the war. After you meet the signora, perhaps we can talk more of this.

"But we must give you a temporary name. Let's see. There is no need to avoid a transparently American name although the signora is not fond of Americans. Who would you like to be?"

"Who I would like to be, Ludo," I replied sounding a little sharper than I intended, "is Blanche Nero."

"I know, I know," he said. "But just for a brief time we shall call you Susan Yates, an American visiting from New Orleans."

"Where did you get that name, Ludo? It sounds so ordinary."

"An invention, mi amore, purely an invention and intended to sound ordinary. The signora and her shop that so intrigues you should be the center of this little visit. The point is to deflect her from interest in you. You will discover soon enough

why that is important. Suffice for now to say that the ruse is
meant to spare both you and the signora unnecessary
discomfort. And myself as well. You would not wish to share
our inevitable discomfort with the signora. That would serve no
good purpose."

Opacity piled upon opacity. But I didn't pursue it. I was
intrigued by the shop and this strange tale of the signora and
her fixations. And resigned to Ludo's byzantine path toward
revealing the story, whatever it was.

The door to the signora's apartment was just around the
corner from the shop front. The space beneath the bell meant
for the occupant's name was blank. When Ludo rang the bell,
the door was answered by a young, rather plain-looking girl.

"Buon giorno, Conte Ludovici," the girl said with a slight
gesture of her body that hinted of a nascent curtsy.

"Buon giorno, Francesca," Ludo replied. "Is the signora
available? There is someone who wishes to meet her."

Although she must have understood Ludo's query spoken in
English, the girl answered in Italian. She motioned us in with
her hand.

"Permesso?" Ludo asked.

"Avanti," she answered.

We entered. Francesca said something more in Italian and
disappeared through a doorway toward the front of the
apartment.

"The signora is in the shop," Ludo explained. "Francesca
will see if she will receive us."

Lighting in the room was very dim. As my eyes adjusted to
the low light, I looked around. Several pieces of heavy
furniture—a chaise or two, a sofa, some chairs—were crowded

into the room. The décor was red, overwhelmingly red. The walls were painted a dark red, a color I associated with funeral parlors and brothels. The velvet coverings of the sofas and chairs were an identical shade of red. The floor was tile of some kind, also deep red. I didn't recall ever having seen floor tiles that color. There was a funereal presence to the room: the redness but also a faint floral aroma (although I saw no flowers), a disquieting stillness, and from somewhere, soft music. I couldn't tell the source, but I distinctly heard the distant soft keen of funeral music.

Francesca returned, leaving the door ajar.

"The signora will see you in the shop," she said in only slightly halting English and gestured toward the door.

"Grazie," Ludo replied, taking my arm.

Francesca led our little procession through the door into the presence of the odd proprietress of The Old Curiosity Shop.

She sat in what appeared to be a permanent slouch in a wheelchair that looked, like its occupant, as though it was near the end of its useful life. She faced the large flag with the threatening black swastika that I had seen through the window, her back to the room and us. From where I stood, she was a mound of drooped shoulders supporting a white tangle of hair just visible above the canvas back of the chair. Francesca took her place behind the old woman, grasping the handles of the chair. Ludo and I waited for the woman to recognize our presence. It took a while.

Finally the old woman waved a hand in the air and Francesca wheeled her around to face us. The signora's head was bowed so that I couldn't see her face. A very old woman hunched in her wheelchair, staring at her lap, her young attendant at the ready. A picture set off against the menacing red and black Nazi mural in the background.

The signora raised her head and looked in our direction. She said nothing. Her obviously sightless eyes were, like her tangle of thinning hair, the opaque chalk-white that veils the aging lenses, protects the elderly from the pain of visual realities, and lends them a certain mystique that intrigues an outsider presumptuous enough to invade their space. Growing old is a personal matter. It is best done at its nether end as privately as possible.

"Who is this woman, Ludo?" she said in English.

Her voice was hoarse and her English was lightly accented but it didn't sound Italian. I couldn't place the accent.

"Buon giorno, signora," Ludo said then in English. "Let me introduce you to my friend, Susan Yates. She is visiting from America and she has been intrigued by your shop."

"American!" She spat the word. "Why do you bring to me a vestige of the enemy, Ludo? American," she repeated, "your people." She appeared to be addressing me. "Your people robbed us of the greatness that was our destiny. Why do you come here? What is it you want from us now?"

I didn't know what to say.

"I am sorry to disturb you, signora," I stammered. "I was attracted to your shop. Can you tell me about it?"

"The shop, as you call it," she replied, "is my small house of relics. A memento of what could have been. You call it a shop. It is not a shop. There is nothing here that I would part with for any price. You!" She waved a hand in my general direction. "You and your countrymen took it from us! No mercy or respect for those whose country you invaded. You took up with the rabble and killed him, Il Duce, slaughtered him and his vision for Italy. Oh, the hands were those of our country's lowlife, but your hands are not without the stains of his blood," wagging a threatening finger, "Americans!" She spat the word again and turning to Ludo said, "Why do you bring this American here?"

"I beg your pardon, signora," Ludo responded, "but our guest that I bring is only curious about your, how do you call it, memorial. We do not wish to disturb you."

"Bah," she answered, "you know very well what Americans are like. Vultures and murderers!"

"Murderers?" I queried. "Why am I a murderer?"

I couldn't help responding to the charge. I was not a murderer. I was quite the opposite.

"Bah," she said. "You are all murderers."

She moved her head from side to side, wagging it as if to taunt me.

"Pardon, signora," I answered, "but I am not a murderer. I am a doctor. I have spent my life on the other side, treasuring human life, saving it where possible. I am not a murderer. I am American by chance, not choice. Do not consider me a child of another generation. I love your country. If there is an unpleasant history, it has nothing to do with me."

"Oh!" she responded. "So our Susan Yates is a woman of spirit! Miss American, you are the child of your forebears and their misbehavior. I can only see you that way. Ludo," she spoke again to him, "why did you bring this American woman here?"

"I am sorry, signora," Ludo answered, "I did not mean to cause you difficulty."

"Difficulty," she said. "You are well aware of my American difficulty. Those people took my Augohus from me. They are a people of no noble intent, Ludo."

"I know of your difficult history, signora," Ludo replied. "I had no intent to complicate your life."

Remembering Ludo's admonition to ignore the signora's idiosyncrasies, I said nothing. But I wondered what lay behind this dialogue. I was obviously an outsider and had the feeling that Ludo intended that to be clear.

"The picture in the front window," the signora said, motioning toward the front of the shop. "There is a picture there. The man by the boat without a shirt, that is my Augohus. That is how I remember him. Before he left to try to consummate his obsession…. and ours. I wished him not to go but he was determined. I feared that he would not return."

"Yes, signora," Ludo responded, "I fear we have caused you difficulty. That was not my intention. I am sorry if we have resurrected troubles, but I very much appreciate your time. We will leave you now with our best wishes."

"What in hell was that all about?" I asked Ludo as we strolled back up the fondamenta toward our homes.

The wind had subsided and the sun illuminated the façade of San Michele as it does in the late afternoon. Ludo seemed somehow invigorated by our brief encounter with the signora of The Old Curiosity Shop. I was not invigorated. I was more than a little confused.

Ludo did not answer but looked out over the lagoon as though I hadn't spoken to him. I fell into the rhythm of our stroll and didn't pursue the question. Ludo was obviously short of breath. Maybe that's why he didn't answer my question. Maybe there were other reasons as well. Of course, there were but I would discover them only later.

CHAPTER 19: FLIRTING WITH THE REAL THING

"Here come da judge," Rasputin Q. Lee (that is the signature that was meticulously inscribed with his familiar flourish on the emergency room admission sheet) boomed at the top of his lungs, his announcement ringing out above the emergency room din.

The sedation was obviously wearing off. Rasputin was a frequent flyer and could get pretty unruly. The staff knew that so he usually got a hefty shot of something to calm him down as soon as he arrived. He had been in the ER long enough to get the shot and get his face put back together as well as I could manage, given its history. We were about ready to ship him out.

"Rasputin," the man said, coming over to the gurney where the patient lay, "what happened this time? Never mind, I know the story by heart. I should know it by now."

I didn't recall having seen the man before. He was nice-looking more than handsome. His longish blond hair was a little disheveled and the blue sport coat was beginning to show its age. I guessed that he was an academic type. Why he would have any connection with Rasputin Q. Lee, Charity ER frequent flyer and Big Easy ne'er-do-well, was anybody's guess.

"Judge Jesse," Rasputin said, reaching up in a futile effort to embrace his visitor, "I knew I could count on you. You the man, Judge. You definitively the man." He lay back on the stretcher but reached for the man's hand and held it for a moment.

The man turned to me and introduced himself. "Doctor, I'm Jesse Pinto. I'll see to Rasputin here when you're ready for him to go."

"I'm Dr. Nero, the ER trauma surgeon on duty," I answered; we shook hands. "Where will you take him?"

"Back to the shelter. He's a regular there as well as here."

"Do you work there?" I asked, my curiosity getting the upper hand.

"Volunteer. I volunteer there pretty regularly. For a day job, I do my best at seeing that Rasputin and his friends get a fair shake from John Law. By night, I help out with cleaning up after them. I'm not sure which of those activities serves the better good."

"So you're an actual judge?" I asked.

"Yes," he said.

There was an awkward silence between us that I didn't understand. We stood there looking at Rasputin. It seemed as though there was nothing more for us to say to each other but that we somehow didn't want to admit that.

"Well," I finally said, "Mr. Rasputin Q. Lee is about ready to reenter his world, wherever that is. The nurse will come by and check him out." I reached to shake the judge's hand again and said something inane like "Take care of him." I don't remember exactly what.

On my way from the ER I ran into Fiona, the head nurse on

the night shift. She and I had struck up a friendship that I'd come to value.

"Who's the judge guy?" I asked.

"You mean Judge Jesse?" she answered. "You don't know him?"

"Don't think I've had the pleasure before."

"I'm surprised. He's here a lot. Picks up the pieces of the derelicts after we patch them up. He's an actual judge, I'm pretty sure. He seems to care about these people. Who knows what the whole story is? Are you interested?"

"No, not really. Just wondered about his connection with Rasputin. Seems pretty unlikely."

"Most of the things that happen here seem pretty unlikely if you think too much about them."

"I hope that's true," I said. "I'd hate to think the whole world was like this."

I was off duty the next day and I called Fiona to see if she'd like to have lunch. Fiona Regan was a remarkable woman. We were about the same age, two single, forty-something women drawn to each other by the gravity of circumstance. I really enjoyed her company. When things got hectic in the ER, she was something to behold. She seemed to thrive on chaos. Her red hair flying, freckles highlighted against her flushed face, she could herd an unruly bunch of residents, nurses, and assorted other personnel into a focused team and get more work done than there was any reason to expect of a human. Away from that scene, Fiona was a charming, witty, and genuinely caring soul. We liked each other. I had had few real friends in my life and I thought of Fiona as a genuine friend. I valued her.

I had pretty much given up men since the trauma of the Brad Palance affair several years earlier. I had decided that men were too much trouble and that sex wasn't that important anyway. Since sex had been the only way I related to men, I no longer had a burning need for a relationship with a member of my opposite gender. And I didn't trust my judgment about men after Brad Palance. I lost myself in my work, enjoyed an occasional lunch or dinner with Fiona. I thought I was pretty satisfied with how things had settled out.

But I admit now that I was thinking of Judge Jesse Pinto on that morning. I didn't know why. I thought maybe I could sidle up to the subject with Fiona without her reading too much into it. I just wanted to learn something more about this unlikely man.

"Look, Blanche," Fiona said.

We had finished lunch and were sipping at the last of a bottle of a really oaky chardonnay that tasted uncommonly good. It was a sunny day with a humid breeze wafting across The Quarter from the river. We sat outside at a small restaurant that we liked.

"If you want to know more about Judge Jesse," she continued, "why don't you just say so?"

I was surprised. I thought I had been subtle enough that Fiona wouldn't get my intent so clearly. She sounded more than a little impatient with me.

"OK," I replied, "so tell me what you know about him."

"Not a lot," she said. "He shows up at the ER with some regularity. He seems to know when one of the really hard-core frequent flyers needs a rescue. They seem to know how to contact him or he gets the message somehow. Maybe there's a network that he's tuned into."

"What kind of a judge is he?"

"I don't know, but the hard-core guys appear to know him pretty well."

"Have you ever asked him about it?"

"Look, Blanche," she said, sipping at the last of her glass of wine. "Just doing my job keeps me pretty busy. Idle conversation with people passing through the ER is not part of the job. I don't have time for it. I'm just glad that somebody is there to haul the patched-up drunks and druggies to some other place once we've done what we can for them. Judge Jesse is a blessing. I don't really care why he shows up. But, thank God, he does."

"Well, it's just interesting," I said, "that he would do that."

"Interesting if you're interested in him. I'm getting the message, Blanche, that you're nursing a thing for the judge."

"Not really," I said. "There was just something about him that made me curious."

"Ah, curiosity." She smiled and looked off into the distance. "I'll see what I can find out."

When Judge Jesse called me at home some days later, I was surprised. It turned out that Fiona had given him my number without telling me.

"Dr. Nero," he said, "this is Jesse Pinto. I hope I'm not intruding. Do you remember we met in the Charity ER a couple of weeks ago?"

I hesitated, not because I didn't remember him but because I did.

"Yes," I said, "yes, I remember you. It's just that I'm surprised by your call."

"Of course," he answered. "Am I intruding?"

"No, no," I said. "I'm pleased that you called. Just surprised."

I could feel my heart racing and didn't like the feeling, didn't understand what I was feeling. My heart hadn't raced like that for a while.

"I would like to see you," he continued. "May I take you to dinner?"

I answered without thinking it through. "Yes. I'd like that."

"Are you free this Friday evening?"

I dredged up my schedule in my head and realized that I was on call Friday night.

"Oh." I sounded more disappointed than I intended. "I'm sorry. I'm afraid I'm on call Friday night."

"OK," he answered. "How about Saturday?"

"Yes," I said, "Saturday would be fine. Shall I meet you somewhere?"

"Why don't I pick you up if that's OK? If you'll tell me where you live, I can come by. Would seven be all right?"

"Seven would be fine," I answered.

I gave him my address and we said goodbye, ending a conversation that would change my life for the next several months…maybe longer than that.

The plans for Judge Jesse and me to share a meal changed. He called later on and suggested that we have Sunday brunch at Broussard's on Conti. Broussard's was a New Orleans fixture and Jesse said their Sunday brunch was nice. I hadn't eaten there. Certainly not Sunday brunch. For me, Sundays when I wasn't working were for sleeping as late as possible, not dressing up and going out to a fancy restaurant. But I awoke early on that Sunday and got dressed up. Interesting in retrospect that this relationship started out with what seemed to me a compromise. Even more interesting that I didn't mind that. I was not accustomed to compromise but I was, in fact, rather happy about this unexpected development.

It was a lovely sunny afternoon and we walked from my place to the restaurant, a leisurely stroll through The Quarter. We didn't talk much, just idle banter about the beautiful spring weather and the flowers opening their brilliant blooms in window boxes and on porches along the way. The conversation was comfortable, a gracious beginning to the dance we were about to do.

"Good afternoon, Judge," the maitre d' greeted Jesse as we entered the restaurant, "I have your table if you'll follow me," then turning to me, "Good afternoon, madam, and happy Mother's Day," he nodded toward me without smiling.

I paid no attention to holidays, no matter whom they were supposed to honor. I had no idea that it was Mother's Day. Except for its effect on ER business, I probably would have been only vaguely aware of Christmas. I wondered whether Jesse had chosen this particular day for some reason, but I was reluctant to ask.

After we were seated, I looked around the room. The tables were full of multigenerational parties. Each table was presided over by a slightly overweight older woman who wore a very conspicuous hat. The room seemed filled with hats of various hues bobbing back and forth in animated conversations. A lot of the hats were red. Red was never my favorite color. Too much red in the OR was rarely a good sign. Behind where we sat there was a platform from which a too-blonde woman played "Mona Lisa" on a white piano.

"I didn't realize that today was Mother's Day," I said.

We sat across the small table from each other and I looked at his face. I noticed the crinkles at the corners of his eyes and that his nose was rather large and not entirely straight. I noticed his eyes, the faded blue color that reminded me of a favorite aging pair of denim jeans that I usually wore on weekends. But more than the color. They were happy eyes.

"Yes," he answered, "I guess it would be difficult not to notice that here."

"And are you ignoring your mother on her special day to fritter away the afternoon with a stranger?" I asked, trying to sound clever.

"Not at all," Jesse answered, suddenly serious. "My sainted mother died some years ago, but I always remember her on this day. Must I do that all alone?"

Our eyes met for a moment and he smiled. We didn't say anything for a few minutes.

"Are we really strangers?" he finally broke the silence.

"Yes, I think we're strangers. And maybe better to stay that way for all I know."

"Here's what I think," he said. "I think that we are no more strangers than any other humans. I'm sure you know better than I do that we humans are all pretty much the same. What is it, like 99.9 percent of our genes are identical?"

"I've heard that number. But I've found that the other .1 percent can make a lot of difference."

A waiter interrupted us with a glass of champagne. He put menus on the table and greeted us. Recognizing that we were more interested in talking to each other, he withdrew.

Jesse picked up the conversation. "I think that other .1 percent is only as important as you decide to make it. That's what I think. But we don't need to talk personal philosophy yet...unless you want to."

The *yet* registered. Like a promissory note. Something more is coming. Better get ready, Blanche Nero.

"What are you doing here?" Jesse asked. "Or, maybe I should ask, how did a beautiful and obviously gifted woman wind up spending her nights patching up the likes of Rasputin Lee in the Charity ER? Seems an unlikely situation."

Interesting that he chose the word *unlikely*, exactly how I had perceived his appearance there and his apparent relationship with Big Easy's less fortunate citizens. I laughed.

"You're amused by my question?" Jesse said, arching his eyebrows and smiling.

"It's not that," I answered. "It's just that when we met in the ER, when you appeared to claim what was left of Rasputin Lee, I thought that situation most unlikely. I said that to Fiona Regan, the head nurse."

"Oh," he sighed. "But what about my question?"

"The story is too long and the path too tortuous to answer this afternoon if you want an honest answer."

"Honest answers are the only ones that count," he said. "They teach you that in judge school."

We laughed together.

I don't remember what I ate that afternoon. Jesse and I continued to talk through the meal and as we walked back through The Quarter toward my place. He saw me to my door.

"I very much enjoyed this afternoon," he said.

Our bodies had not touched through the afternoon, not

even a handshake, and still didn't on our parting. Jesse stood a little awkwardly with both hands in his pockets, his jacket open.

"I did too," I said.

"Can we do something like this again?" he asked.

"Yes," I said. "I'd like that."

I didn't ask him in and he made no indication that he expected or wanted that. I watched him stroll off down Iberville and closed the door.

My relationship with Jesse Pinto developed slowly over the next few months. He was a native of the city and had a long menu of favorite places—restaurants, bars, galleries. Many were off the beaten path, some with more local color than I would have been likely to discover on my own. He was known everywhere and always heartily welcomed. I was impressed that Jesse was attracted and attractive to all kinds of people. He seemed equally at home with a glass of wine chatting with the elegant clientele in a fancy art gallery and with a Dixie beer in a seedy blues bar. With him, I began to feel comfortable in those places too.

Although I had outfitted my kitchen fit for a gourmet chef, I had never developed any significant culinary skills. It turned out that Jesse was an outstanding cook. It also turned out that he lived in The Quarter and as we got closer, he would often come to my place on the weekends and cook something absolutely wonderful. He was in his element in the kitchen. We'd share the meals along with a good wine and a lot of laughter. Jesse liked French wines and knew them well. Although he was especially proud of his Creole creations, he seemed able to cook almost anything without a recipe. He said that his mother had taught him how to cook.

Jesse talked sometimes of his mother. She was a New Orleans cop (another unlikely fact). He never knew his father. He was an only child. His mother put him through college and law school at Tulane. He revered her for a very long list of reasons.

We had been seeing each other for a couple of months before we made love. I think now that we were in love well before we made love. Before Jesse, I had never thought of the act of sexual intercourse as making love. My attitude toward sex had always been more pragmatic than romantic. And I had lost interest in that. Sex with Jesse revived my interest. If our coupling didn't create love, it certainly embellished the experience.

At some point during those several months, it finally dawned on my conscious that I loved Jesse. That was a new realization for me. I had spent a lot of time and effort avoiding loving anyone and had been rather proud of the emotional independence that keeping a distance from other people afforded. After all, I had done what I had done pretty much on my own. I wasn't about to risk the vulnerability that loving another person was likely to involve.

But I was in love with Jesse and surprised myself by telling him so. We were in bed, afterglowing together. My head lay on his shoulder and he caressed my hair. Without planning it, I spoke the three words that I had studiously avoided saying my entire life.

"I love you," I said.

He replied, "Of course you love me. I love you too. If we don't love each other, what are we doing here?"

As I write this sitting at the table in my little flat late on a cold Venice evening, I feel again some of the warmth of being with Jesse Pinto. The feeling makes me very sad. It was unlike anything else that I have felt in my life.

CHAPTER 20: SHORING UP THE WALLS

What I remember most from those few months with Jesse are conversations. We talked. We talked about a lot of things. I think it was all those shared words as much as anything that drew me closer to Jesse than I had ever been to another person.

"Your time must be pretty valuable," I said. "Why do you choose to spend so much of it with such lowlife?"

"Lowlife? I wouldn't call people with limited opportunities lowlife."

There was sharp impatience in the tone of Jesse's reply. And the ends of his sentences often sounded querulous, his tone tilting upward.

"I'm sorry," I answered. "I didn't mean it to sound that way. It's just that it seems like a strange way for you to spend your time and energy. So many of them are apparently hopeless repeat offenders. At least that's the way I see them. They keep coming back in the same condition."

"But does that mean you give up on them? If you really think that, why do you keep putting them back together? Why not just let nature take its course?" The querulous tilt again.

"Because I'm a surgeon. I deliver care to anyone who shows up and needs it. I fix bodies. I don't need to touch souls."

"I suppose that's a difference between us. Care is something you deliver but it's something I do."

"Maybe it's not so different. Maybe we just express caring differently. It's easier for me to do it than to feel it."

"I find that strange," he said. "You're capable of such strong feelings."

"Strange," I pondered the word. "What I feel with you is strange to me. I haven't felt like this before."

"I know what you mean," he answered, trailing the *mean* upward.

"Why surgery?" he asked.

"Why not?"

"That's no answer," he chided. "Why did you choose a profession that seems, at least on the surface, so unfeminine. You're so feminine. *Unlikely* comes to mind again."

"You mean you don't think one can be tough and also feminine?"

"Not really that. I don't know what I mean. It just seems unlikely. Do you enjoy cutting on people, all that blood and gore?"

"Actually I enjoy that very much. It excites me."

"I tend to faint at the sight of blood." He smiled and reached for my hand across the table.

We had finished dinner and were sitting at the little table I had put on my balcony.

"Violence frightens and angers me," he continued. "My mother would often recount her daily experiences to me when I was young. She was a policewoman, a cop, on the front lines. I hated the stories. They gave me nightmares. But I never told her. I loved her too much to let her know that she was causing me trouble."

"I've always been attracted to violence," I answered. "A morbid attraction I guess. But I made the best of it."

"What is it about violence that attracts you?"

"The sensuality," I answered. "Pain and pleasure aren't that far apart you know."

"Where did that notion come from?"

"Experience, my dear," I said, "experience. A lifetime of experience. I learned that lesson very early and I've found no reason to change my mind."

"Do I…our relationship, I mean…cause you pain?"

"Not yet. Just pleasure," I said.

I took his hand and we went inside.

"You are the most nonjudgmental person I know," I said. "Why did you decide on a profession that requires that of you?"

"Judges don't judge people. If we do our job right, we judge, or discern, the law. I have a lot of respect for the law. The law is supposed to see everybody the same. I don't judge people. I try to see that they all get a fair shake. If I can do that, I've done my job. And it's a job I am proud of when it works. Unfortunately, it doesn't always work."

"Do you sentence people to death?"

Something that I didn't understand flashed in his face for a moment before he spoke.

"Not if I can help it," he said, looking off into the distance.

We sat on a bench, watching people and the passing river

traffic, holding hands.

He continued. "How about you? You don't save the lives of all your patients, do you?"

"Unfortunately not," I answered. "I'm quite good friends with the Death Angel. Actually, there is something pretty exciting about the balancing act you have to master to do my job."

"Balancing act?"

"Yes, I think of it that way. Skirting carefully the edge of the abyss without falling in. Maybe it's like pain and pleasure. I mean that the territory between life and death where I do my job isn't very big."

"It often feels like the territory where I do my job is bigger than the whole universe. There seems to be no end to the possibilities. You only have to deal with life and death. There are precious few dichotomies like that in what I do. The shades of gray are infinite."

"I rather like to think that most things are pretty much black or white, right or wrong. You don't think so?"

"I know that's not so," he said, although the statement sounded a little quizzical.

Then his face broke into a broad smile and he laughed.

"Why do you laugh?" I asked.

"Blanche Nero," he said. "White and black. I hadn't thought of your name that way. Maybe it's your fate to deal with life as a dichotomy, either-or."

"It's worked all right for me so far."

"Has it really? Is it still working?"

"I think so. What do you think?"

"I think, my love, that what's happening with us doesn't fit comfortably into a black and white world. What's happening with us is infinitely richer than that."

And so it went. The conversations multiplied and the intensity of my feeling for Jesse grew as well. We talked of almost everything. I had never known anyone so interested in me as a person. It was performance that got me to where I was, not my person. And I guess I had avoided knowing myself very well beyond me as performer; I had certainly had no inclination to share such an exploration with anyone else. Before Jesse, that is. I told him a lot about myself, sometimes discovering things as I said them. Feeling such freedom to talk was so new that I came to say things without thinking. I told him things that I had never said before, excited by the newness of it all. The feelings that grew inside me were new as well.

At some point, I got scared. I can't explain it even now. I had never felt so good in my life. But I began to fear that I could not bear such feelings that depended so completely on another person. And—this was really scary—I began to dream of hurting Jesse, physically hurting him. Sometimes the dreams were mixed up with the recurring dream of my father's conviction and death. One time Jesse was the judge who sentenced my father. In another dream, Jesse was strapped in the electric chair and I was pulling a huge black handle that closed the circuit. There were a lot of other variations on the theme. I was terrified by the dreams. They started coming too often. I didn't tell Jesse about the dreams. And I never told him about my father's death either. I mean, I told him that my father died when I was fifteen, but I didn't tell him how. I avoided the subject as much as possible. I just couldn't deal with that.

It seems almost silly of me when I reflect on it now but Jesse's proposal of marriage came as a total shock. The thought had never crossed my mind. Fear had already been incubating a while and the thought of marriage terrified me. I think that I did love Jesse as much as I could. I wasn't fooling myself or him about that. But not marriage. There is something too final about that. And the only marriage that I knew anything about firsthand had not made anybody happy, including me. My response baffled Jesse.

"Blanche," he said, "I won't believe that you haven't thought about it."

"Believe what you want, Jesse, but that's the truth," I said. "I'm just not the marrying kind. If that's what you need, then you need somebody else, not me."

"I don't need somebody else," he answered. "And I don't need to get married. I'm forty-nine years old and I've made it fine living alone until now. I don't need to marry. I want to marry you. This is a very specific feeling, my love. It hasn't happened before, so maybe I'm not handling the situation very well. But this is the most real thing I have ever experienced and I want to write it in stone. I want to spend the rest of my life with you. I want us to grow old together."

It seemed that the more he said, the more frightened I got. I believe that I shared a depth of feeling with Jesse. But the thought of an unknown future depending on someone else scared me nearly to death.

My response at that time was the biggest mistake of my life. The fear so engulfed me that I broke off with Jesse then and there. I told him that we were never to see each other again. That we should get on with our lives.

I broke both our hearts that afternoon. Jesse pleaded with me to think this over but I obstinately refused. If I thought it over, I would only get more frightened. I wanted that hollow space deep in my chest where fear had settled in to go away. And that meant that Jesse had to go away, out of my mind and out of my heart. This thing might have started with a pleasant compromise, but I would not compromise now. Black or white. Right or wrong. Either-or. The decision had to be made and I made it. I have made a lot of life-and-death decisions but this was the worst one I ever made.

"So," Fiona said, "You broke it off with Judge Jesse? That surprises me. You guys had gotten pretty thick. I was starting to hear some wedding bells tolling in the distance."

We were lunching at that little place in The Quarter that we liked so much. It had been a while since we had done that. I'd been spending most of my free time with Jesse for the past few months.

"No wedding bells for me, Fiona," I feigned a casual attitude toward the topic. "That's not in the cards."

"So he popped the question and you said no?"

""You could put it that way, although it was a little more serious than you make it sound. And not so simple."

"I'm not surprised that it wasn't simple," Fiona responded. "You two invested a lot of time and energy in each other for the past little while. And from what I could tell, you seemed to be enjoying yourselves."

"That's certainly true."

"So what's your problem, Blanche?" she asked leaning toward me, her elbows on the table, looking directly into my eyes.

"So you're the expert on marriage?" I responded looking aside to avoid her gaze. "Is staying single a problem? Doesn't seem to cramp your style particularly."

"My situation is different from yours, Blanche." She sounded pensive now. "But we don't need to go into that. You made your decision. I'm glad to have you back. Eating alone all the time and talking to one's self isn't a lot of fun."

So that was it for my attempt at falling in love for real. I fell in all right but my fear of drowning sent me scurrying to the safety of my private shore as soon as the water started getting too deep. I got on with my life, as they say, immersed myself in my work and the logistics of living. I came to appreciate and value my friend Fiona Regan again, feeling a little guilty for neglecting her. But she was fine with it.

The troubling dreams about Jesse gave way once again to the troubling dreams of my father. Back to my real world.

It was never the same after Jesse.

CHAPTER 21: GATHERING STORMS

"This thing started..." said a youngish man with slicked-back hair and a jacket that strained across his generous paunch. He waved his arms about gesturing at a large weather map and marking periodically on it with a black magic marker. "...when a tropical wave clashed with Tropical Depression Ten here," pointing to some obscure remote place in the Bahamas. That created Tropical Depression Twelve."

"It seems so far away and technical," I said to Fiona.

We were taking a short break from the ER action. We sat in what passed for a lounge, a small windowless room with dirty green walls. It had been a storeroom that was cleared of supplies and furnished with a steel table, several dilapidated folding chairs, a coffee pot, and a small television. No one had bothered to repaint the walls. The TV was tuned to the weather channel. Everyone was watching the weather.

"Yes," she replied, "but looks like it's getting bigger and closer."

"Here is where we think Hurricane Katrina is headed," the man said, pulling up another map displaying a large part of the southeastern U.S., the green of Florida jutting into the blue expanse, a priapic barrier holding apart the waters of the Gulf and the Atlantic. "This is our best guess at the moment," he continued. "Things can change rapidly with storms like this."

The red and yellow dots that marked the projection of Katrina's path tracked across the south end of Florida and arced through the Gulf, hitting land somewhere east of New Orleans.

It was late August. I was fond of August in New Orleans. I thrived on the heat that others found oppressive. The heat of August in New Orleans warmed me to the core. There was also something stirring about hurricane season. None of us took the threat of an impending natural disaster very seriously. There were so many false alarms. So we were intrigued by Katrina's development and watched it with interest but without the drama so vigorously nurtured by the TV meteorologists. They obviously thrived on their moment in the spotlight of public attention and did everything possible to make the most of it. Let them have their fun. We had more serious work to do.

"I've seen this kind of thing before," Fiona said. "We all have. It'll blow over."

We laughed at her unintended pun.

It didn't blow over. It blew through.

Over the next few days, it became apparent that the Big Easy was in for some rough time at the hands of Katrina. The alarms gained volume and intensity as Katrina built into a hurricane of major proportions and headed for landfall close to New Orleans. The National Weather Service began predicting catastrophe for the city—widespread destruction of houses, no electricity, no potable water. The objective descriptions of technical details gave way to dire predictions that the resulting human suffering would be"incredible by modern standards." Evacuation orders for the city were broadcast and a mass exodus of those residents who had a way out began.

We knew, of course, that most of our customers at Charity had no way to evacuate and we had to get ready to deal with the consequences of whatever happened for the ones who were stuck in the city by either circumstance or sheer obstinacy. Our clientele were not prone to yielding their independence to the whims of nature. If you were too afraid of Mother Nature, you wouldn't be living in a place the very existence of which defied natural phenomena.

Little Easy was in charge of assembling the cadre of professionals who would stay at Charity and deal with business until the storm was over. Little Easy must have been close to seventy by then but if he had slowed down any it wasn't apparent. He still looked to me pretty much like the penguin-frog chimera that I had imagined him to be when we first met. And he was as arrogant and ironic as he had always been. He seemed to take to his role as Master of Disaster for Charity. Maybe it reminded him of his distant battlefield days. Maybe it was an anamnestic response.

Little Easy had a group of us assembled in the auditorium on the second floor. He strutted back and forth in front of the group.

"You've heard the predictions," he said. "It looks as though we are in for some serious excitement. Although we know from long experience here that these things are not really predictable, we have to prepare as well as we can for the worst case."

It seemed to me that his strut gained energy as he spoke. He was the Master of Disaster and intended for that to be apparent to the assembled group. He was taking charge.

"You are the skeleton crew," he continued. "Although I sincerely hope we will avoid as many skeletons—either real or metaphorical—as possible."

Neither Little Easy nor anyone else in the room so much as smiled at his feeble flirtation with black humor.

"There are three things to remember through what could be a very trying time in the next few days," he went on, continuing his Master of Disaster strut. "First is that your job is to take the best care that is possible of those for whom you are responsible. That is, as always, our job and our commitment. Second is that if this thing really blows up, you will be under a media spotlight the likes of which you have never experienced. Every move we make, every decision, every action will be examined, dissected, and second-guessed by a gaggle of reporters who have no way to understand your challenges. And they will not always be sympathetic. Remember that. Finally, again, if this thing gets as bad as the doomsayers are predicting, you will be physically challenged beyond anything you can imagine. You will be called upon to do things that you have never conceived of in your roles as medical professionals. You'll have to do that when you are physically exhausted, pushed beyond anything that could be reasonably expected of a human being. Believe me, my colleagues, it is quite likely that you are about to have what we old warriors know is a life-changing experience. There is no way to know whether you are up to the challenge. I have personally chosen this group because I believe that you are the best hope for Charity to survive this thing with at least a modicum of the respect and honor that we strive to deserve every day that we come to work. Only time will tell whether that will be what happens. It is up to you."

I had never known Little Easy to refer to his war experience before. I was moved by his little speech. I was even proud to be a part of the chosen group. After all, it was the chaos of medical emergency that drew me to the profession to begin with and I hadn't lost touch with the thrill of that. As misanthropic as it may sound, I was looking forward to taking on Katrina. Let her give us her best shot. We would handle it.

"Little Easy is in his element," Fiona said as we left the auditorium.

"Little Easy," I mused. "I've become rather fond of the old guy."

"Yea," she said, "he does grow on you."

I was looking forward to Katrina at the time, hyped by Little Easy's inspiring pep talk. It was in retrospect a naive and inappropriate feeling, the anticipation, the excitement. Little Easy turned out to be right. There was no way to anticipate what we were in for. There would be some excitement for sure, but it wouldn't last long. Extreme exhaustion pretty much trumps any other feelings.

Storms gather in different ways. Sometimes, like Katrina, they start small and build rapidly to something of major proportions and then blow themselves out, dying with a whimper, a faint echo of their climactic bang. But there are also quiet storms that smolder along, gathering intensity slowly, almost imperceptibly, advancing with sure and certain deliberation toward an inevitable and destructive end.

It was a cold morning in late December. I awoke early, had

some coffee, and wrote for a while. Ludo was supposed to come by at one. We were going to have lunch at D'Alvise. I closed my writing notebook and sat staring out the window toward San Michele, thinking of Ludo.

He was looking less and less well. I could see the change almost daily. Ludo was going to die and it wasn't going to be that much longer. The viral storm incubating in Ludo's body was surely and deliberately advancing toward its ultimate goal. The candle of another human life snuffed out. Another notch etched in the handle of the virus's bloody sword. If I had ever been tempted to believe that there was a God, the existence of the virus would have convinced me otherwise. Nature has no concern for what is right or just. What *is*, is. That's all there is to it.

By the time I mused away some hours, had a shower, dressed, and drank another cup or two of coffee, I noticed that it was almost one o'clock. I fed Violetta and sat down to wait for Ludo. By quarter past the hour he hadn't arrived. Ludo was usually prompt lately and I was surprised that he hadn't shown up. I waited until almost two and since he still hadn't arrived, I decided that I'd better go and check on him. Maybe I had misunderstood our arrangement for lunch.

I put on a coat, went around to the door to Ludo's palazzo, and rang the bell. There was no answer and I rang again several times. Still no answer. I was worried that something was seriously wrong. Ludo had given me a key to his place earlier as a precaution and I let myself in.

"Ludo," I called his name as I ascended the stairs. "Ludo, it's Blanche. Are you here? Are you all right?"

There was no answer.

I entered the *piano nobile* and looked around. I recalled thinking when I first saw that room that it looked like a place where the decadent rich might choose to hole up and die. When I looked toward the large window that faced the lagoon, I saw the top of Ludo's head above the back of the large sofa. Just the back of his head was visible and it appeared to be bent forward. I walked round to the front of the sofa. Ludo sat slumped over. His hands lay in his lap. I could tell that he was breathing, raspy short breaths. He looked even paler than usual. He held a blood-stained handkerchief loosely in one hand.

"Ludo," I said, placing a hand on his thin shoulder. "Ludo."

I could feel the sharp shoulder bones even through the thick sweater that he wore.

"Ludo," I repeated, louder; I shook him gently.

"Oh," he said, struggling to raise his head up and staring at me with hollow eyes, "Oh, Blanche."

"It's almost two o'clock," I said. "Weren't we going to have lunch?"

"Lunch," he said, clearing his throat and shifting about. "Yes, lunch. I am having lunch with Blanche," he said.

"Yes, Ludo," I replied. "I'm Blanche."

"Yes, yes, of course you are Blanche," he said. "I am sorry. I must have dozed off, mi amore."

I sat down beside him and took his hand in mine.

"Ludo," I asked. "Are you all right? Should I call your doctor?"

"No, no," he answered. "That is not necessary. I am fine, or as fine as you can expect me to be under the circumstances. Are we too late for lunch?"

"No," I said, "but are you sure you're up to it?"

"I am not sure of much of anything, Blanche," he said. "But let us have a try at it."

I helped him up from the sofa. He walked unsteadily toward the closet and got out his cane and the green overcoat that I had come to think of as a kind of icon of his persona. I helped him on with the coat, arranging its bulk as best I could over his gaunt frame. We made our way down the stairs and with some effort navigated the short distance down the fondamenta to D'Alvise.

CHAPTER 22: LUDO'S HISTORY LESSON PART II

As Ludo's health deteriorated, his need to talk to me about the distant past increased. I confess that my curiosity, especially about my father's place in that history, grew. But I was so concerned about dealing with Ludo's condition and his obviously impending fate, dealing with it myself, I mean, that curiosity about my father's history often seemed a distraction. My father was long dead. Whoever he was and whether that sordid history would offer the explanations that I came here looking for wouldn't change the present reality. Probably wouldn't change anything really.

Ludo was no longer strong enough to go out very often, especially when the weather was cold. Late December in Venice can be very cold on gray days when the sun hides behind heavy clouds and a fresh, mean *laguna* wind blows hard against the fondamenta. What was left of Ludo's never-robust body wasn't up to that kind of punishment.

I spent a large part of most days with Ludo, usually in his palazzo, sitting on the sofa overlooking the lagoon, drinking coffee with grappa. I also prepared food for him and we ate together. I was concerned about his appetite and tried to make food that he liked and also tried to pack in as many calories as possible. That seemed to help some. But I knew full well that the Death Angel was calling the shots now. We both knew that.

"We near the end of the story, mi amore," he said. "And we begin the most difficult parts of it."

It was late morning. I hadn't slept well the previous night. The dreams had never gone away entirely, but lately they were recurring with more intensity. They came almost every night. I was tired.

"Really, Ludo," I said. "You needn't talk about this now. Why don't you take a rest for a while?"

"No, no, Blanche," he answered. "I must finish this tale and we are both aware that there is not much remaining time. I do not relish it, but I could not die in peace if I did not finish telling you the story."

"Very well, Ludo," I said. "As you wish."

"There is an old saying, mi amore, '*Se i desideri fossero cavalli mendicanti avrebbe cavalcato,*' or in your English, 'If wishes were horses beggars would ride,'" he smiled. "The story is not what I wish, Blanche. I very much wish there was a different story to tell and a different one to live. But I am burdened with a story that I cannot wish away. Perhaps it is that I need to share that burden with you."

"I understand, Ludo," I replied, although I didn't fully understand at the time.

Ludo stood with some difficulty and walked over to the window, gazing out at the water. I sat on the sofa.

"You see, Blanche, it is that war is chaos. Or at least that war was chaos for my country. And as the end neared, there was a building crescendo of confused passions and loyalties. I was but a lad, trying as they say to 'come of age' and having trouble with that. So my confusion was perhaps greater than most."

He coughed. He came back to sit beside me.

"How does one decide loyalties when presented with such contrasts? How was a troubled adolescent to distinguish between the rabid fascism of his father and his mother's passion for the partisan cause?"

Ludo had not spoken of his mother before. I had wondered about that but hadn't asked him for an explanation.

"Your mother took up with the partisans?" I asked.

"This is difficult, Blanche. It is difficult to relive such a painful experience." He paused and cleared his throat.

He continued. "Yes, that is true. I last saw my mother when I was probably in my fifteenth year. I came home from school one afternoon to find her sitting in the *piano nobile* of our palazzo on the Grand Canal. My father was not at home. My mother had a small suitcase beside her. She was wearing a heavy coat. She called me to her side and told me that she could no longer endure living in the house with my father, that she must do whatever she could to oppose the fascist evil that he represented. She was going to join the partisans and fight for her country against Il Duce and his henchmen. I begged her to take me with her but she refused. She said that I should stay here, grow up in the safety of Venice. She said that she hoped that I would grow to understand what she was doing and that it would help me to come to know right and wrong. She held me for a few minutes, told me that she loved me, and left. I never saw her again.

"My father was enraged. He ranted, calling her some very unkind names, accusing her of chasing after a lover among the partisan fighters. I don't know whether there was any truth to that. I prefer to think that she was following quite another kind of passion.

"For whatever reason, my mother's departure fueled my father's fascism. He had no intention of risking his own life for any cause. My father was perhaps as great a coward as I have been. But he sought out like-minded Venetians. They plotted ways to serve the cause of Il Duce. They had resources and Venice, even as the war ended, was an ironic place of refuge for all kinds of people. My city's irony is legendary."

"How sad, Ludo," I said. "How very sad."

"The time was very sad for me. And confusing. My father, you must understand, was a very strong-willed man. I did not love him, but I feared him. I did not even understand at the time why the passions were so intense, what these consuming causes were about. You must understand that I was preoccupied with my personal ambiguities. The war, Il Duce, fascism, the *partigiana*, the partisans, they were words that didn't stir me. Although the feelings were not there, I made no effort to resist my father's insistence that I go along with his fascist doings. I see now that it was a compromise, but I didn't see it at the time. I feared my father and I saw no option but to do his bidding."

"But you, Il Duce, as you call him, lost the war, didn't you? Wasn't that the end of it?" I said.

"Ah, my dear Blanche Nero," he replied. "Forever parsing the world into two contrasting categories, black or white. Surely you are coming to realize how much that oversimplifies our race and what we do?"

"It does seem to me, Ludo," I answered, "that if there is any human activity the results of which are unambiguous, either-or, it must be war. Somebody wins. Somebody loses. Spoils to the winner."

"You cannot appreciate the ambiguities of war from a distance, mi amore, but there are ambiguities. There are casualties on all sides. The space that separates victory and defeat is not a large space and it shrinks with time."

He stood again and began to pace slowly about the room, leaning heavily on his harlequin cane. He stopped occasionally in front of one of the pictures that hung on the wall and stared at it as though searching for something that he couldn't quite put his finger on. He stared for a few minutes and then hobbled on to confront another picture. He said nothing more for a while and I sat quietly waiting to see what he would do next.

After a bit, he joined me again on the sofa and continued.

"The death of Il Duce," he said, "his murder, my father called it. You must know something of that event. It will become important to you."

Another of Ludo's vague references. But I didn't respond. I would let him tell this tale in whatever way he chose.

"It was the spring of 1945. Il Duce had lost most of his power and retreated to the north of Italy hoping to control a region there with the help of his Nazi bedfellows. But the cause collapsed under the weight of Allied support and the commitment of the Italiana. Il Duce attempted to escape through the mountains to Switzerland disguised as a German officer and hiding in the back of a German truck going north."

"I don't understand," I interrupted. "Weren't the Germans the enemy? How would he be safe with them?"

"That is true, mi amore. But the partisans had agreed to give the Germans safe passage to the north as long as there were no Italians among them. The partisans were determined to destroy the Italian fascists. That was their obsession. The fascists had done some very brutal things to their countrymen who opposed them. Il Duce's brutality was contagious. There was much intense anger. Much desire for revenge.

"Il Duce was discovered by a suspicious partisan guard when the German convoy passed through the village of Giulino di Mezzegra in the Como region, near the beautiful lake. He was taken into custody. Clara Petacci, Il Duce's mistress, had followed him there and she too was taken captive by the partisans."

He paused and looked at me, apparently expecting a response of some kind.

When I didn't respond, he continued. "Do not you recognize the name, Blanche?"

"The name?" I said, "You mean the name of his mistress? Why should I recognize it?"

"It is the name of the signora at your curious shop. Signora Petacci-Flaherty. The signora is the sister of Il Duce's mistress. Could that perhaps explain the signora's odd fixations?"

But Petacci was not the name that shocked me. It was Flaherty. A lump formed in my throat.

I cleared my throat and spoke but my voice was shaky. "And Flaherty?"

"Oh yes, the signora's married name," Ludo said. "Aughus Flaherty came from Ireland to fight with Il Duce's army. He shared the signora's fascist passions. He was, in fact, present at Il Duce's capture and execution. At least he claimed to be. Claimed to have witnessed the entire scene, barely escaping and finding his way back to the safety of our ironic Venice refuge."

I was afraid of where this story was going. I couldn't see how the rest of the story could possibly go with any coherence to where it appeared to be headed. I was afraid of what was to come. I half wished that I had never come to Venice, never met Ludo, satisfied myself with what *is*, abandoned any notion that knowing what had been would make a difference. I was frightened now of what the rest of the story would bring. But I was drawn to it. I wanted to hear it through. The familiar attraction-repulsion dilemma. I had felt it before.

"I realize, mi amore, that you wish to know more of Mr. Flaherty. I will finish his story for you at another time. For now, he will only serve as the source of what we know about the ignominious demise of Il Duce and those unfortunate enough to have committed to him."

The more Ludo talked, the more apprehensive I became. I tried to calm myself and just listen. My mind strained to race ahead, put together the rest of the story, but I resisted that. I should just listen to the firsthand account. The developing real story promised more insight into the mystery than any story I could invent.

"I must say, Blanche," Ludo continued, "that there are several accounts of what happened at Dongo Bongo. Flaherty's account is the one my father and others of the remaining Venetian fascists chose to believe. Whether it is true is impossible to determine. But it is of significance to you nonetheless. We spoke earlier, I think, of truth and perception?

I believe that you will agree when the story is finished that the latter is of more consequence than the former. The truth of Dongo Bongo was, in fact, irrelevant to what followed. It was perception that drove history. That is often the case, I think."

I sat deathly still. My palms were sweating. I couldn't speak. I just wanted Ludo to finish the story. I was not interested in resurrecting any philosophical discussions.

"According to Flaherty," Ludo finally continued, "a small group of the partisan leaders decided to execute Il Duce, Clara Petacci, and fifteen others of the fascist group. The fifteen were in retaliation for fifteen of the partisans who had been executed by the fascists in Milano earlier. Five partisans were selected as an execution squad. The fascists were lined up and shot by the five gunmen firing simultaneously.

"What happened afterward is well documented. There was much hatred, high passions. The bodies were taken to Milano and hung upside down in a public square where they were reviled and desecrated by an angry mob. It was not my countrymen's finest hour."

I remembered being at once drawn to and repulsed by pictures of that scene in a book that I read in college.

"How gruesome," I finally regained my voice and began to calm down some. "How absolutely awful."

"That is true, mi amore. It was awful."

He paused again and walked toward the window looking out for a moment, then turned to look directly at me.

"There is another fact you must know," he said. "Signor Flaherty carefully recorded the names of the five partisans who were the executioners. One of those names was Giovanni Nero."

CHAPTER 23: APOCALYPSE

With the rest of Little Easy's designated disaster-activation team, I arrived at Charity at seven on Sunday morning. The news was that the hurricane wouldn't hit the city directly, but close enough that we could expect some significant action.

I entered through the first-floor ER. Most of the city had been evacuated. For the first time in memory, the ER was completely deserted. I stood there for a while, reflecting on the chaos that was typical of the place and thinking how strange it was to see the place empty and eerily silent. There was something ominous about the scene, a calm before the storm perhaps.

We were to be prepared to spend a few days at the hospital and I had brought some necessities in a backpack. I made my way to an on-call room on the nineteenth floor and deposited my things.

All but about two hundred or so patients had been evacuated from the hospital. Our instructions were to work together as a team to take care of the patients who remained, ignoring the usually rigid specialty boundaries. I was teamed up with an intensivist, an emergency medicine specialist, and my friend the ER nurse, Fiona Regan. We met and began rounding on the group of patients that we had been assigned. That included the patients in both the medical and surgical intensive care units.

The patients who remained were a mixed bag of frail elderly and seriously ill. Several depended on ventilators. Heart monitors beeped in the background. We spent the day getting familiar with the cases and taking care of whatever needed to be done for them. It was a pretty routine day. No surgery. Not much excitement.

"So far so good," Fiona said.

It was evening. Fiona and I were sitting in the little lounge off the ER and drinking coffee. The Weather Channel was on the television but we weren't really watching it. Katrina was going to do whatever she chose. Watching her progress on the weather map wasn't going to change anything.

Fiona looked apprehensive. That was unusual. I had rarely seen anything like concern on her face. In her professional role she was a veritable machine. But her brow was furrowed and she was quieter than usual.

"Are you all right?" I asked.

"Yeah," she replied. "It's just that I have a really bad feeling about this. Maybe it's just the uncertainty, not knowing what to expect."

I was a little tired from the long day spent doing routine stuff. That's not how I usually spent my time at the hospital. There was little routine about my usual day and I liked that. So I was tired, but I was actually anticipating Katrina's arrival. At least we were not likely to be bored.

"I'm ready for more action than we had today," I said.

She looked at her coffee cup, massaging it between her hands.

"Some action would be fine, as long as there's not more than we can handle," she said.

I felt pretty confident that we could handle Katrina. We'd handled some pretty tough situations together.

The wind hit during the night. I didn't sleep very well anywhere and the drab on-call room with its lumpy cot was never my favorite place to spend a night. When I finally drifted off, the dream intruded. There were variations on the dream, but always the terror that awoke me. The bedside clock read four a.m. and the wind was picking up, rattling the small window in the room. The wind made a high-pitched keen that didn't sound at first as powerful as I expected of it. But as I lay there the sound took on a deeper tone and came in sharper thrusts.

I got out of bed and looked out the window. It was raining heavily, but the wind blew the rain in odd directions, sending much of it back skyward, defying gravity's earthward pull. The city was dark and I couldn't see anything moving. The rain pounded the small window with intermittent blasts as the wind whipped it about.

Finally I dressed in scrubs and went down to the ER. A few stragglers had managed to get there. They appeared to be mainly just escaping the weather rather than looking for any particular medical care. They sat in the waiting area and stared vacantly into space. A resident was seeing to them.

As my team rounded on the hospital patients over the day, we could tell that the wind was dying down. Word was that the hospital had lost electricity but the backup generators in the basement had kicked in so we had power everywhere. By afternoon, it appeared that Katrina had given us her best shot and Charity had taken it in stride. A few broken windows and water leaking in in a few places, but nothing major. The old girl was a tough nut. The patients were warm and dry and as well as we could make them. And Charity Hospital, icon of care for the poor and needy of Orleans Parish, stood as proud and incongruent as ever.

Late in the afternoon, Little Easy's entire disaster team met with him in the second floor auditorium. There was an urn of hot coffee and we stood around with plastic cups of the strong coffee smiling and congratulating each other. It seemed to me that the whole experience was something of an anticlimax. I thought Katrina was a going to be tougher girl than she turned out to be. I was more than a little disappointed.

"Ladies and gentlemen." Little Easy raised his voice above the group and pounded on the folding table that held the coffee urn. "First, let me thank you for your efforts and congratulate you on a job well done. But, lest we get carried away with ourselves, please know that our jobs may not be finished. Be prepared to stay here at least another day or so until we're certain that the patients are cared for and the coast is clear." He hoisted his plastic cup and continued. "To Charity and to you, her guardians," he said.

"Hear, hear!" we chanted in unison, raising our cups.

My memory of the next few days is of a jumble of events without a clear chronology. While I remember with frightening clarity many things that happened, they do not fit together into a story, a narrative with any coherence. The events I remember are in isolated fragments. They are horrible memories. They still haunt me.

When the levees broke, the game was over. What had stoically withstood the ravages of Katrina's winds was no match for the consequences of human failure. The flimsy levees, token barriers against the power of the deluge, gave way and the water came. It flooded the Charity basement, shorting out the auxiliary generators.

Darkness. Sudden and penetrating darkness. And stillness. The heave of life-sustaining ventilators silenced. The comforting hypnotic beep-beep-beep of heart monitors gone quiet.

And then chaos of an order I could not have imagined. Screams of fear and desperation. Patients clinging desperately to what shards of life and hope remained in the still and dark of the ER, the ICUs. Doctors, nurses, technicians screaming fear and desperation at each other, cursing the cards that fate had suddenly dealt us. Frantically searching in the dark for Ambu bags to replace the dead breathing machines. There were too many patients who needed ventilating and too few hands to do the job. Some stood between two patients, alternately compressing a black rubber bag in either hand.

Smells. The acrid smell of fear and desperation. And as the days passed, the overpowering smell of human excrement as the plumbing failed and the irrepressible urges of biology played out wherever they found opportunity.

A stairwell that led from the first-floor ER to the second floor sticks in my memory. A stairwell I had taken often in calmer times now reeked of urine. We lugged patients from the ER on makeshift stretchers, struggling up the dark stairs to the second-floor auditorium as the water threatened to flood the first floor. One after another, we lugged the leaden bodies up those stairs with tags of red, yellow, or green tied to them to indicate how urgently they needed help.

I remember the auditorium, with row on row of the sick and dying wedged in head to toe like helpless dolls, a warehouse of humanity waiting for God only knew what. An old woman with white hair fingering a rosary and moaning. A young man coughing up blood. A pretty young woman trembling with fever and fear and shock.

I crouched in a flatboat beside an old man, compressing the rubber breathing bag to keep him alive until we could get to Tulane Hospital where the evacuating helicopters were supposed to be picking up the patients. We got the patient to the helipad. I turned the job over to an exhausted emergency medicine resident and headed back to Charity. I had to walk those few blocks through fetid water almost up to my neck in places; unknown things floating in the water bumped against me in the dark.

The flap-flap of the Death Angel's wings awoke me. I finally had time to catch a couple hours of sleep and went to the roof trying to escape the stifling heat and the other sensations that assaulted the senses, making the hospital an unfit human habitat. I fell into the sleep of the dead. A rhythmic whop-whop sound awoke me and a strong breeze blew down from above. In my half sleep, I imagined the huge black silhouette of the Death Angel descending upon us. His arrival was overdue.

"You!" A person dressed in black and barely distinguishable in the dark yelled at me, snapping me into consciousness. "You!" he repeated, pointing a menacing-looking automatic weapon of some kind at me. "Get up and stand against the wall!"

It slowly dawned on me that my imagined Death Angel was a helicopter—a Blackhawk I was told—and these were army people of some kind. I later learned that it was a SWAT team come to hunt for snipers who had been spotted on the hospital roof.

There are many other fragments of memories. The most vivid of them is the last time I saw Jesse Pinto, looking considerably older than I remembered him from almost two decades earlier. He appeared, soaking wet, at the Charity ER, struggling to wrestle the near-lifeless body of Rasputin Lee into the room and onto a gurney. Rasputin was barely breathing, short staccato breaths that often come for a short time before there are no breaths at all. I tore open his shirt. The left side of his chest was prominent. I percussed the tympanitic note that means air in the chest, outside the lung. He had a collapsed lung and wouldn't last more than a few minutes from the looks of him unless I could fix it.

"Fiona!" I yelled. "I need some help here, pneumothorax." Then I turned to Jesse. "Jesse, I've got to put a tube in his chest and there's no time for anesthetic. I don't even know if we have any. Can you help hold him down?"

Fiona appeared with a scalpel and a Foley urinary catheter. I have no idea whether they were clean or used. But it didn't matter at the time. It's all I had to work with.

"Hold him down," I said, and cut a clean hole just over a rib, inserting the catheter. The familiar whoosh of air under pressure released into the outside world, making space in the world inside for the lung to reexpand.

Rasputin bucked some when I made the cut but he was too weak to make much of an effort at objecting. When the air whooshed from his chest, his breathing gradually slowed and evened out. He opened his eyes but didn't say anything.

"Fiona," I said, "get an IV started. Jesse, can you stay here with him?"

"Sure," Jesse answered.

"Dr. Nero!" a resident yelled. "Dr. Nero, we've got a code here."

As I turned to head over to help with the code, my eyes met Jesse's for the briefest moment.

As I write this I fear I may have imagined it, but I distinctly remember hearing Jesse say as our eyes met, "I still love you, Blanche."

CHAPTER 24: TAKING LEAVE OF THE BIG EASY

Charity Hospital, L'Hôpital des Pauvres de la Charité , the Big Free, benevolent Queen Regnant of the Big Easy who had ruled my life for almost three decades was dead. She was no victim of the elements. She was too obstinate and determined to give in to those. She had seen the elements come and go for more than two centuries in her many incarnations, taking their best shots in stride. But she was no match for the human perfidy that cut corners with the levees so that they gave way and flooded her or for the exigencies of Louisiana politics. It was human failures that dealt the fatal blows. She did not die of natural causes.

Charity could have been saved. After the patients were all evacuated and the flood receded, the military came in and cleaned the place up. Little Easy and the rest of us made a resuscitation plan. We could patch things up enough to get back in business while awaiting the more extensive repairs that would have to be done eventually. It was a good plan, and workable. The place had never been ideal. We knew how to work without a lot of the niceties. And our clients were still out there. They still needed caring for.

Before we could get the plan underway, we got the word from on high that we were to stop. Charity would not be resurrected. The decision was made by the people in charge, few of whom had ever set foot in the place, that Charity was dead once and for all. There were plans for a fancy new facility in the city that would enable state-of–the-art biomedicine, they said. We should lay any thoughts of a Charity renascence to rest. They did not say what was to happen to the thousands of the poor and needy of Orleans parish to whom we had dedicated our professional lives. They were still out there. They were neither less poor nor less needy.

When I finally got back to my apartment after those interminable five days at the hospital, I slept. I didn't eat. Some days passed, I'm not sure how many. I was often frightened awake by the terror of a new nightmare added to my repertoire. In one recurring dream scene, I am trying to cut my way into Rasputin's chest to decompress his pneumothorax. His raspy gasps get shorter and more labored. But the scalpel is too dull and I can't penetrate his chest. I keep trying, stabbing at his thorax over and over but with no effect. I panic as his breaths get shorter and faster, frantically stabbing at him with all my strength. Just as Rasputin appears to gasp his last, I wake up sweaty and trembling.

There were also the more familiar terrors during those days of disorienting sleep and waking and something in between those states when I thought I was a teenager back in Almsboro arguing with my mother over something trivial or sitting at a troublingly nonverbal dinner with her and my father. My father's face floated ghostlike through a lot of my dreams.

When I finally regained a semblance of consciousness and sanity, I tried to think what I was going to do. I opened a bottle of Knob Creek bourbon that I found in a cupboard. I don't know where it came from. I didn't remember buying it. I had never been a bourbon drinker. Single-barrel bourbons had not caught my fancy. I took the bottle and a glass to my balcony and sat down, placing the bottle deliberately on the table with a resounding thunk. I poured the glass full to its brim. I sat down and took a long swallow, relishing the sensation of the bolus of hot liquid traversing my upper gastrointestinal tract, throat through esophagus, and settling into a very warm place deep in my abdomen.

My world, the life that I had made for myself, that had brought me professional and personal equanimity, had evaporated in a sudden cataclysm of events that I could not possibly have anticipated. It seemed to me that everything I had done was wasted. What difference did it make? All those long days and nights doing my best to fix the consequences of people doing violence to each other. Who cared? All that time and effort spent learning medicine, developing the skills, learning how to use the knowledge and skills of medicine and surgery to lessen suffering, preserve life. What difference did it make in the end? Rasputin Q. Lee and his like were still out there, still inflicting harm on each other and looking for my kind of expertise to fix it, patch things up so they could do it all again. Well, good luck, guys. We tried like hell to keep your game going, and ours. Both our games were over. Charity in New Orleans, Louisiana, USA, was dead.

I refilled my glass.

What now, I thought? I was almost sixty. Money wasn't an

issue. I had saved up. But my life was so inextricable from Charity Hospital that I didn't see a future without her.

I had finished a second glass of bourbon at that point. I was abysmally depressed. For the first time in my long life, I considered ending it. I wasn't afraid of death; the Death Angel and I were well acquainted, intimates you might say. What difference would it make whether someone discovered my dead body half-decomposed in a week or two of New Orleans heat or if I stayed around, an anachronism hovering in the wings while the powers-that-be plotted a very different course for medicine in the Big Easy, a course that would probably have little use for the likes of me.

I must have dozed off sitting on the porch because my head was resting on the table when the sound of the ringing telephone from the open door to the living room awakened me. I aroused myself and walked, a little unsteadily, into the house and answered the phone.

"Where the devil have you been, Blanche?" Fiona's voice lashed out at me before I could even say hello.

"I'm here, Fiona," I answered. "Just been catching up on sleep for a day, I guess."

"I rang your home several times," she continued, "and no answer. I left messages. Haven't you checked your messages? I've been trying to reach you for three days."

"I guess not. Has it really been that long?" I said.

I hadn't even thought about messages and I also hadn't heard the phone ring. I had spent the last few days in another place.

"Are you okay?" Fiona asked.

"I think so," I answered. "I'm more than a little drunk right now and before I fell back to sleep I was thinking about killing myself. But I'm OK now, I think."

Fiona and I had always dealt pretty straight with each other so I told her the truth.

There was a long silence.

"Have you eaten anything?" she finally asked.

"I don't remember. I don't think so."

"I'm coming over, Blanche, "she said, "Be there in a quarter hour. Sit tight. I'll bring food."

I went back onto the porch and poured some more bourbon.

"Were you really contemplating suicide?" Fiona asked.

We were finishing up the Chinese takeout she had brought over. I had wolfed down most of it while Fiona played with her food like a picky child. She had also brought several bottles of water and I had polished off a couple, suddenly aware that I was terribly dehydrated. I was starting to feel a little better.

"The thought crossed my mind," I answered, "but I could never do it. It was just that I had this overwhelming feeling of futility. Like everything we've been doing all these years was a royal waste of time and energy and resources. Isn't that what the politicos have decided? Charity? Oh well, let's just forget about it. Those people don't really matter that much."

"The politicos aren't going to tell me what's important," Fiona said. "I'll decide that for myself."

I pondered that. I suspected that Fiona meant what she said. She made her own priorities and stuck by them. I admired her for it. But at the time I just didn't feel all that strong.

I have no idea how he arranged it, but Little Easy organized a wake. He somehow got permission to hold it in the abandoned Charity ER and invited mainly the disaster team. I hadn't seen any of them except Fiona since the apocalypse. Little Easy meant for the occasion to be a celebration of the Big Free's long and dedicated life. I think he was pretty serious about it.

Unfortunately, Little Easy's wake was a disaster. There was still no electricity at Charity and for lighting, a row of tiki torches was arranged around the room's perimeter. That started out OK but as the evening progressed, the smoke from the torches began accumulating and we all started coughing and tearing up, trying hard to play the roles that Little Easy had defined for us but without much success.

And the tone of the party was anything but celebratory. It was a very sad occasion. I was almost overcome with sadness in the middle of the very space where I had plied my trade for all those years—the place now desecrated by a bunch of my colleagues pretending to pay homage to the memory but not sure how to do it. Not sure what to feel.

I found a relatively quiet corner and stood looking into the room. I didn't feel very sociable. As I stood there, I thought about my father's death. I remembered that I had trouble then knowing what I was supposed to feel. I also thought about the fact that he had brought his fate upon himself and that my mother said that there was something in his blood that made him do it. In his blood. In my blood. What did that mean?

Fiona came over and stood beside me for a while.

"Let's take a tour," she said.

"A tour?"

"Of the hospital, I mean."

She found a flashlight somewhere and we felt our way up the stairs. We had last used those stairs when we were moving patients from the ER up to the auditorium, fleeing the water. There was still a hint of urine in the air, but nothing like when we were last there. And it was quiet and still and dark.

We wandered around the second floor. A lot of equipment—ventilators, heart monitors, IV pumps—was scattered about, useless and cast aside when emasculated by the loss of electricity. I remember being struck with the quiet. A silence like death. The Big Free was dead and could not, or would not, be resuscitated. I just had to live with that.

Fiona and I must have wandered around for an hour or so before returning to the party downstairs. That was my last encounter with Charity Hospital.

I'm not sure exactly when I decided to go to Venice in search of my father. I don't think there was a specific time. I think that as I reflected on my life and thought about what to do next, the decision gradually developed. However it came about, at some point I decided to do it. I petitioned the university for a year sabbatical. I had that coming and I think they were probably happy to see me out of the way for a while. They didn't quite know what to do with me anyway. I was tenured so they were stuck with me but I suspect they needed some time to figure out what to do.

I leased my house, furnishings and all, to a psychiatry resident for the next year. I seriously thought about selling it, but it was not until later that I realized that I could not imagine going back there. I could always sell it later. I found a relatively inexpensive flat in Venice by going online and Googling Venice apartments for lease. It was a small flat but the location looked good from the map and I didn't need much room.

I didn't have a lot of things to take with me. My wardrobe was mostly jeans and scrubs with only a couple of nice things. I could get everything I wanted to take with me in a single suitcase. I gave the rest to Goodwill.

So I packed it all up. I taped the lid to the urn containing my father's ashes firmly on and decided to carry it with me on the plane in a shopping bag. I took a taxi to the airport where I murmured to myself some last goodbyes and took my leave of the Big Easy.

CHAPTER 25: LAST DANCE IN PARADISE

I moved in with Ludo. He didn't ask me to do that, but when I suggested it, he didn't object. It was time. Ludo was so frail now that I feared he would have a crisis of some kind during the night alone and helpless, or fall and be unable to get up. I was spending most of my time at his place anyway.

I packed the suitcase I had brought with me with some clothes, toiletries, my writing book, and several jars of the Sicilian tuna to which Violetta had become addicted. I also put the urn with my father's ashes in the suitcase. I spent most of that sunny morning getting things together. I made a pot of coffee and sat for a while looking out the window at the brightly sunlit façade of San Michele. It was a Sunday and a few brave souls were rowing their lacquered wooden boats about the lagoon.

I gathered Violetta in my arms, took up the suitcase, and left the flat, securing the door after making certain that I had the keys with me. I walked around to the door of Ludo's palazzo and rang the bell. When there was no answer after several rings, I let myself in with the key he had given me and went up the stairs. I set my case down and put Violetta down as well. She trotted directly to the sofa by the window and curled up, settling in as though she completely understood the change of venue.

"Ludo," I called.

He didn't answer.

A man I didn't recognize came into the room from the direction of Ludo's bedroom.

"You must be *Dottore* Nero," he said.

"Yes," I answered, a little confused.

He walked across to me and extended his hand. "I am Dottore Petrino," he said. "Ludo has told me of you. I am a medical doctor here in Venice. I have been caring for the Conte during this difficult time."

"Is he all right?" I asked.

Ludo hadn't told me that he was expecting a house call from the doctor.

"Yes," the doctor answered. "That is, there are no major new developments in his condition."

Dr. Petrino appeared to be in his early middle years, fortyish, I guessed. He wore an impeccably tailored dark suit and a red tie. There were flashes of gray in his black hair that curled down over his ears. He looked the part of the affluent Venetian doctor that he undoubtedly was.

"Ludo tells me that you are an American doctor," Petrino continued. "Is that correct?"

"I am a surgeon, actually," I answered. "Or I was in another life. But my caring for Ludo has nothing to do with that. I am his friend."

"I understand," he said. "Ludo is very fortunate to have such a friend. He is in great need of a friend at this time."

"Are you sure he's all right?" I asked.

It seemed to me that the doctor was engaging me in a conversation that had some purpose yet to be revealed. I suspected that something was wrong and he was preparing me for the news. I was familiar with the tactic.

"Yes, yes," he said. "It is just that he is starting to have pain. That is not a good sign as I am sure you know."

Ludo hadn't mentioned pain to me although I had suspected that there were times when he was hurting.

"You are, of course, aware," Petrino continued, "that your friend is dying. There is nothing that can be done about that."

"I know," I answered.

"But he should not have to suffer the pain," he continued. "I have given him some morphine today and he is resting now. But the pain will return and will worsen. Since you are a doctor, perhaps you could give him the morphine shots when they are needed. Is that possible?"

"Yes, of course," I said.

"Good," he said. "I will leave some vials of morphine and syringes. Do not hesitate to give him whatever it takes to keep him comfortable."

"Thank you," I said. "I will do all I can to keep him comfortable."

"It is also possible," Petrino said, "that he will rally some. There are often highs and lows as the process plays out. On a sunny day, he might feel up to a tour around the area. I will have a wheelchair sent. He will not be strong enough to walk, I think, but a little tour in the wheelchair in the sunshine could be pleasant for him."

"That is very kind of you," I said. "I'm happy to do that."

The doctor put on an overcoat that was thrown over a chair and picked up his black leather bag. The scene seemed to me like something from a remote place in medical history. I imagined the picture captured in a Norman Rockwell painting with the title *House Call*.

He shook my hand again, holding it gently for a few seconds and looking with genuine sympathy into my eyes.

"I will check in occasionally," he said. "Ludo has the number of my *telefonino* if you need me. I will let myself out."

Dottore Petrino departed down the stairs and I suppose out into the Sunday sun to pay a visit to others for whom he cared. There was much recent talk in America of what was called personalized medicine, matching treatments to one's genetic makeup. It seemed to me that Dotorre Petrino was the real face of personalized medicine.

When the doctor was gone, I looked in on Ludo. He appeared to be sleeping quietly.

When we discussed my moving in, Ludo had shown me a second bedroom with an adjacent bath that would be mine. I took my things there and unpacked the suitcase. I placed the urn on a small writing desk by a window and lined up the jars of tuna there as well. I sat down on the bed. Violetta joined me, curling up in my lap and purring softly. As I sat there dreading what lay ahead for the next little while, it dawned on me that in all of my adult life, I had never before lived in the house with a man.

Over the next few weeks, Ludo did have some good days when I would bundle him up in his big green coat and scarf, help him down to the wheelchair that we kept in the small foyer at the bottom of the steps, and take him for a tour. He liked to go up to Campo Sante Giovanni e Paolo and rest there in the sun watching the children at play or admiring the grand façade of the church and the palazzo that was now the city hospital. I could occasionally coax him into having a gelato from Rosa Silva, which claims to be the oldest gelateria in the city. He seemed to enjoy those afternoons.

Late one afternoon, Ludo came into the *piano nobile* where I was sitting with Violetta and writing in my notebook.

"Blanche," he said.

I thought that he looked considerably more chipper than he had for a while.

"Could we take a stroll to the piazza, mi amore?" he said.

I couldn't believe that he intended to walk there.

"Stroll?" I said.

"Well," Ludo answered, looking a little sheepishly down at the floor, "a stroll as we do that lately. I have become rather fond of the ride in the chair, the wheelchair. I have become accustomed to being wheeled about by your gentle hand."

"Of course, Ludo," I said.

I bundled him up and we made our way down the stairs.

The late afternoon sun spilled a soft light across the Piazza San Marco. People milled about, but there was not the pressing crush of the summer crowds. I wheeled him across the piazza toward the *bacino* and we looked out across the water. Gondolas bobbed about at their moorings. A half-empty vaporetto clacked past. I pushed him along the perimeter of the piazza, skirting the café tables. Music from the band at Caffè Florian floated into the crisp air.

Ludo brightened, his eyes darting about.

"Shall we dance?" he said.

"Most certainly, mi amore," I said.

I wheeled him about in circles in rhythm to the music for some time, transported for a while by the warm sun and the music and the magic of this most beautiful place in the world. Ludo began to laugh for the first time in my recent memory. I joined in his laughter as we wheeled about. A small group of people gathered watching us and when the music stopped and we came to rest, a smattering of applause broke out. Ludo, with some effort, stood, bracing himself on the chair and bowed with a sweeping gesture to the crowd.

It was our final venture together from the elegant confines of Ca' Ludovici.

And it was, to my knowledge, the last time Ludo laughed.

CHAPTER 26: LA VENDETTA DI IL DUCE

If I said that I was uninterested in the rest of the story, I would not be telling the truth. I wanted to hear the rest of it, but Ludo was getting so weak, and needing such frequent morphine injections to control the pain, that I hated to see him have to go through the obviously excruciating effort it took to finish telling it. Dying was difficult enough for him. Why complicate it? But he insisted.

"Il Duce was dead. The war was declared over and he was on the losing side," Ludo began, heaving a deep sigh and grimacing.

It was early evening of what had been, it seemed to me, a very long day. Ludo had slept away most of it. I had spent several hours sitting with Violetta on the sofa in the *piano nobile* and staring out at the lagoon. I should have been writing, I thought. I was nearing the end of that effort and would be glad to get it done. But for some reason, I was not in the mood. I looked at Violetta, screwed into her usual tight spiral and sleeping peacefully.

I envied the sleep that seemed to come so easily to the cat. And to Ludo as well, although the morphine may have been responsible for that. Since moving in with Ludo, I had slept even more fitfully than usual. There were, of course, the dreams, but often I would just lie in the bed in the elegant guest room wide-awake, staring at the ceiling, my mind a kaleidoscope of thoughts and memories.

I began to fear sleep. What if Ludo needed me in the night? And then, too, if there was no sleep, there were no dreams. Sleep had never been my friend. But I was more and more exhausted as the days passed. I had not been at my best for a while now and that particular day was one of my worst in some time.

That early evening, we sat next to each other at one end of the long table in the large dining room. I had prepared dinner and we had lingered over the meal for some time. Ludo's waning appetite seemed to be a little better than usual that evening. We were sharing a bottle of Soave. Most of it was gone when Ludo launched into the final segment of his tale.

I remembered those conversations with my mother after dinner, still sitting at the table, conversations that were the sole source of my understanding of where I came from up to now. Ludo was adding to the story begun those years ago after a much simpler dinner in a much simpler space and perhaps, at least for me, in a much simpler time.

"But," he continued, "the war was not over. It was never over for those who had sworn their allegiance to Il Duce."

As he spoke, he didn't look at me. He looked blankly at the vacant space in front of him. It was as though he were testifying, recounting something for the record rather than revealing anything to me. He stifled a cough. The morphine was helping with the cough as well as the pain, but the cough still intruded on occasion.

288 | THE LIFE AND DEATHS OF BLANCHE NERO

"My father was a leader of the Venice fascists after the death of their leader. My father and Signora Petacci-Flaherty and her Irish husband. There were more of the fascists remaining here than you may think. Some were Venetians, but many came to Venice to escape the retribution of the partisans and others. You see," he was talking too rapidly and had to pause for a few seconds to catch his breath, "my city has always made room in her bosom for those with no other place to be. She is—my city—proud, I think, of offering herself without conditions to those who choose to come here."

He paused for a while, still not looking in my direction, still testifying for the record.

"They met in my father's palazzo to make their plans," he continued. "There were maybe twenty of them, more or less. Most of them were not the kind of people (men except for Signora Petacci-Flaherty) who would ordinarily have been welcome in my father's house."

"Plans?" I queried. "What plans did they make?"

"You see, mi amore," he said, "It was Il Duce's death—his murder, they insisted on calling it—that enraged them. And the desecration of the corpses in Milano. They made copies of those pictures of the desecration and pored over them, fueling the fire of their rage. They swore vengeance for those heinous acts, swore to each other and to God. Yes, they believed, or seemed to, that their cause was not only just but righteous. Even then, I found the righteous part a trifle hard to swallow. But I didn't protest."

"You were at those meetings?"

"Yes, I was there. My father insisted on it. I was there but I was nauseated by the pictures and frightened by the vehemence with which these grown men spoke of vengeance."

"Did they just meet to wallow in the ignominy of their defeat and to rail at the injustice of it? Did they do anything about it?"

"I am afraid so, mi amore, and this final chapter in the story is the most difficult for me. And for you as well although it may provide you with the explanations that you came here seeking.

"These men, bonded together by their fascist passions, fancied themselves a band of, how would you say, avengers. *La Vendetta di Il Duce*, they called the group. Recall Flaherty's list of the partisan execution squad? They swore to kill each one of those five men regardless of where they were to be found and regardless of the time required to accomplish the task. The sole purpose and passion of La Vendetta di Il Duce was to seek out and destroy those five men and as many of their loved ones as they could locate. They had resources, my father's and others. It became a life's work for those misguided persons. Passions..." he paused and turned to look at me. "Passions are so readily put to bad use. Are they not?"

I tried to get the chronology straight in my head. Ludo was talking about something that happened near the end of the war, around 1945. My father died twenty years later.

"This was right after the war ended, right?" I said.

"Yes, yes," Ludo answered.

"But my father's death was twenty years after that."

"Yes."

Ludo struggled up from his chair with some difficulty and walked to the window, looking out with his back to me, resting his hands on the sill for support.

"The vows of La Vendetta di Il Duce were not limited by

time, mi amore. The deaths of the first four of the partisan executioners were accomplished over a few years, before my father's death. The group enlisted the aid of some criminal types to hunt them down and dispense with them. But executioner number five, Giovanni Nero, eluded them. There were rumors that he had escaped to America, but your country is large and there was no knowledge of exactly where he had gone, no specific information."

"How in the world did they find him after two decades?" I asked.

"I would call it coincidence, but those of the group who remained thought it divine providence. You see, we Italians are tethered to our country, even the specific parts of our country from which we come. Going to another place does not break the tether; the connection is far too strong and deep. So, although your country is a great distance away, there remains a network of Italians there who are still Italians, still connected to this land and its people."

Calibrini, I thought. It had to be the Haightsville lawyer, Calibrini. I knew of no other Italians who knew where my father was. It had to be him.

Ludo sat back at the table and didn't speak for a while. He was breathing heavily.

Finally he spoke. "Word came quite unexpectedly from someone, an Italian who had himself been in the war, and not on the winning side. I think his connection was through the Signora Petacci-Flaherty. I am not sure. The word was that Giovanni Nero was living with his American family in a small town masquerading as a farmer. I do not know how the news arrived, but the ones of the group who remained believed that it was accurate."

Another long pause. A cough that he could not suppress, its crimson produce spat into a handkerchief.

"I am sorry, mi amore," he said, then continued. "It was Flaherty and his Irish passions that convinced the others of his plan. He insisted on doing this himself. The signora argued with him at great length. But he insisted. The others—there were only a handful remaining—were caught up in the chance to complete the work of La Vendetta di Il Duce. Flaherty's enthusiasm inflamed them."

I hesitated but then asked, "And you, Ludo? Were you party to this plan?"

"I have told you, Blanche, and I am sure that it is obvious. I was never a strong man. You see, as my father lay on his deathbed, his heart failing, victim of his many excesses, he extracted from me two promises. You must undersand that this man whom I feared and on whom I depended for sustenance was dying. I sat by his bed in the *ospedale*. He looked at me with those stern dark eyes that had struck fear in my heart from when I was a child. 'Only two things, Ludo,' he said, 'that you must promise me. You must never reveal your fondness for other men. You would disgrace the Ludovici name. And you must carry on the work of La Vendetta di Il Duce. You must see that the work is finished.' He grasped my hand and pleaded, 'You are all that is left of the Ludovicis, Ludo. You owe this to me and to your blood relations who made for you a life that you could not have had but for our strength and commitment.'

"I agreed to keep those promises. When my father's will was read, I was named his sole heir. But there were two conditions. The two promises.

292 | THE LIFE AND DEATHS OF BLANCHE NERO

"So, you are correct. Although I was a passive party to Flaherty's plan, I did not object."

My heart raced. This man whom I had come to love in a way that I had not known before was party to my father's death. I couldn't speak.

We sat quietly for a long time. The sun had fled to the west and the room was dark now.

It was Ludo who finally broke the silence.

"When we first met, Blanche," he said, his voice trembling, "you said that you watched your father killed. But the word that came back to us was of a murder and a legal execution, both Nero and Flaherty dead. Flaherty had finished the work of the cause and paid the ultimate price for the deed. The group celebrated him as a martyr to the cause, a hero. If you were present when he killed your father, how did you escape? Flaherty left Venice determined to massacre the entire Nero family. His plan was to ingratiate himself with Giovanni Nero to create the opportunity and then to carry out his bloody work. How did you escape?"

It was now clear to me. My father must have learned of Flaherty's plan somehow. He must have known that there would be other avengers who would come if Flaherty's mission failed. He must have felt that he had no choice but to kill Flaherty and martyr himself to protect me and my mother.

Ludo listened intently as I unfolded for him the truth of the entire gruesome story. He said nothing. When I finished, Ludo struggled to his feet.

"I am very tired, mi amore," he said. "I must take to my bed."

He grasped the harlequin cane that he had propped against

the table and leaned heavily on it as he hobbled toward the door to his bedroom. At the door, he turned to look at me. Tears ran down the hollows of his gaunt cheeks.

"I was never a strong man, Blanche," he said.

He turned and left the room.

I sat for what must have been hours in the dark. It felt as though a black shroud was drawn across my mind. The story ended. The dark curtain descended on the final act.

At last I stood and went to my room. Violetta curled beside me on the bed. I could no longer hold back the wracking sobs.

I did not sleep.

CHAPTER 27: HOMAGE TO THE ANGEL OF DEATH

I killed Ludo. Although I had been party to death, I had never before deliberately ended the life of another person. When my patients died, it was the victory of the Angel of Death that took their lives, not my doing. I had spent my life fighting, often desperately, for the other side and winning my share of the battles. But I killed Ludo, conspiring with him to steal the Death Angel's thunder.

After our night of revelations, Ludo's condition rapidly deteriorated. The pain worsened. Dottore Petrino provided us a generous supply of morphine and I administered it in increasing doses as the effect began to weaken. Soon Ludo was never free of pain, the drug only softening the sharp edges some. He spent most days in bed, struggling up only to tend to the essential functions of his disintegrating body. He still arose in the mornings and spent long periods in his bathroom, presumably washing himself, accomplishing, no doubt with great difficulty, his ablutions.

"Ludo," I said one evening, sitting on the side of his bed after injecting his pitiful buttocks with a generous dose of the drug. "I'm happy to help with your baths and whatever else you need. I'm a doctor, you know. I have a lot of experience with the less pleasant sides of human biology. I'm not offended by those."

"Oh, no!" he responded with as much energy as I had seen from him in a while. "No, mi amore. I appreciate your generous offer, but when I can no longer deal with those private matters, I will know that the time has come."

I didn't raise the matter again.

Christmas came and went. I would not have known that except for the calendar, which I now watched with regularity, and the decorations in the city that I saw when I went out for food and other necessities. Venice is very festive at that time of year. Strands of tiny fairy lights strung across the narrow *calle*. Bakery windows stacked high with *panatone*. Red Santa Claus dolls climbing rope ladders toward the upper-level balconies. And throngs of happy people decked out in their finest, laden down with shopping bags, chattering loudly and waving their arms about.

I didn't share the festive feeling. I was doing what needed to be done. Going through the necessary motions.

I continued to prepare meals for Ludo. I started serving his breakfast to him in bed, sitting with him and trying to coax him to take in some nourishment. His appetite continued to decline. He was steadily wasting away.

On the morning of December thirty-first, New Year's Eve, I was awakened by Ludo calling to me. A trembling, plaintive call.

"Blanche," he called. "Blanche."

I went to him. He was propped up on a pillow and continued calling my name as I sat on the bed beside him. I took his hand in mine. He looked at me. His look was hollow and I noticed the deep dark spaces beneath his eyes.

"Blanche," he said, "I find that I am unable to rise from my bed this morning."

"Here," I said. "Let me help you."

He made no effort to cooperate with my halfhearted attempt to help him up.

"No, no, mi amore," he said. "I do not wish to rise this morning," reclining back onto the pillow, "I wish instead for you to keep your vow. It is time."

I knew what he meant, of course. I would keep the promise I had made, a promise that betrayed that other oath that I had taken all those years ago. Those Latin words, *primum non nocere,* the Hippocratic oath's proscription against harming the patient came into my mind.

There was plenty of morphine for the task. I retrieved the remaining vials of the drug and a large syringe, which I filled with the contents of several of the vials.

"Are you certain of this, Ludo?" I asked.

"Mi amore," he answered, "we must not allow the Death Angel his ghoulish victory. You are my Angel of Mercy, mi amore. You have brought me pleasure in my dying days that I could not have imagined. I am too aware of the irony; La Vendetta di Il Duce has played many tricks on us. But you taught me love apparently unfettered by conditions. I would have died without the knowledge of such a possibility were it not for you. It is time for its consummation."

I knew he was right.

I placed a tourniquet that Dottore Petrino had left with the other supplies around the skeleton of Ludo's arm, wondering for a fleeting moment if the doctor was a coconspirator with us. I gently inserted the syringe needle into a vein in his forearm.

"Goodbye, mi amore," I said.

"Arrivederci, Blanche," he responded.

I released the tourniquet and slowly emptied the syringe into his vein. He smiled at me and breathed his final breath.

I sat with him for a while, holding his hand as it turned cold and lifeless.

There were many ironies. I had just done the most difficult deed of my life but I felt a strange relief, as though a burden I had carried for a long time had been lifted from me. I could not explain the feeling, but it didn't frighten me. I felt sad as I could not remember feeling sadness. But there was also a sense of freedom mixed in the complex of emotions that I felt.

I thought of my father.

CHAPTER 28: CEREMONY AND CELEBRATION

Ludo had made detailed arrangements for his interment with one of the many *salone di funerale* in the neighborhood. There was to be no lying in state, no viewing of the body of the deceased. No funeral. He wished the final journey of his meager remains to the Ludovici mausoleum on San Michele to be via the traditional gondola. (I remembered Ludo saying to me once that weddings and funerals were the only occasions when it was appropriate to ride in a gondola; this very private celebration of Ludo's person and his troubled life was the occasion of my first and only such experience.) He wished his body to be placed in the mausoleum without ceremony of any kind. When we discussed his preferences for what was to happen after his death, he said something like, "There is nothing more eloquent than silence when one must endure the Death Angel's victory dance."

Ludo also specified that there was to be no public announcement. No posting of the white computer printout sheets with pictures and announcements of his death on walls about the city as was the custom. Ludo specified to those arranging the affair that I was to be the only person other than the professional funeral attendants to be present for the occasion. He had further specified that he was to be interred as quickly after his death as was possible, preferably the following day.

The two glistening black gondolas were tied up alongside the Fondamenta Mendicante, next to the *ospedale*. I walked there, wearing a black dress and a black hat and veil and carrying locked securely between my two hands the terra cotta urn containing the remains of my father. I had managed to find a shop open the previous afternoon to purchase an outfit appropriate for the occasion. I had never attended a funeral so that my wardrobe didn't include mourning clothes.

Strange, I thought, that death had been so much a part of my life but I had never attended a funeral. And neither was Ludo to have one. I had been spared most of the ceremony that usually accompanies death. I appreciated that. Death just happens and is usually an anticlimax. The ceremony that accompanies it is often superfluous and contrived.

It was a short walk, just over the bridge and a block or so along the canal that emptied into the lagoon just by Ca' Ludovici. As I walked, I looked across the canal at Ludo's palazzo. It appeared less elegant than I had come to think of it over the months. The windows were dark. The canopy over the balcony was fading, streaks of faded pink among the deep regal red. Life was gone from the palazzo.

The procession to the cemetery was just the two gondolas, each a solid black without the shiny metal trim and gold braiding favored by the commercial *gondelieri*. And unlike their commercial colleagues who catered almost entirely to the tourists, the gondoliers, two in each boat, one fore and one aft, were dressed completely in black. Even their shoes were the traditional black velvet ones rather than the more practical running shoes that many of them now wore. The bier in the lead gondola was draped in rich black velvet.

As I approached the place where the boats rested, two men in dark business suits stepped toward me. A red carpet lay alongside the gondolas. The *gondolieri* stood straight, their long oars held erect. One of the attendants helped me into the rear gondola. I sat down unaided in the single seat in the center of the boat. I placed the urn carefully beside me.

When I was seated, the attendants resumed their stations. Four additional attendants appeared carrying the ebony casket. They set it on the bier in the lead gondola and retreated. As if on signal, the four *gondolieri* placed their oars in their locks and slowly moved away from the fondamenta into the canal toward the lagoon.

It is not rare in Venice for the various modes of water transportation—vaporetti, water buses, water taxis—to declare a strike, usually for only a few hours. The strikes are often completely unanticipated; the canals and the lagoon just go suddenly still, completely devoid of the usual teeming traffic. That must have been the situation on this bright Sunday afternoon as Ludo and I made our way to his place of final rest. The canal and lagoon were eerily still, the flat water disturbed only by the muted swish of the oars and the smooth slice of the elegant boats through the water.

We emerged from beneath the bridge that spanned the end of the canal into the mirror-still lagoon. Our elegant small procession crossed the lagoon and pulled up to the siding at San Michele that was used exclusively for such occasions. More suited attendants appeared and removed the casket from the bier.

As they stood holding the casket, an attendant helped me from the boat. I clasped the urn tightly to me. I followed Ludo to his final place of rest, past the grave of Ezra Pound, to the garish Ludovici mausoleum. The men carrying the casket disappeared inside the mausoleum for a few minutes and then reappeared, shutting the door with a loud, decisive clang.

No one spoke. As we walked less formally back to the landing, a dark cloud obscured the sun and a harsh breeze arose. I began to shiver with the cold and probably with the intensity of other emotions that were struggling into my consciousness. An attendant placed a heavy coat around me.

I sat again in the trailing gondola on the return trip. The water was still quiet. There was something very moving about the vacant bier in the leading gondola, a return to the land of the living without one who had completed a journey there and had been transported to his final residence in a separate place.

I held my father's urn in my lap. After we were clear of San Michele and gliding gently back toward home, I removed the cover to the urn and slowly scattered the ashes it contained alongside the boat into the placid water of the lagoon.

CHAPTER 29: *SERENISSIMA*

Closure is an overworked word and heavy with too much expectation.

Ludo was dead and buried, his terminal event accomplished at my hand; a promise broken, a promise kept. The mystery of my father's death was solved and his remains were scattered in the waters upon which floated his native land. I was finished with my effort to write down my history, a try at reliving the journey, at coming to grips with who and where I was and to learn something from it.

I went back to my little flat. I rummaged through a small case I had brought with me, finally locating an old address book. I thumbed through it to a particular page, unused and unobserved for almost two decades. I located a number and punched it into my cell phone.

"Hello?" a voice answered after several rings; the querulous upward tilt of how the word was spoken brought a rush of familiarity from a distant place and time.

"Jesse?" I said.

Silence. A dense silence of time and space and circumstance.

Finally a tentative "Blanche?"

I felt a heavy sob building deep in my chest.

"Will you marry me, Jesse?"

ACKNOWLEDGMENTS

This book owes its most important debt to Venice, the most interesting and beautiful city in the world, and one that has rewarded the author's visits with inexhaustible reserves of beauty and mystery over a period of nearly two decades. Jan Morris's book, *Venice*, is a superbly written and illuminating guide to the city's history.

.

ABOUT THE AUTHOR

Ken Brigham is emeritus professor of medicine at Emory University. His medical degree is from Vanderbilt. He completed his medical residency at Johns Hopkins and had additional training at the University of California San Francisco. He has edited three science books, and has published over 400 original works in the scientific literature. Most recently, he was associate Vice President for Health Affairs at Emory, a position from which he retired in 2012. Ken has coauthored two novels with Neil Shulman (*Spotless* and *The Asolo Accords*), published a short account of his personal experience with cancer (*Hard Bargain*), and most recently, coauthored a nonfiction book, *Predictive Health*, with Michael M.E. Johns. He lives with his wife, Arlene Stecenko, in midtown Atlanta. Details of his interesting and more remote history may be found at www.kenbrigham.com.